Dear reader

Happy reading :)

K Bake

MAID
OF
STEEL

KATE BAKER

The Book Guild Ltd

First published in Great Britain in 2023 by
The Book Guild Ltd
Unit E2 Airfield Business Park,
Harrison Road, Market Harborough,
Leicestershire. LE16 7UL
Tel: 0116 2792299
www.bookguild.co.uk
Email: info@bookguild.co.uk
Twitter: @bookguild

Typeset in 11pt Minion Pro

Printed and bound by CPI Group (UK) Ltd, Croydon, CR0 4YY

ISBN 978 1915352 699

British Library Cataloguing in Publication Data.
A catalogue record for this book is available from the British Library.

For Edward, whose faith in my ability never wavers

Chapter One

1911, Manhattan

Bright sunshine made no difference to the March temperature, nor did it dry the puddles which covered the surface of Brooklyn Bridge in a rash of reflective measles. Enormous motorcars weaved their way between the more traditional hansom cabs, an army of dark metal monsters chugging their way to a takeover of city life.

Emma pulled her heavy woollen coat more closely round her body to keep out the chill wind whipping up the East River.

'Hey, you okay?' Martina stepped back to where Emma had paused at the handrail. They both leant over to watch the wakes left by barges wash to the river's edge.

'I'm fine,' Emma replied. 'We always hurry across and I just want to enjoy the view for once.'

Martina held up blistered fingers, raw from the scissors she used to cut material into shapes that made up long skirts at the Joseph Cobb factory where they both worked. 'Try braiding your little sister's hair with fingers so raw they feel like they're on fire.'

Emma knew all about agony and today was particularly acute, being the anniversary of John's death. Her twin brother from whom she'd been inseparable until they'd reached sixteen, and he'd joined the army. Everyone had laughed when she'd expressed an interest to do the same. Everyone except John.

On the day he'd left with his kitbag, he'd hugged her tight and told her he'd be fighting for the both of them. While he'd avoided physical injuries as a soldier, on each – somewhat rare – occasion he came home on leave, another piece of him was missing. When he'd come home on leave, their parents had put his unusually quiet demeanour down to being tired. But on the day they received the telegram to say John had taken his own life at his barracks by throwing himself off the roof of his accommodation block, three days before what would have been their nineteenth birthday, Emma knew she'd been witnessing his deterioration.

After a while Martina pulled Emma away. 'C'mon, we'll be late.'

Emma kept losing Martina's words in the snatched jumble of strangers' conversations as they weaved their way along crowded sidewalks. 'Apparently Sylvia's talk at Hotel Astor last month was incredible. I wish I could have gone to watch. Those English girls are really giving it to them *and* risking arrest, it's brilliant.'

Emma kept her eyes on Martina's worn black heels and walked faster to keep up. 'Would you go to prison for the cause?'

'For sure I would. You would too, I know it.'

They turned down a side street where there was more room to walk next to each other. 'But did you read the reports on Black Friday? Some were hospitalised with broken bones. So many were arrested, and now they're even force-feeding them. Can you believe that?'

Emma had known little about the American Women's Suffrage Association until she'd met Martina. Emma's mother, Maggie, had been horrified and told her to stay away from the growing movement, which had reminded Emma of the time she'd not been allowed to go with John to the Boys' Club in the church rooms when they were seven. It was always the boys who got to go places.

'It's precisely why we've got to keep going,' Martina said, and put out her hand for Emma to grab hold of as they ran across the road. The wheels of a hansom cab swished dirty puddle water onto their skirts and Martina yelled at him. Her exclamation was met with a sneer from the driver, who snapped a whip on to his horse's flanks. Three motorcars chugged past, wheels slicing through piles of horse manure like knives through butter.

Pushing open the doors under the Joseph Cobbs sign on the corner of Green Street and Washington Square, they made their way to the lift. Martina pressed the brass button and Emma eyed the enormous clock whose stern hands warned they had two precious minutes to reach the eighth floor.

It was their boss, the imperious Mr Joseph Cobbs, who walked out when the doors opened. He stood for a moment before he registered he was looking at two of his own staff.

He pointed his cane at them. 'You two had better to take the stairs, and save yourselves from that middle-aged spread which will arrive all too soon.' He pulled a watch from his breast pocket with his free hand, his expression eliminating any possibility that he might have been joking. 'In fact, by the time you've walked up, you'll be late and therefore you'll both stay an extra hour this evening.'

Emma's fury escaped her lips before she could stop the words forming. 'But sir, why should we do a whole hour extra if we are only a minute or two late?'

'Insolence too? How dare you answer me back. You are lucky I knew your father and gave you this job. I can just as easily take it away. Now get up those stairs and start your work before I change my mind and add a second hour to the end of your day!'

They raced up the newly carpeted stairs and arrived breathless, falling into the room on the eighth floor which housed three rows of tightly packed treadle sewing machines used for making the panelled skirts Joseph Cobbs was famous for.

The sound of Joseph's doorman, Douglas, turning the key behind them was drowned by the buzz and roar of too many women in the confined space. Blood, sweat and tears were the price the girls paid to be in work. There was a sign above the door which reminded them in capital letters, '*BE QUIET AND GRATEFUL*'.

Martina faced the locked door and stuck out her tongue. 'I hate it here.'

Chapter Two

Emma cut around the tissue-paper pattern and the green fabric reminded her of her grandmother's stories of Ireland: nostalgic tales of grass meadows and trees never starved of moisture.

She pinned the pattern to the next section of fabric, but it caught a breath of air and flapped around her wrist. She looked up to see Martina leaning out of one of the windows, inhaling a lit cigarette. Smoke billowed back into the room and some of the women were starting to grumble.

Martina looked at them over her shoulder. 'Oh, stop your moaning – you want to start living a little.'

Emma used her scissors as a paperweight before walking over. 'They're right, though. What if Joseph smells it?'

'Have you seen the holders the socialites are using now? I really want one.' Martina ignored Emma's question and offered her the cigarette. Emma declined and Martina inhaled theatrically as the door to the factory opened and banged against the wall. She threw the cigarette outside and fanned the smoke with her hands in a desperate attempt to hide the evidence.

'What's all this?' Joseph filled the doorway, his face red with anger.

'There was a bird trapped, sir, I was just letting it free,' Martina said.

A few of the women sniggered. Martina held up empty hands. 'Just a poor, helpless bird, Mr Cobbs.'

'I smell smoke!' He pointed at each of them in turn, taking his time. 'You all know the rules: the windows stay closed. Leave the smoking and drinking to people who know what they're doing. Now get on with your work.' He pulled the door to with a bang, which sent a shockwave of air across the tables, scattering patterns onto the floor. He turned the key to lock them in, as was his daily practice.

'Boring man,' Martina mumbled as she moved between the tables, bending to retrieve the wafer-thin papers. Snakes of discarded threads built up beneath the treadles on a daily basis and once a week she carried full sacks of discarded material and thread down the metal fire escape on the outside of the building to place them in huge bins in the narrow alley between the buildings. Joseph refused to allow refuse to be taken out through the main entrance, and the rear doors to the building had been jammed closed for months, so the fire escape was the only way.

They worked on without speaking for the next couple of hours and were so engrossed that at first no-one noticed the tiny curl of smoke coming through the floorboards. A machinist pushed back her chair and called out, 'What's that noise?'

Faint but terrified screaming could be heard from the floor below.

Another pointed to the floorboards. 'Is that smoke?'

Gradually the machines slowed as realisation spread through the room that something was amiss. Further wisps of smoke appeared between the floorboards and rapidly joined forces to form a mist which wrapped itself around table legs.

The women deserted their stations and called to each other, their sudden movements twirling the smoke into a fog. The bitter stench of burning wood squeezed through the boards and spread easily through those still oblivious.

Emma ran to the door and turned the knob. Surely Douglas would set them free? She banged against the panels. 'Help! Douglas!'

She banged the door harder, ignoring how much it hurt her hands.

Martina joined her and together their fists rattled the heavy wooden door. 'Hey! Hey! Let us out!'

Valerie, a woman with four children and two grandchildren, had opened the window and stepped out before helping others who hitched up their skirts to escape from the room. 'Come this way, quick. Down the ladder.'

Martina moved away from the locked door. 'Come, Emma.'

Outside the window, women gripped the railings, petrified to look down through the lacy metal platform to the ground eight floors below.

The room went dark as a mass of bodies flocked to the windows. Flames followed the smoke and now tickled the floorboards as women pushed and shoved each other, desperation robbing any attempts to get in line. Emma felt sweat running down her spine as the heat increased.

She grabbed for a chair and hurled it against the door. Legs splintered, but she did it again and again until one of the panels cracked. Dropping the remains of the chair into the now waist-high smoke, she pushed at the panel with the heel of her hand repeatedly until her arm spliced through the wood, tearing through her skin.

Ignoring the pain as a shard of wood dug deep into her flesh, she withdrew her hand and forced her eyes to search through the smoke to the corridor beyond. It was filled with screaming people, even thicker smoke and an orange glow from the lower stairwell.

Emma reached through the gap to feel for the doorknob on the other side. Amazed, she found the key in the lock and turned it.

'Door's open!' she tried to shout, but her throat had dried up.

Her lungs contracted as they fought in vain for clean air. Behind her, a few of the women who'd been hoping to get through the windows only seconds before now scrambled over burning furniture to reach the doorway. Tripping on upturned chairs, their heavy clothing became an easy target for hungry flames.

She pulled the folds of her own skirt close. The newly installed lift was designed to carry twelve people. The crowd jostling in front of the doors would simply not all fit.

'The stairs?' Martina's question reached Emma across the din of shouts and the roar of approaching fire, but the flames licking the banisters in the stairwell told their own story of impossible passage.

Emma coughed and shook her head. 'No, Martina. We've got to use the window.'

Martina turned and held out her hand for Emma to grab hold of, but this time Emma tripped as she reached for it. A layer of smoke covered the floor and Emma struggled to stand up when her boots pinned her skirt to floorboards no longer visible. When she finally managed to pull herself on one of the stools, Martina was ducking through the open window.

Flames leapt and danced, delivering lungfuls of poison. Emma's path to the windows became barred when the sewing machines – faithfully lubricated in oil – were consumed in a new wall of flames.

Martina looked like she might come back inside, but Emma waved her away. 'You stay there!'

Martina disappeared into the melee of bodies waiting to descend the fire escape, and Emma's view between the flames became obscured.

She hurried as best she could towards the door and the stairwell.

An older woman knocked Emma off her feet. 'Sorry, girl, get up. The lift is back.'

'No – we've got to take the stairs… it's our only chance.'

But the woman ignored Emma and pushed into the crowd surging forward as the lift doors separated. The screams intensified when the occupants realised, too late, that their bid for escape had led them into a lit oven. The doors closed and the illuminated triangle above the doors went out, as did the lights in the corridor.

Two bodies with flame-covered, wind-milling arms fell backwards down the stairwell. The lift would not be coming back and Emma was swept along towards the stairs. Someone's elbow caught her throat; another's hand tore at her ear as they tried to overtake. The stairs led up to the ninth floor.

Her feet searched for steps she could not see. Instead, bodies already succumbed to the smoke covered the ground beneath the smoke, causing her to trip.

The smell of burning flesh made her gag.

One of the young machinists who wore a frame around her leg from polio had collapsed at the edge of the stairs.

Emma tried to pull her to her feet. 'I've got you, Rose.'

'Leave me. I won't make it...'

'Don't be silly. C'mon... up you get.'

'It hurts!'

'I know, but Rose, you've gotta try!'

The slap took Emma by surprise. Rose's hand hovered in the blackening stench between them. 'I'm sorry, Emma. But save yourself. I tell you... I won't make it.'

For a moment, Emma hesitated. To leave Rose was unthinkable, but to die here, now, when her family needed her...

Blind from thick smoke, Emma felt for the curve in the wall at the top of each flight. She was a monster and did not deserve to survive, but her legs moved of their own accord.

Then there were no more stairs, only the roar from below and pungent air.

She felt a door, a bar across it. The fire door onto the roof.

She glanced back but could see nothing, her eyelids refusing to open fully. There were no other moans or calls in the dark.

She was alone.

She pushed the bar with what was left of her strength. Daylight welcomed her as she fell through the space and onto the roof, gasping for air.

She kicked the door closed and shut in the fire. For a moment she lay on the gritty surface in disbelief facing the sky. Up here, she was nearer to God. Was it too late to talk to him now, so that he might welcome her with open arms?

It was too late to read that final chapter to her young brother, Henry, which he'd asked her to do for days. Perhaps her mother had been right about the city being a dangerous place. She gulped back tears, a childlike desire for her mother's arms leaving her lungs even tighter.

A grating sound came from somewhere and with it, a distant chorus of screams.

Smoke billowed in thick plumes up the sides of the building and she turned her head a little to watch it feather and disappear into the blue sky beyond. The roof's surface was surprisingly cool beneath her hands, but she knew it wouldn't be so for long. She crawled to the edge of the building and pulled herself up on the low wall to peer over the edge.

She watched, transfixed as three people – then a fourth – hurled themselves from windows below. Bodies like discarded rag dolls littered the street. Her belly contracted just before she was sick.

Eager flames consumed the door through which she'd come and now staggered their way across the roof's surface like a fierce blind animal searching for food, bobbing in every direction.

She slumped behind the low wall in defeat. At least this way she'd be with John.

You can do it. Who cares if you're a girl – prove them wrong, had been her twin's assurance, from when he could ride a bicycle and her balance had remained elusive. From the time he'd taught her to throw apples overarm. From the time he'd given her bricks to lift when she'd been watching him building his strength in the yard. The other half of her had always encouraged, told her she could turn her hand to anything. *See, you can do it if you just try.*

She wasn't sure how many minutes had passed when a man's voice called out and Emma wondered if she was dreaming. When it came again, it sounded closer.

'Miss? Miss, can you hear me?'

She turned and saw three firemen standing on the roof of the next building. They were feeding a ladder across the gap to form a bridge.

'We can't come to you, it won't take both of us. You *have* to try.'

He'd read her mind. He knew she couldn't do it. He was simply doing his duty and would go home later, shrug his shoulders and tell his family he'd tried.

She thought again about John. He'd be shouting at her now, had he been there. *You can do it!*

The firemen beckoned her. 'Come on, Miss – don't stop to think about it.'

She pulled herself up, grabbed the wooden slats and lay along the ladder on her tummy. The ground was miles beneath her and after a tentative few inches, she started to sob. 'I can't do it.'

'Yes, you can.' The fireman was sitting astride the ladder at his end to keep it from moving. 'Sit like this and pull yourself slowly across.'

She was sure to topple off to one side and drop to her death, but there was no alternative.

She wiped her face.

She unhooked her skirt and stepped out of it before easing herself astride the ladder in her white cotton drawers, her bare knees shaking. The fire hissed as it devoured the roof's surface.

It was now or never.

'That's it, good girl. Look at me, don't look down… that's right.'

Emma focused on the fireman's face, beaded with adrenalin, kind yet full of urgency for her to succeed. She searched for strength in arms which raged with pain.

'Keep looking at me. Slowly does it…'

Her breathing faltered and she shuddered. The wooden rungs gave a little and bounced when she moved. Her thighs started to wobble and she felt lightheaded.

'Not far now, keep coming.'

The fireman's hand was reaching out to her.

'You're nearly halfway, good girl.'

She focused on the soot-smudged fingers and inched herself closer. Clouds of smoke closed in, wrapping their warmth around her, not wanting to let her escape. Snapping and crackling behind found her digging deep for a final effort John would have been proud of.

'Don't look back. I've nearly got you.'

She saw the fireman's sooty hands, the sweat on his own face, felt her lungs pulling life from the tiny breaths she was taking. It hurt, and she thought about giving up and letting her body fall.

'Hey!'

She gritted her teeth and pulled her aching body once more along the ladder. When he could finally reach her, the fireman pulled her from the lifeline and wrapped her in a blanket, supporting her body when she collapsed. She turned in time to see the flames crackle towards them and watched the ladder as it fell away like a box of lit matches.

A few minutes later, she was led out of the building and onto the street. Her left arm had blistered, little weeping domes of red flesh. The slash on her right wrist where she'd forced her hand through the door had stopped bleeding, but splinters stuck out at crude angles, embedded in muscle. The pain was pulling her towards death, of that she was sure.

The policeman steered her past bodies, charred limbs twisted.

'Oh, my God… I saw these people jump.' Emma covered her mouth with her hand.

'Don't look.' He was taking her to where the horse-drawn ambulances were queuing across the end of the alley, waiting to take the injured to hospital. 'Poor things jumped, but some are from the fire escape.'

Emma stopped walking. 'The fire escape?'

'That mangled mess.' He pointed to a skeleton of bent and twisted metal. Torn fabric pieces hung from spikes of broken steel. 'It broke under the weight of too many people.'

Physicians and nurses were busy covering bodies with blankets as police tried to keep the crowds back. The cries and sobbing which filled the air were testament to the unfolding horror. Emma scanned the walking wounded, praying.

Then she stopped.

Strands of hair stuck to her face and she had to drag it away from her eyes three times before she could be sure that the skirt was that of Martina. It lay in ripples across unmoving legs, one of which no longer had a foot. *Use the window!* Emma had told her, convinced it was the safest route out of the fire.

They had a lifetime of shared memories yet to make: the vote to win, husbands to find, children to bring into the world.

How could this be the truth?

Emma slumped to her knees, but the policeman pulled her back to her feet. Even the nurse's kind attentions could not console her or stop the howling sobs. Life wasn't life without Martina in it. Her presence had made the loss of John more bearable – she couldn't possibly have lost her too.

Chapter Three

Alice searched for an empty compartment. Usually, she loved nothing more than to be recognised, but tears were gathering momentum behind her heavily made-up eyes and today all she craved was privacy.

The dismissive tone of the director had played on repeat in her head since she'd left the audition, and failing was an experience she was not familiar with. *I'm sorry, Alice. You're simply not the look I had in mind for this part.* He'd waved her away, and the walk back to the station had been humiliating. She'd felt invisible while negotiating pedestrians intent on getting in her way and had pulled her felt hat further down, hoping it would shade her face – hardly the actions of the screen goddess she yearned to become.

The train pulled out of Dublin station and picked up speed as she dabbed beneath her eyes with the corner of a handkerchief. Kohl pencil was a bugger for smudging and she'd used a fair amount, knowing it complemented her green eyes. With red lips and her trademark waves of glossy black hair, the look had never failed. Until today.

Mr Bassinger, a producer of fine plays across Europe, had travelled from London to Ireland to oversee a week of auditions. He had barely looked at her twice.

Through the train's windows, Alice looked at the buildings rooted forever next to the train tracks and shuddered. Her acting career should be taking her away from the slow pace of life in Ireland and into the cities around the world where exciting times were to be had. And now she had failed to impress. What would she tell her husband? Dull, dutiful Thomas. Alice sighed and pictured him back home running their hotel on the south coast, the place where she'd spent her childhood waiting to escape.

'Ticket, please?'

A conductor steadied himself against the door to the compartment as the train swapped tracks. He waited while Alice fished in her bag and pulled out the return ticket she'd bought in Queenstown the day before. Holding it up to him, she returned his smile.

'Been somewhere nice?' he asked.

She could tell by the way he couldn't look her in the eye, and the red patches on his neck, that he found her striking.

'The Castle, actually.'

'You're someone important then?' He pulled his collar away from his neck with a finger.

She leaned forward, old habits pushing the morning's disaster to one side, touched his sleeve and whispered, 'I'm a touring actress.'

His eyes widened. 'A pleasure to have you aboard, Miss. Anything I can get you, please just let me know.'

He reversed from the compartment and she watched him through the glass panel retreat along the corridor, the moment of fun slipping through her fingers just like the part she'd been poring over for days. An unwelcome feeling of panic sizzled beneath her feet and she moved to the window seat in an effort to regain firmer ground. Her boots dug into her ankle bones and the heels had made her back ache, but beauty and stature came at a cost. One she was prepared to pay.

She retrieved the script from her bag. Tearing the pages in half felt good. She smiled to herself and raised an eyebrow as the pieces fluttered to the carpet by her feet. Perhaps Clive had been right, yet she'd been determined to find out for herself. Her agent had advised against the audition, reminding her he had a part lined up in Scotland. Even as she'd dragged her nails down his hunched back, he'd begged her not to go to Dublin. She had moaned in his ear, and he'd become putty in her hands, yielding to her touch and her demands. *But darling, you know if there's something I want, I will have it.*

The hedgerows blurred at the edges of her vision. She'd simply have to lie to Thomas and claim she had secured the part or he would think she was past her best. She pulled off her gloves and tried to remember the last time her husband had shown an interest in one of her plays. She squeezed her lips between her teeth and could taste the pungent wax of the lipstick which gave her mouth ruby glamour. Clive had bought it for her on their last tour and begged her to wear it in bed, and nothing more. Obliging him was a small price to pay for the doors he'd promised to open. She would travel to Edinburgh and do the provincials for three weeks. Thomas need never know of the deception.

But it was neither Thomas nor Clive who filled her thoughts. She rested her head back against the seat and closed her eyes, allowing herself to dream. The eyes of her true love had bored into her own after that first kiss, a kiss like no other, and Alice's tightly knit facade had become unravelled as they'd explored each other's faces with fingertips and kisses. The passion which had soared within seconds had left Alice breathless, as if they were the only two people left in the world. While her lover lived in constant fear of discovery, Alice had promised to protect their affair with her life. She needed it to remain a secret. After all, illusion was everything.

Chapter Four

Emma threw the newspaper across the room, where it flittered through the air. 'They're reporting they don't know what happened. Why don't they come and speak to *me*? I'll damn well tell them what happened.'

Maggie put a tray of food down on a table and tried to console her daughter. 'Now, stop this. Calm yourself. You shouldn't be up, get back in bed. Remember, the doctor told us—'

'I don't care what the damned doctor said.'

'Oh, Emma, please.' Maggie straightened up and took a deep breath. 'There's something you should hear. Your father has had an idea.'

'Oh?'

'Yes, he thinks you should go away to recover. Just a few weeks – somewhere nice and quiet. Perhaps with my sister on the west coast?'

'I can't. When there's so much going on here?'

'What's going on?'

'The Women's Federation rally in May, and it's even more important now that I be there, to show Martina…' Emma shivered as she said her name, 'that her fight for equality will continue.'

'We've been through all this before, Emma. You're wasting your time.'

'How can you say that? Surely you wanted more than to look after us and Dad?'

'I didn't, actually. It's always been enough.' Maggie moved to an oval mirror hanging from a picture rail and checked her reflection, avoiding her daughter's eyes. 'Anyway, your father thinks a trip away will be good for your health.'

'And you? Have you got any ideas about what would be good for your daughter?' Emma squeezed her fists tightly by her side.

Maggie said nothing and poured out tea from the pot.

Emma ran from the room.

Maggie called after her, 'You'll come back and realise we all just want you to be happy.'

Going to buy supplies with her father at least meant Emma was out of the house. The atmosphere inside bristled with things unsaid. There was no way she was going to miss the biggest rally the women of New York had ever organised. She owed it to Martina to demonstrate and be counted, even if it meant falling out with her own mother. The fire had shown her that attitudes needed to change, and that the old habits of a few should no longer dictate the lives of the many.

'You can't do everything you want, Emma,' her father said as they walked along the sidewalk.

'What's that supposed to mean?'

'Even this…' he paused to raise his top hat to a woman pushing a pram, 'this defiance you've started showing. It doesn't suit you. And any husband worth having won't like it, you can bet your bottom dollar.'

Emma stopped walking. Her father's words took her breath away, and she was about to respond when a hansom cab driver snapped his whip to encourage his horse down the middle of the road. An attempt to overtake the line of queueing cars. The driver did not see the streak of spaniel chasing a cat. But his horse saw it.

Spooked, the horse snorted and lurched sideways, forcing the cab briefly onto one wheel. Its agile design stopped it from tipping over, but screams from the occupants drew attention to the near-disaster.

The driver stood and swore at the horse, reprimanding it. Emma saw the whites of the animal's eyes and blood on its lips where the metal bit had torn at the corners of its mouth. The animal threw up its head in alarm and felt another sting of whip against its neck, the knot at the end hitting it squarely in the eye. Sparks flew as shod hooves scraped the road. The horse skidded to a stop before rearing on its hind legs in an effort to escape the barrage of pain.

'Stop!' Emma forgot about her father's words and ran the few feet into the road. She grabbed a rein, yanking it from the driver's hands, unbalancing him.

'Whatya doing, ya dumb broad! Let go!'

'No, I won't. This animal does not deserve such treatment.' Emma glared at him, adrenalin surging through her body.

'I'll lay this whip on *you* if you don't let go.' The man's face had turned puce and one of his passengers leant out the cab window. The queue of motorcars behind Emma began to edge forward and she found herself wedged between them and the terrified animal towering above her. She stroked the quivering neck muscles, soaked through with sweat. A policeman's whistle pierced the air from somewhere. The horse blew air from its nostrils, covering Emma with wet flecks. She remembered an apple core in the bottom of her bag. At first the horse flinched before snatching it from her flattened palm. The froth turned pink in the horse's mouth where blood mixed with its saliva.

The policemen appeared and pulled the driver down onto the road, issuing warnings about dangerous driving. Emma talked in soothing tones and the horse started to relax.

The passenger from the cab got out and ran his hands through his hair, the colour drained from his face. 'My wife had asked him twice to slow down.'

'You can't use this horse, look at its mouth,' Emma said. 'You're right.'

A second policeman intervened and took the reins from her. 'I'll take it from here, Miss. Now, you get back to the safety of the sidewalk.'

The passenger retrieved his tearful wife from the cab before turning to Emma. 'Thank you for stopping him, that was brave of you.' The man held out his hand. She hesitated before accepting the gesture. It was the first time a man had treated her as an equal.

Shivering, Emma walked back to where her father had rescued his office supplies and was encouraging onlookers to get on with their day.

'What the hell was that all about?'

Emma's heart still hammered in her chest. 'Didn't you see him hit that horse?'

'How dare a daughter of mine disrupt a man engaged in his work? I was wrong to secure that job for you at the factory. It was that useless twin of yours persuading me to let you try something—'

'Stop it!' Emma turned and ran, ignoring the pain caused by material stretched over her scars. There was no way she would agree to go west to some ailing uncle's whom she had never met.

As she went around a corner and slowed to a walk, she thought again about Ireland and the tales her grandmother had shared. It was there she would tell them she could go. Putting some ocean between herself and her parents seemed like the only chance she'd have to be herself.

Chapter Five

After the final dinner guest had wished them goodnight, Thomas retreated to the garden. Alice watched him go and shuddered when she noticed he still wore the sagging tweed jacket she so hated. She couldn't recall if it had been his father's or perhaps even a grandfather's. Either way, it needed burning.

She said goodnight to the staff and went up to her private study which overlooked the back courtyard. Outside, light from an outside oil lamp reflecting off the bonnet of the car her father had treasured, a 1904 Mercedes Simplex, and she had argued when her father told her he'd be leaving it to Thomas in his will. It had been, and still was, the only car in Queenstown that she knew about, and she liked the status its presence gave the hotel, but also when she was taken out by Thomas, people stopped to stare, wave at and admire her.

If only she could learn to drive it herself, then she could take her lover away, smuggled in the vast space behind the doors of the luxury saloon. She allowed herself to dream a moment before lighting another cigarette and noting how dirty the windows still were.

With the Atlantic only a few yards from the front of the hotel, saltwater residue on windows was a year-round problem. Thomas had been instructed on numerous occasions to get them cleaned, and yet each time she came home she found he'd not done them. Alice watched her lazy husband for a moment through the murky glass, his cigar smoke spiralling in a straight line where he stood by the stupid rowing boat at the edge of the garden. It was a rare night when the air in the port was still. He turned and looked up, and she jumped back from the window.

Perhaps her outburst in the dining room had been unwarranted and unwelcome, but she felt particularly grisly today. *Your standards are slipping, Thomas. It's revolting.* They were short-staffed, which didn't help, but what had disappointed her more than anything was the person she'd dearly hoped to see was too busy looking after an ailing mother to spend any time with Alice.

She'd met Thomas at the rowing club on the banks of the River Lee one summer. Her father had taken her with him to help with some catering for a regatta. Astonishingly, growing up, she'd never before set eyes on him even though Thomas and his mother had kept the run-down boarding house right next to her father's hotel. But looking back, she'd probably not have noticed a grubby little boy playing with all the other grubby little boys on the quay.

At the club, she'd found the sight of half-naked men preparing to row somewhat repulsive. It was sporting gear, her father had reassured her when, aged fifteen, she'd been unable to carry the tray of sandwiches through the clubhouse.

Thomas had spent every summer at the club in the days before his mother became too unwell. After that first regatta, Alice's father encouraged her spending time with 'the boy next door', telling her she could do much worse. So, to appease him, she'd agreed to a handful of dates with the quiet man while she planned how to end it. Then, one day, her father had dropped the bombshell.

'We're buying them out.'

'Buying who out?'

'Thomas's place. His mother is gravely ill and has had to close her business. I've offered to incorporate her rooms into our hotel extension. My builders are planning it already and we've got it for a song. But there is one condition.'

Alice had looked at him warily. 'What condition?'

'I need this place to be successful. To expand and grow with the times. We need a man at the helm and you need a husband.'

'I do *not* need a husband!' Alice stepped back and banged into a table in one of the bay windows of the dining room. Waiting staff moved respectfully to the other side of the room and placed cutlery for breakfast. 'This is the new century, Father. You cannot arrange a marriage for me. I won't have it. I want to be an actress and be free to travel.'

'That's a silly dream and you know it,' he said, gesturing grandly around his empire. 'This is where your future lies, and you'll be very good at the entertaining and front-of-house. Consider it your stage. However, every ship needs a captain, my dear, and Thomas is perfect. He knows the trade, albeit on a smaller scale. He's local and very soon, he won't be bothered by family ties.'

Thomas was twenty when he married the beautiful daughter of the grand hotelier next door. It saved his mother having to work through an illness which had been silently and slowly stealing her away, cell by cell. Within weeks, the rooms he'd known as a child had been incorporated into the confines of The Admiral, newly designed and wallpapered, no expense spared.

His mother had been well looked after in a private room which had once been their scullery. Before pneumonia finally took her, she spent her last evenings listening to Thomas reading out loud to her. It had been his greatest pleasure to see her smile and his greatest pain to watch her tiny frame sinking further into the pillow.

Alice's parents paid for a funeral festooned with flowers at the Sacred Heart church overlooking the sea, the place where Thomas's mother had worshipped for seven decades. Alice's father had taken Thomas to one side and assured him in quiet tones that love for his daughter would come in time. That all he had to do was dedicate his life to Alice. That they would find common ground and passion would grow. Thomas had no reason not to believe him.

'I'm off now, Mr Thomas.'

He turned and waved. 'Thank you, Aoife. See you tomorrow.'

He watched the head housekeeper pull her bicycle from the wall and wheel it away. With the tip of a finger, he pushed the little cardboard tray of matches through its outer casing and retrieved one. He inhaled the sweet smoke of his pipe, the flame drawn down into the tobacco. His finger secured the small mass into the bowl and heard the sizzle of partly charred tobacco reigniting. A smoke was one of life's small pleasures.

Perhaps 1911 would become the year when boats might feature once more in his life. In his ten-year marriage, he'd missed the companionship of the men at the club. His promise to Alice's father had been harder and harder to keep. His assumption that when Alice was home from tour, she would at least *try* to look like she was happy to be home, had been misplaced. He felt despised, and the notion was catching. And as for that eejit of an agent, with his greasy skin and belly full of beer. Thomas could only assume that Clive would deliver on his promise of making Alice famous. Why else would she spend that much time with him? Alice was a beauty and Thomas knew she turned heads but had always prayed his wife would have enough self-respect to not play into the hands of men who wanted more. He dropped the end of the cigar on the floor and stood on it, twisting it into the ground so there was nothing left.

He'd met Alice when he was twenty-three, and quickly become besotted with her confidence and lipstick. She'd taken an immediate shine to him, and swift approval was given by her father. Thomas had been swept away on a tide of what he now concluded was lust rather than love and agreed to propose after she'd insisted they become official.

The day she'd run her fingers down his thigh, his insides had fizzed. She told him that no-one had made her feel loved like he did and she hinted they would start a family as soon as they were married. She'd even expressed a desire to teach drama in local schools if time at the hotel allowed.

He'd believed it all.

His toes had cooled while dew soaked through the soles of his shoes. He reached out to the canvas covering the rowing boat and lifted a corner. A pot of black paint had long since dried up. The little brush was stuck fast to the rusted rim. As he ran his finger over the capital 'A', he recalled how his plan to name the little craft and surprise his wife had failed so spectacularly. *What the hell is that?* Alice had spat the words when she'd found him, paintbrush in hand.

She'd left him in no doubt that she hated small boats. In fact, she wouldn't be seen dead in one and went on to declare that her father had not left the hotel in her capable hands for it to be ignored in favour of silly pastimes.

Thomas dropped the cover and swallowed the hurt which still niggled like an itch after sunburn. In a few days' time Alice would be gone again, chasing her dream. Yet he worried about her still. He sensed she was no happier now than when she'd first insisted she wanted to try making it big on the stage. He'd been shocked at his wife's sudden change in direction. *I thought you wanted to run the hotel. Your father thought that's what you wanted?* She'd argued her father had never listened to her desires or bothered to find out what she wanted from life.

Back in his office, Thomas slid open his desk drawer and felt for the hip flask which he kept nestled behind the accounts books. The whiskey caught in the back of his throat and made him cough. He'd never been a drinker, not like his father-in-law, who'd been able to down half a bottle after dinner and still oversee breakfast the next morning. This was not another pleasure, more a necessity to dull the unhappiness which filled his days from morning to night.

He stared at the papers on his desk. Invoices needing cheques, letters from hopeful suppliers wishing to supply the well-known, highly respected hotel on the quay. He should be content with this life, but the gaping hole might one day consume him. Alice's father's prophecy had yet to come true.

Chapter Six

'Here you go, Miss. One more step.' The gangplank swayed slightly as Emma inched towards the dock at the end of her voyage across the Atlantic. An outstretched hand came into view and she took it, careful not to drop the luggage label in her hand. 'Welcome to Queenstown.'

'Thanks.' She smiled at the man with wiry sideburns and smudges on his cheeks. 'Could you please point me towards the main street?'

'The start of it is right 'ere, Miss,' he said, pointing to the ground a few yards in front of where they stood.

Emma was cheered. 'I'm looking more specifically for the hotel called The Admiral?'

'You'll find it on the left. Can't miss it – got huge lamps hanging either side of the door.'

'I have a trunk onboard.'

He pointed to a single-storey building behind them. 'Go see the harbourmaster, give him your ticket and he'll arrange to have it delivered when it's unloaded.'

The road into town widened and passengers dispersed, giving Emma a chance to take in her surroundings. The fog and drizzle of Ireland's welcome had not deterred her from standing out on deck during the ship's final approach

– she'd wanted to savour her arrival at the place her grandmother had left so long ago.

Previously hidden by the weather but now clearly visible high on a hill, loomed a building that appeared to guard the town with silent authority. She walked past the shops in the harbour, paint peeling from weathered signs. A row of coloured houses nestled against each other like stripes on a deckchair, their doorsteps anchors on the path.

A sign for The Admiral came into view and she paused at the wide stone steps between curved iron railings. There were steps up to a black-painted door, the hotel's name etched in the glass panel above.

The door was heavy and swung closed behind her as she stepped into a large round hallway, its floor a sea of black and white tiles. The door banged, making flames in an open fire spit and crackle behind an ornate fireguard. Stairs to the first floor hugged the curved wall and a reception desk had been built into the space beneath them. On a central mahogany table stood a porcelain vase filled with daffodils. Her mother had brought daffodils for her room in the hope their cheery colour and mild scent would help sweeten the stench of antiseptic and blistered skin.

A door she hadn't noticed and painted the same colour as the walls opened behind the desk. She prayed the man stepping through it and running a hand through his hair, wasn't going to tell her off for disturbing the guests.

'Sorry about the door.'

He looked up and smiled. 'Sorry, miles away.'

She thought about offering her hand as she removed her gloves. 'Emma Quinn.'

'Ah, the three-month booking.'

She nodded.

'Yes, of course. I'm Thomas, by the way.' He smiled. 'How was your crossing?'

'Calm, mostly. But after ten days, it's a relief to be here.'

'You must be exhausted.'

'A little.' She signed her name where his fingertip indicated.

'Three months is quite a stay.' The statement carried a question.

'It's what my mother thinks I need to help me recover.'

Thomas raised an eyebrow. 'Recover?'

The words had slipped out and now she'd have to illuminate. 'There was a fire in the factory where I used to work, I'm sure you won't have heard of it.'

'The one at Joseph Cobbs? I read about that.'

Emma dropped her gaze. If she left now, he'd have no need to find out what an awful person he was about to host.

'We have newspapers delivered daily so we do read about life in America, though it's at least four days old by the time we see it,' he added, then appeared to struggle for what to say next. 'I'm so sorry you were involved, but looks like you were lucky.'

Emma opened her eyes wide against the familiar sting. 'I lost my colleagues and my best friend, so it's not luck I feel. But yes… I did survive.'

She would no doubt be rewarded with a cutting reply for sounding petulant and waited for the comment.

He moved out from behind the desk, his voice soft. 'I'm really very sorry. I hope your stay here helps. If there's anything you need, you only have to ask.'

Buoyed by the empathy, she said, 'I'm hoping to learn about my grandparents actually.'

'Ah, left in the mass migration, I'm guessing?'

'Yes.'

'Right, well, first things first. Let me show you to your room.' Thomas picked up her bag and she followed him to the staircase.

'I've given you a sea view so you can watch the big ships arriving. It can be quite dangerous, though, I have to warn you.'

She paused, one foot on the patterned carpet of the first step. 'How do you mean?'

But Thomas was making his way up the stairs, unaware his words had worried her.

He turned at the top and grinned. 'Very time-consuming. You can waste a lot of it staring out of south-facing windows here.'

She laughed for the first time in weeks.

The room was spacious with a high ceiling and two sash windows framed by velvet curtains. Lined with cream linen, they were the colour of the wine her father drank each evening. Tiebacks edged with jaunty bobbles. The room had a woman's touch.

Light rain from earlier had worsened and now lashed against the panes of glass. Emma felt a draught and noticed a wooden panel fitted against one of the squares.

Thomas placed her bags down. 'I've got someone coming this week to replace the glass in the window. I could have given you a back room, but the view here is far superior, and he'll take no longer than an hour to mend it.'

'Oh, it's fine, thank you for the view. Accidents happen.'

'We had some trouble last month and stones were thrown.'

Emma looked out at the street below. 'What trouble?'

'It's political. Most of the Irish want to be free of English rule.' He drew the curtains, perhaps to hide the reminder. 'I have all nationalities stay here and that night, an Englishman started a conversation about the Royal family with a nationalist.'

'What happened?' She laid her coat over the end of the brass bed.

'They'd been drinking. Disagreed about something and I asked them to take their dispute outside, where it escalated into a scuffle. Alas, my window was the local's final word.'

Emma walked back to the window and peered between the curtains. 'Is this local someone I should be worried about?'

Thomas laughed. 'No, he's moved on. You'll be quite safe. Everyone loves Americans. Many have ancestors who came from these shores, just like you.'

She thought of her grandmother and lifted the gloves to her nose. She had taken them from the trunk still filled with her grandmother's clothes, but the wisps of her scent Emma had enjoyed at first were no longer there.

'Perhaps tomorrow I can ask you about the workhouse where my grandmother lived before she left?'

He moved to the door. 'There were so many, do you have its name?'

'The details are in my trunk which is still with the porters.'

'We have a library in the town full of journals about such things.'

'Thank you.'

He glanced back to where she stood at the window, still looking out into the dark. 'I'll bring your trunk up when they deliver it, but now I'll leave you to rest. If you feel hungry later, I can arrange to have a meal brought to you. Alice often has supper in her room when she's home.'

'Alice?'

'My wife.' Thomas gently closed the door and left her to settle. Still fully dressed, she sat on the edge of the bed, then laid back on the eiderdown and fell into a deep sleep.

In the bedroom directly above, sleep was the last thing on Alice's mind.

'A little lower, no, further… oooooh, that's it.'

'We really need to go through these scenes again.' Clive pressed his fingertips in small circles against Alice's shoulder blades, only the silk of her robe a barrier to her skin. 'There'll be no time once we board the train and the audition is Friday.'

'Relax.' She turned and trailed a finger down the side of his cheek. It revolted her that his skin was permanently blotchy, red and shiny with sweat. Worse than that, he never sported a moustache like her previous manager – not even a whisker – and if she had to shape her future in this manner, then Alice would have preferred a moustache.

'There, my love, now be a darling and rub my toes. Then, I promise, I'll go through the lines, just for you.' She employed her most seductive tone and tilted her head to one side. 'If you want, I'll even do it naked.'

She doubted Clive could even grow a moustache as she looked down at him from her height advantage. But what he lacked in facial hair, he made up for in contacts, and she wasn't going to let another woman step into her shoes for all the opium in China.

Clive's sigh filled the room and he checked his pocket watch.

Twenty minutes later, cigarette holder between her fingers, Alice left a ribbon of smoke along the corridor as she walked from Clive's room, where she had left him exhausted and snoring, and opened the door to her marital bedroom.

Chapter Seven

The next morning, Emma ate eggs and toast for breakfast at a table in the window overlooking the quay. Clouds still haunted the sky and rain left tiny dashes on the windows while boats bobbed about on the choppy water of a spring tide in the harbour.

A ginger dog lay sleeping. White hairs peppered his muzzle and long legs reached across the patterned carpet. Emma wished John was there to tell her what breed it was. He'd always wanted a dog, but their father had forbidden it, declaring the shop enough work. John had shared a secret with her, that he would own his own dog before he was twenty-five, and they'd giggled into cushions so their father wouldn't hear.

She'd known all of John's secrets. She'd never told a soul that on their ninth birthday, when their father had belted John for bringing the neighbour's dog into the back yard, he had cried himself to sleep that night. The neighbour, Mrs Wilson, had happily let her old beagle attend the twins' yard party and had been confused to find a red-faced George on her doorstep only a few minutes later.

The waitress paused as she passed the table. 'Is everything to your satisfaction, Madam?'

Emma looked up. 'Oh, yes, it's delicious. Thank you.'

The rich yellow egg yolk shone on her spoon, and the salted butter melting in little mounds on home-made bread – turned golden on the top of a range – were making her tastebuds zing.

She watched people through the window setting up market stalls opposite the hotel. Customers hovered close to buy their daily supplies and women held up fresh crabs and silvery white fish in pieces of rag. Now and then, a horse clopped past pulling rickety carts, the likes of which Emma had never seen.

At the edge of the road, last night's rainwater tumbled over itself, teaming beneath wooden boards placed bridge-like to provide safe passage across rudimental gutters.

A shriek came from somewhere in the building, dragging Emma's thoughts back inside. The sound of raised voices was unmistakable: those of an hysterical woman and the deeper hum of a man's reply. Emma reached for a newspaper from the next table and decided it was what she and Martina would have assumed was an argument. Flicking through the pages, she spotted a headline and a name she recognised. *Emmeline Pankhurst has hit back at Census Officials.* The English suffragette had encouraged women to be away from their homes on the night of 2nd April in a mass boycott of the census. Government officials were angry that their efforts to register everyone had been thwarted by a group of vengeful females, claimed the author of the article. There was a quote from a woman who'd been jailed for a week for throwing stones: '*If women don't count, neither shall they be counted!*'

Emma's heart skipped a beat. Here was the same passion, the same belief in the cause, that she'd seen in Martina.

The waitress came to clear the table and Emma moved the paper to one side. The girl smiled, colour rising on her cheeks. 'I was going to ask what that article was about but didn't want to disturb you.'

'That's okay. It's about the census which took place earlier this month.' She folded the paper and held it up, but the girl took a step back and shook her head.

'Oh, I can't read that well yet.' She glanced behind her. 'Just, I recognised the woman in the picture.'

'Emmeline Pankhurst?'

The girl looked longingly at the photograph but said nothing more.

Emma filled the silence. 'What's your name?'

'Aoife.'

'Eefie? That's unusual, and so pretty.'

'Thank you. I was named after my grandmother.'

'Aoife, do you know if there are any suffrage meetings in Queenstown?'

'I don't, but Aunty Babs ran off down the allotments and hid on the night of the census. It caused uproar when the enumerator went round, so as my cousin told me at church.' Her eyes darted towards the door once more, the shrieking woman audible from the hallway. 'I shouldn't be talkin'.'

The girl had turned and was hurrying towards the kitchens.

The arguing couple had left the hotel and Emma looked back through the window. They were standing on the pavement outside. The wife's hands gestured wildly, her eyes outlined in black and a shade of lipstick brighter than the roses in any florist. A calf-length skirt followed the contours of her hips; her brown leather laced-up boots had a high heel. She had shiny black hair which lay in beautiful waves, on her shoulders. She poked her husband in the chest with a finger and Emma wondered what the argument was about. Finally they turned and walked across the road, the husband lagging behind with a large brown leather case in each hand and smaller bags under each arm.

'Sleep well?' Thomas was beside her.

'Oh! Yes, thank you. I did.' He'd been right about the windows being dangerous for stealing away your attention.

'Will you be here for lunch? We make the buffet fresh every day.'

'I was thinking of taking a walk to explore. Nothing too strenuous, but yes, lunch sounds lovely.'

'You'll do the whole town in an hour if you get a brisk walk on.' Thomas laughed.

There was a clatter outside.

'Oh, dear,' Emma said. 'They look heavy.'

Two men were shouting at each other, as they began retrieving planks which had fallen from another ramshackle cart pulled by a heavy horse.

'It's the McGuire men. They've been bringing the planks in for days now. They collect them off the train,' Thomas said. 'They're making the scaffolding for the spire.'

'The spire?' She looked back at him and noticed his hazel eyes didn't quite match.

'The new spire for the cathedral.'

'The big church on the hill?'

He grinned. 'St Colman's is a bit more than a church. It's taken over forty years to build. And this year is special, because they're adding the spire. It's going to be nearly three hundred feet high, they say. You won't miss it then, so you won't!'

When Emma left the hotel later that morning, she could taste salt on the wind and looked up at clouds being swept from the sky.

She made her way towards the square and very soon noticed the ginger dog trotting towards her and Thomas by its side.

'It's bracing out here, Emma. Stay warm.'

'I have gloves, and this scarf.' She pushed the woollen folds closer against her neck. 'I'm used to the cold in New York, so this is no worse!'

He nodded and smiled. 'Have you met Oliver?'

She leant and tickled the side of the dog's muzzle. 'Is his eye alright?'

'He's old and it's cataracts, I'm afraid. Nothing we can do.'

'Oh, no.'

'He doesn't seem to worry. He knows his way around here.'

'He's sweet. What is he?' White whiskers tickled her fingers.

'You're an Irish terrier, aren't you, lad?'

Oliver's ears were darker than the rest of his coat and twitched on top of his head like triangle radars. 'He was a wedding present from my wife's parents, ten years ago.'

Emma scratched the dog's head again. 'Well, I won't keep you. I'm off to find that library.'

Thomas grabbed her arm and startled her. 'Careful!'

Another cartload of planks on its way to the cathedral thundered past, pulled by a horse with hooves the size of dinner plates.

'Forgive me, I forgot about your arms,' Thomas said, his face ashen with worry.

'It's okay, it's my wrists that were injured.' She smiled at the relief on his face.

The library provided useful information about workhouses and Emma filled a small notebook with details. She learned name registers were still kept at the houses which had not been demolished. Many had been converted to hospitals or homes for the elderly.

She thought about how she might travel further inland, having not seen a hansom cab since her arrival. Only simple carts full of local produce, planks or garbage. Back out in the cold wind, she pulled her coat close and stepped carefully around puddles and horse manure. Men in cloth caps congregated around doorways to public houses even though it was not yet past noon. Laughter and the smell of beer filled the air as Emma moved past them.

She worked her way towards the cathedral, between rows of tiny cottages wedged into the hillside. Catching her breath at the top of the hill, she leant against some railings. Behind her, builders moved through and round a skeleton of planks which looked like the towers of cards John used to build from playing cards. In front of her was the harbour mouth, the sea beyond, and although out of sight, New York and home was on the other side of this expanse of water over which she'd sailed. The morning light on the water reminded her of the story her grandmother had told.

About the day she'd finally arrived at the port after four days of walking, starving, having escaped the workhouse.

'I'd been travelling four days when I joined a small group of people going in the same direction. There was talk of big wooden ships bringing timber in from Canada that would take paying passengers back across the Atlantic. I had no money but knew if I could make it to the port, I might somehow earn enough for a ticket. It took over a week to arrive in Queenstown and I prayed. A lot.

'We arrived in the port early in the day and walked down the hill through some houses, our energy renewed by excitement of seeing the sea. I remember the sun was rising and the water was like a mirror reflecting the most beautiful pinks and oranges. I'd never seen anything like it. We kept walking until we reached the harbour. Fate was looking after me. I spent that first night in a back yard of one of the boarding houses and a boy came outside to fill a dustbin and spotted me. I gave him such a fright that he screamed and the rubbish he was holding fell all over the ground.

'I helped him collect it together – peelings, eggshells, cigarette stubs. He took pity and offered me a space to stay on the larder floor but let me in only when he was sure the owner was asleep and I wouldn't be discovered. I was allowed a few hours' rest in relative comfort on sacks of flour before he removed me the next morning.

'I was glad he didn't get into trouble on my account while I slept on those flour sacks every night. It was *the most luxury I'd known. He gave me leftovers to eat and told me that he, too, was planning on travelling to Canada for a better life. His name was Peter.*

'After two weeks, we'd become good friends and I knew he wouldn't leave Ireland without me. Three days later we were queuing to board a ship, but it filled up before we got anywhere near the gangway. Rather than wait two weeks for the next Canada-bound ship, we boarded a different one and took a chance. It was headed for New York.'

The wind off the sea was icy and Emma pulled her scarf up to cover more of her face and thought of her grandmother trying to keep warm without the luxury of a coat, scarf and gloves. The chestnut horse from the harbour was standing next to the cathedral and stamped occasionally on the ground, the echo bouncing off the walls.

A woman wearing a floral apron and a wide smile appeared from a tumbledown shed to one side, carrying a cup-laden tray. The men deserted their tasks and gathered round her.

The woman looked over. 'Hello, dear, are you alright?'

Emma checked behind her, but there was no-one else there.

'Come on over, I've hot tea. Not much milk, mind, that blessed goat keeps going walkabout.'

Emma followed her to what was little more than a shed. She had never had goats' milk and wasn't sure she liked the sound of it.

They walked past the stone wall, and she felt tiny beside it. Coloured glass of biblical scenes portraying themes she didn't understand towered above her, sunlight from behind the cathedral finding its way through from windows on the other side. The colours mingled. The shapes appeared to move as the sun's rays reached through the panes.

'I'm Mary. Mary O'Connor, by the way.'

Emma gratefully accepted the cup of hot sweet tea, and her palms tingled with the heat coming through the sides of the cup. 'You're very kind, thank you.'

'And what do I call you?'

'Emma.'

'Is that an American accent?' Mary moved a book from an old wicker chair so Emma could sit down.

'Yes, New York.'

Mary's eyes sparkled. 'That big darn city. I've heard so much about it, what with my boy itching to emigrate.'

'He is?'

'He's been learning to write, would you know. I never knew how to write, but you young'uns want things we oldies did without.'

Mary wiped plates and cups and told her all about how the cathedral had started with just a few stones being laid in the hillside. The shed was larger than its entrance suggested. A table and three chairs nestled against one wall, and further back, beneath a window overlooking the sea, a bed.

'Is this your home?'

'We have a cottage on the edge of town, but when the bishop is here or now the builders, then I like to be here to keep them fuelled up with cake and tea. People donate their spare coins to keep me going.'

'This tea is good. You should sell it.'

'Goodness me, no. It's made with love and that's fine by me.'

Mary wiped her hands on a tea cloth tucked into the waist of her apron.

'I hear they're building a spire?' Emma said.

'That they are. Can't picture it myself, some silly height they want. But I like to do my bit. It's fun having them around, and once my Harold leaves, I'll be glad of their company. Some of them come from miles away each day and bring nothing to eat.' Mary offered her a bun. 'But more to the point, what brings you here, Emma?'

She took a bun and smelt its freshness. 'I arrived yesterday. I'm here for a few weeks to look into my grandmother's past. My grandparents met in Queenstown.'

'Oh, isn't that the loveliest thing. Tell me more.'

'There's nothing much to tell, really. They both had plans to leave Ireland and ended up here in the port at the same time. They're dead now, but my grandmother told me how she'd had to leave a piece of her heart behind when she left. I guess that's what happens when you've grown up in one country and move to another.' Emma broke the bun into small pieces and recalled the ritual where she and Henry and sat by her grandmother's feet while she repeated the story of walking for days to the port. 'She lived in a Kilkenny workhouse for a while and I'm hoping to go and find the very one.'

Mary screwed her face up in disgust. 'Terrible places, so they were. My sister worked at a hospital a few miles inland which had been a workhouse. I went there to have Harold.'

'Was it really that bad?'

Mary rested her arms on her ample belly. 'With all the death and disease those places endured, I was surprised the floors hadn't upped and walked away themselves.'

Mary laughed, and Emma joined in.

'And how long are you staying? Because I'd love to show you inside the cathedral sometime.'

Emma's heart skipped a beat. 'I'm not sure yet. A few weeks. But I'd love to see it.'

Mary beamed. 'That's settled then. You must meet Harold too, you can tell him about America?'

'Of course I can.'

'Where are you staying?'

'The Admiral on the quay.'

'Dear Thomas's place. I know it well.'

'You do?'

'Yes, I clean there on Fridays, go right through the place. Alice get off okay?'

'Sorry?'

'Thomas's wife. I'd heard she was back in town for a couple of days. Dark hair, lipstick. Stands out like a pig in an aviary.' Mismatched plates clattered as Mary stacked them in a cupboard. 'Think there was talk of Paris next, or was it London? I can't recall.'

Emma stared at the brown curled leaves which had found their way in from somewhere and scratched circles in the breeze. 'I think I may have seen her leave this morning, but she was with someone. A man.'

'Hard to keep up, eh?' Mary reversed out of the cupboard and winked again.

'I haven't met her to speak to.'

'I've said too much. Me and my big mouth.' Mary shook her head while she folded cloths. 'That dear Thomas, I've watched him grow up, see. Me and his mother went back a long way. It's such a shame.'

'What's a shame?' Emma ventured.

'No, I mustn't say another word against the lass. Now, let's go and see if the bishop is ready for his tea.' They walked together back past the scaffolding and Mary leant in close as if she might be about to whisper, but her words were perfectly audible to the builders. 'You call in again – any time, Emma, dear. I do teas daily, ten 'til three, although the boys here would like me to open up five days a week, would you believe the cheek of them.'

'You make it, Mrs O'Connor, we'll drink it!' came a shout from the scaffolding.

The bishop, who'd been discussing building progress with a stonemason, waved. He'd just taken a step towards them when two teenage boys started to yell in the road. When one took a swing at the other the bishop ran over and intervened.

His long robes hid a surprisingly agile figure, and he was soon marching them off down the hill.

'Oh.' Mary sighed. 'He won't be wanting his tea just yet then.'

'Where's he taking them?'

'Soldiers' Home, I shouldn't wonder.'

'What's that?'

Mary put her hands on her hips and shook her head. 'A place where they can have a little… shall we say… quiet time. Somewhere other than the public houses, which is probably where those two have been.'

'Is the home close by?' Emma watched the heads of the bishop and the two boys disappearing down the hill.

'On the quay, right next to the butchers. You'll have walked past it, but they don't make a song and dance about it. It's not for the ordinary folk of the town, only soldiers and sailors. I go down to listen to 'em sometimes, there's a few of us take turns. All they want is just somebody normal to talk to, not those colonels and the like.'

'Normal?'

'Well, you know… someone out of uniform, someone who isn't barking an order. They're all so young, first time away from home. Missing the comforts of being surrounded by family. It's only natural they go a bit doolally, but I think a few hours spent at the Home can really help. It's lovely to watch them leave with a smile on their face again.' Mary frowned. 'What's wrong with you, child? You look pale.'

'I'm fine.'

'Do you need to sit down?'

Emma shook her head.

'You could go and read to them sometime if you've time on your hands, or just knit and listen as sometimes all they need is to talk and get stuff off their chest.'

'I can't believe such a place exists,' Emma whispered.

'There's one in most barrack towns across Ireland, set up by Elise Sandes.'

'A woman?' asked Emma in surprise.

'Yes.' Mary laughed. 'She started with one or two a long time ago. Married to an army officer and offered his young recruits tea on their days off. To give them a taste of home when they were far away. Mind you, I suspect her afternoon teas were better than some of those poor boys had ever seen in their lives!'

'That's so kind.'

Mary nodded. 'With the naval base out in the harbour, we've seen many a young lad saved from his own mind.'

Emma looked at Mary. 'I'd like that. To volunteer, I mean. I'd really like to help them.'

Chapter Eight

As April turned to May, the twisted skin on her wrist no longer stung unless she dressed too quickly, when clothing would drag and pull the scar, reigniting memories as well as pain. The temperature started to rise and Emma had discovered the bandstand on the promenade was the perfect place to write letters in private to her mother while enjoying the view of the sea.

She'd learned that the year her grandparents left Ireland building on the cathedral had not started, which explained why Emma had not heard of it. One evening, she was describing the iconic building in a letter home, when a familiar snuffling told her Oliver was closing in, and she turned around, ready to greet him. Through the white ornate iron railings of the bandstand, Oliver's nose sought her affection. The old dog had made it quite clear from day one that Emma was expected to fuss him whenever they shared the same space. She'd come to love his misty eyes and pink tongue which very often hung out the side of his mouth over worn-away teeth.

At the other end of the leash, Aoife pulled him back. 'Oliver, down! Let's find the steps…'

They walked round and up to join her and Aoife let him go. He pushed his wet nose against Emma's hand.

'Are you having a lovely walk, young man?' She protected her half-written letter in a folder made of card and wound the ribbon around the button to hold it closed. His better eye focused on her own and she ran her finger down the top of his nose where the ginger fur parted slightly.

'I hope we're not disturbing you – he seemed to know you were up here as soon as we turned onto the promenade.'

'It's always a pleasure to see him.' Emma smiled. Oliver moved away to sniff the bandstand floor before ambling back down the steps.

'I love this place. It's so sweet,' Aoife said.

Emma pointed across the water to square grey buildings. 'I've meaning to ask, what's that over there?'

'That's Haulbowline, the naval base. My brother's been there over a year now. Comes ashore sometimes.'

Emma wondered whether Aoife's brother had ever had need to visit the Soldiers' Home Mary had mentioned.

'Those buildings look spooky, like they're haunted.'

'I know.' Aoife turned. 'He told me once that over four thousand men live there, and ghosts in uniform are spotted regularly. Boys who died on the island over two hundred years ago, they say. They float up from the deep basin and evaporate on the wind, that's what he told me.'

'The deep basin?' Emma pulled her shawl more tightly round her shoulders.

Aoife beckoned her to follow. A bronze plaque was displayed near the harbour's edge and told visitors about Queen Victoria's visit in 1849. She used a fingertip to draw an imaginary map on the surface of the bronze. 'So, here, you've got the island, and here' – Aoife drew a smaller square within – 'is a large area that can be drained so a ship's hull can be worked on. Warships come and go all the time.'

'I see,' Emma said. 'So, your brother's in the navy?'

'No, He's been working on the dig to build the basin. He'll be home soon. Said he can't wait because it's horrible over there.'

Emma tried to picture such a huge number of men living and working together and thought again of John. His letters had taken weeks to reach her, and hers back to him the same. If only there'd been a way she could have made contact on those long dark nights when he was suffering in silence. Some way she could have told him he was loved and missed, then maybe he'd have hung on just long enough.

She turned away, mumbling about getting back, the words leaving her mouth strangled with emotion.

'Emma, did I say something wrong?'

'No. No, of course you didn't. It's just that—'

'Don't go. What is it? What's wrong?' Aoife asked, and Oliver stood in Emma's path, wagging his tail.

Emma tried and failed to stop the tears. 'I'm sorry, you don't need—'

'Come and sit down.' Aoife led them to an empty bench and placed a hand on the dog's back. 'Lie down, there's a good boy.'

They sat with their backs to the sea, facing the hotel and the row of shops which had closed for the day.

Emma blew her nose.

Along the road, two uniformed men entered a building through a door.

Emma noticed, for the first time, the letters carved in stonework above the door. Her shoulders sagged; she hoped Aoife couldn't read her mind. She didn't want to have to explain the reasons behind her sadness – that she'd been unable to help two of the most precious people in her life.

But Aoife was no mind reader. 'Ma always tells me that when I'm feeling a bit blue, I should have a good cry. Do you need to do more crying? Because we've no reason to hurry back. Oliver will wait for his tea.'

Oliver heard his name and lifted his head from where he'd been resting it on his paw.

Emma smiled, despite herself. 'I'm sorry, it's hard for me to talk about it…'

'You don't have to tell me anything.'

But Emma found herself telling Aoife everything. About John, and the fire. It all came tumbling out as the evening sun gave way to the blue-grey light of dusk.

'I feel responsible for her death because I sent her to the window. Not one of them made it. Eventually I managed to break the door which had been locked. We tried going up the stairs.' She sniffed. 'But the fire caught us up so quickly. Yet somehow I made it to the roof.'

Aoife was shocked. 'I can't believe you had the courage.' She twisted on the bench before adding, 'But I'm so pleased those firefighters helped to save someone as brave as you. I think you're amazing.'

'I'm not, though, I'm a terrible friend, Aoife.'

'I don't believe that for a minute.'

'I was led away, past all the bodies that had fallen from the fire escape.' She pushed her fist against her mouth. 'It fell away from the side the of building. And that's when I saw her. I knew it was her. I'd know her clothes anywhere.'

'Oh, Mother of God.'

Fresh tears ran down Emma's cheeks. 'So, you see? I don't deserve to be alive. My brother and Martina, both gone, and all because I didn't do the right thing by either of them.'

Her shoulders shook as she sobbed. She scratched at her wrists, delicate scabs giving easily. Fresh trickles of blood seeped onto the cuff of her blouse. Aoife swiftly pulled a handkerchief from her pocket and covered the wound. She helped Emma to her feet and, with an arm around her shoulders, steered them back to the hotel.

The weight of a blanket being laid gently over her body reminded Emma of her childhood and her mother's care. A damp cloth against her forehead darkened the world in front of her eyes and the reassuring pressure of fresh bandages took Emma to a sleepy place.

As the pain dulled, she relaxed to the soothing tones of quiet voices, and by the time Thomas and Aoife backed quietly from the room, Emma was dozing, back by her grandmother's bed, listening to the story of when she'd left Ireland.

'I'd had to leave my pillowcase of possessions behind in the rush to leave the workhouse. Inside were one or two items of clothes, a book and a shawl of my mother's with a brooch. A special brooch my mother had been given by her own mother. She wanted it to stay in the family. And I lost it. Peter could not console me.

'It was stupid. I'd hidden the pillowcase in a small shed to the side of the workhouse assuming I would

go past it when I left just before dawn. But when the time came, I spotted three guards leaning up against the shed before their day's work started. I had no choice. I left it behind and crept away into the dark.

'Peter was amazing, telling me we would find a replacement brooch at some point in the future after we'd settled in our new life. I had to learn to let it go or I'd have been consumed with regret and guilt. Your grandfather and I kept each other alive on that ship and by the time it docked at New York, we were in love.

'Over time the sentiment faded. I had Peter and then I had your mother. They became my world and the love I had for my mother lived on in my heart. Life is about what's coming, not what's been.'

Emma didn't even know about the tears that dripped from her cheeks to the pillow while she slept.

Chapter Nine

And get father's car looked at! Alice's parting instruction still rang in his ears as Thomas drove out of the city two weeks after his wife had left on tour. Her father, Victor, had preferred the finer things in life and the car had quickly become the status symbol in the port he'd hoped it would be. Thomas couldn't help but appreciate the luxury presently surrounding him as he drove. The will had clearly stated Thomas would inherit the car, but Alice had a canny knack of making him feel like a failed custodian.

The smell of leather mixed with new linen – curtains, made to order – folded on the back seat, collected earlier and another of Alice's wishes.

The road followed the river, and Thomas slowed when it narrowed, squeezing between rows of tiny cottages. It wasn't long before he left the dwellings behind and the river came into view.

Less than a mile later, Thomas turned into the entrance of the rowing club and parked the car. The very person he'd hoped to bump into was moving about on the grassy slopes that led down to the water's edge. Oars made of ash lay parallel on the grass, wearing a new layer of varnish and drying in the sun.

'Good God, am I seeing things?' The man in his twenties sat back on his haunches and put down a varnish-covered brush. He wore a striped vest top, cotton trousers rolled up to his knees and a curly black moustache. 'Good to see you, Tom. Here for some pre-season training?'

Thomas laughed and shook his hand, ignoring the flutter of excitement at the prospect. 'I'd love to, Patrick, but—'

'You need to delegate some of that work and come back out. We need all the oarsmen we can get. If *I* can manage it, I'm sure you can.'

'Still studying law?' Thomas opened the back door of the car and let Oliver jump down onto the grass.

'My God, he's still alive! I remember you as a puppy.' Patrick bent down to stroke the terrier's head. 'Yes, only a year left, then I'm a fully-fledged solicitor.'

The men had been friends since their school days and had joined the rowing club on the River Lee as teenagers. Within months, they'd been taken out and taught how to row and both had enjoyed success in regattas each summer.

'Is that yours?' Patrick nodded towards the car.

'It was Victor's.'

Patrick peered inside then knelt beside the running boards, mumbling to himself at the marvels underneath. He stood up and continued his perusal around the perimeter before letting out a whistle. 'What the hell did this cost?'

The question did not require an answer.

'You know he insisted on the best of everything.'

Patrick wiped his fingers on a rag that smelt of turpentine and glanced sideways at Thomas. 'To the detriment of his life.'

It was true. Two years after Thomas had married Alice, her parents had died in a terrible accident on the roads outside Paris during a particularly harsh winter, where they'd been looking to open a second hotel.

'Well, we still benefit from his business efforts. The Admiral does okay.'

'And what's that wife of yours up to nowadays? Still treading the boards?'

'She's good on the stage, Patrick. If it's what she wants to do, I have to support her.'

'But doesn't that moral support work both ways?'

Thomas knew that it should. Oliver crept down the bank, his ears cocked and his good eye focused on a family of ducks swimming past, little balls of fluff bobbing close to their mother.

'Sorry, none of my business,' Patrick said. 'Come inside, it's nearly twelve. We'll have a beer to mark this rare occasion.'

Black and white photographs of winning teams through the years dotted the panelled walls like portholes into a past Thomas remembered with pride. Patrick poured a small glass of ale and pushed it across the bar, then poured another for himself. 'So... what does bring you here?'

Thomas knew the truth would sound nostalgic and his friend would think him wet. He licked the froth from his top lip. 'I was in the city having the brakes checked so thought I'd pop in and see if you wanted Bertha back.'

'God, not that old thing? I'd have thought you'd have broken her up for firewood by now.'

Thomas smiled. 'No, she's too good for that, but Alice didn't want to be rowed round the harbour, up the river...

61

or anywhere come to that.' Thomas swirled the ale in the glass. 'Think I've been misjudging her since the day we met.'

'You old romantic fool.' Patrick roared with laughter and then checked himself.

Thomas continued, 'Anyway, I'm having a sort-out at the hotel, inside and out.'

'So, you're saying you need Bertha moved? I'll pop down next week and check her over. See if she's worth bothering with.'

Thomas nodded. 'I think the garden could become an outside space for the guests to relax. It's wasted at the moment.'

'I thought Alice like guests in and out. Quick turnaround. Do any of them have time to relax outside?'

'Alice's business views are those of her father, and anyway, we occasionally have guests who stay longer than just a night who might appreciate more outside space.' Thomas moved to the window. Outside, dark clouds billowed over the tops of trees lining the riverbank on the other side of the river.

'Since when?'

'We've had a guest staying since the start of last month in fact. A young woman from New York. She likes to read outside, write letters home, that sort of thing, and I'm embarrassed by the state of the garden.'

'You're spurred on to do a garden makeover, for just one person?'

'For everyone.' Thomas lowered his voice and took a gulp of beer. 'This autumn I could even host a celebration bonfire for Samhain.'

'Ah, now you're talking. I'll help with the fire.' Patrick came round from behind the bar. 'Looks like rain coming, help me in with the oars, will you?'

They put the oars safely in the hut, just before the early spots of a downpour grew to the size of marbles and smacked against their shoulders.

'You're gonna get wet in that,' Patrick said.

'You think?' Thomas ran to the car, the dog following slowly behind. He lifted the black roof from its folds behind the rear seat, pulling it forward and clipping it in place on both sides of the windscreen.

'Bloody hell, a roof? I've seen it all now.'

Chapter Ten

Alice stretched beneath the sheets and watched a pigeon take advantage of another on a rooftop opposite her Paris hotel. Clive had gone ahead to the theatre, leaving her to enjoy her morning routine.

After untying the scarf, then unwrapping rollers from her hair – in which she slept each night – she pulled the open letter across the marble table to read for the hundredth time. Her lover's handwriting covered the paper embossed with the hotel letterhead and Alice smiled at the audacity. Thomas would never have noticed that sheets of paper had been taken, but nothing got past Alice. Anyone else would have received short thrift, stealing from the office, but she'd never deny a thing to the one person in the world who knew her so intimately, who loved her with abandon and who forgave her everything.

Later, in the wings at the Théâtre Impérial du Châtelet, Alice watched in awe the dancer Loie Fuller perform her famous Serpentine display, with silk wings billowing in huge circles as her arms guided the wooden poles inside the material. Alice had always hoped to perform at the same venue as the dancer and later she would ensure they shared a cocktail at the bar. Loie was American, and America was where Alice had been wanting to perform for as long as she could remember.

Later, after a successful performance, Alice and Clive were eating dinner and in discussions with the director who'd been side-eyeing Alice since he'd invited himself to sit and dine with them.

'I'm taking my company to Dusseldorf next week. Why don't you come along? I think you would be a great asset to me.'

'She can't. She's booked to do the Palladium in London,' Clive said quickly.

'But Clive, *allez!*' Antoine reached out a chubby hand and handled Alice by the jawbone, tilting her head this way and that. 'Don't you think they deserve to see this creature in the flesh? I know I'd like to very much.'

Alice's heart thumped against her ribs in disgust, but a well-practised habit found her smiling at him, trying a little too gently to peel his hand away. 'You can't mean that—'

'Oh, but I do, my dear. Say you'll come to Dusseldorf and I'll make it worth your while.'

Clive coughed into his napkin and pushed his chair back, summoning the waiter for the bill. 'I think it's time we left, Alice.'

'So soon?' Antoine leaned forward and brushed his smoky thumb across Alice's lips.

'Yes. We have songs to rehearse. But thank you for your hospitality.'

'Yes, thank you,' agreed Alice.

'But you haven't heard what I could do for your girl, Clive. Surely you'd like her to appear for the King?'

'What!' Alice gasped and sat back down.

'We've tried that. His itinerary won't allow for more acts. That's what I was told.'

Antoine stood up and released his coattails. 'My dear man. It's not what you know but who. You should know that by now.'

Clive flushed and put out his arm for Alice to pass in front of him away from the table. But she stood firm and turned to Antoine. 'What are you saying? Are you saying you could get me in?'

'Alice. You are by far a more superior actress than many who are booked. I have taken the liberty this morning of sending a telegram to my friend,' he paused to look at Clive, 'whom I know will secure you a slot. I'm sure I will have heard back by Friday and would be honoured if you would dine with me so I can go through all the details.'

'Well, I'm not so sure...' Clive stammered.

Alice hesitated.

'You wouldn't break an old man's heart, now surely?' Antoine's hand flew to his chest in dramatic fashion.

'Of course I wouldn't let the King down!'

'Ha! Ha! You see, Clive? We have wit *and* beauty in this package. You really should let me take her on.'

Chapter Eleven

The workhouse was a few miles north of Cork. Aoife had been insistent Thomas should drive Emma there on one of his shopping expeditions, although the debate had continued for three days. Emma had no desire to put Thomas to any trouble.

'Aoife's right. It makes sense as I'm going that way. Look, I'll drop you off and then pick you up a couple hours later,' he had concluded.

'I don't know what to say.'

'You don't need to say anything. Well, perhaps idle chat on the way may be preferable to silence, but honestly, I'd prefer to help out and ensure you get there.'

They left the town behind and below them, climbing inland to a rural landscape criss-crossed by stone walls. Emma had never seen so many fields of sheep in which skipping lambs played and grazed near their mothers. At one point, Thomas slowed to crawl past two sheep nibbling at a verge while the rest of their flock were crowded on the other side of a gate, jostling, hoping to join the renegades.

'I want to apologise, and to thank you for the other day,' Emma said. 'For my outburst.'

'Don't mention it. I'm glad Aoife was there. We keep plenty of bandage wraps.'

She turned to look at him. 'It wasn't so much the bandaging I was referring to.'

He glanced briefly at her.

'It was the fact neither of you judged me.'

There was a moment of silence.

'I only judge you on your courage, Emma.'

Pale green leaves had started to unfurl, decorating the hedgerows and altering its appearance from the sombre mode of winter to the excitement of spring. Emma thought of the small yard back home. It would be showing its own little signs of spring. The little apple tree that she and John had loved to climb to spy into the next-door garden would definitely be covered in blossom and she pictured her nana as she used to sit beneath it.

She opened the notes she'd made in the library a few days earlier. Woodleighs workhouse had been taken over by the hospital trust in 1881 and had been renamed Ballyned Hospital. It specialised in looking after the elderly who hadn't fled the country.

Thomas slowed again for more sheep, this time being herded by a farmer and his dog from small farm buildings on one side of the road, towards an open gateway on the other.

Emma sat forward a little to watch the woolly backs huddled in front of the bonnet before they scuttled away, the dog weaving back and forth behind them.

'They say there are more sheep here than people, a legacy of the famine, I shouldn't wonder,' Thomas said.

She wound down the window and smelt damp grass and stagnant puddles where the concrete frayed into verge.

The signposts for Ballyned confirmed they were headed in the right direction.

When they entered the village, it was little more than one farmhouse, a row of broken cottages, a public house and a church. They pulled over to park and found a shop in a glorified shed. It sold pots of local honey, muddy vegetables and week-old newspapers. A woman stood behind a glass-topped desk and pulled her cardigan closer around her bosom. She barely broke a smile when Thomas asked for directions.

Once they were back in the car, Thomas checked over his shoulder. 'Our friendly neighbour says we go down this road for two miles and it should be on the right.'

'I'm terrified.'

'Why?'

'This could be the very place Nana ran from and it feels a bit like digging up ghosts.'

'Perhaps it's not fear. More trepidation and excitement.'

Emma laughed nervously. 'We've probably driven the same route she spent a week walking.'

'She wouldn't have had these modern surfaces, either. Just the stony old lanes used by horse and cart back then.'

Emma felt a lump in her throat as she thought about the journey her grandmother had described. 'You know, I'd love to hug her right now.'

They wound their way up a narrow hill through woodland and the wheels swished through water that cascaded down one side of the road. At the top of the hill, the trees became less prolific and the view opened up. A tumbledown wall ran for a few yards before stopping.

'Is this it?' She checked her notes, then peered back at a plaque next to the car as Thomas stopped. *Woodleighs.* They turned in and approached a long two-storey building with rows of identical square windows on both floors.

Thomas pulled the handbrake from the dashboard and got out to talk to two men near a central door. Emma watched him shake hands with one, while the other glanced at the car. A moment later he returned and opened the passenger door.

'They say you can go in and talk to the manager. She'll have historical records of who was here.'

'What are you going to do? The last thing I wanted to do was hold you up.'

'Why don't I come in with you and check we've got the right place?'

A modern porch had been added at the entrance, with a pillar either side, an attempt to give a mundane building a sense of importance.

'Looks like a prison,' Emma whispered.

The lady behind a reception table looked up and smiled. 'Good morning, can I help you?'

'Good morning. I'm not sure where to start, but I believe my grandmother was here before she left Ireland in 1850.'

A toe-curling howl came from somewhere unseen.

'Oh, don't mind Reg, he thinks he's a wolf. Call me Eva, I'm manager here and senior matron.'

'I've been told you might have records of names?'

Eva turned to a wooden cabinet and pulled out two heavy files. 'I'm quiet today so you've timed this well.'

Emma looked at Thomas. He checked his pocket watch, then nodded. 'The shopping can wait.'

They followed Eva into a back room with simple furnishings and a long rustic table. At one end sat two elderly men focusing intently on a game of cards.

'Here, sit this end. They won't disturb you,' Eva invited.

'Okay, so, we're looking for…?' Thomas asked. 'What was your grandmother's maiden name?'

'O'Reilly.'

'Right,' he said. 'You check this book and I'll do this one. It'll be quicker with two.'

She pulled the heavy leather-bound book towards her and opened the cover. Her heart sank when she saw the lists had been written with a fountain pen, in swirly letters and in no particular order.

'We don't need to check anything later than 1850, but I wonder what month she actually left? She didn't mention and I never thought to ask.' Emma put her head in her hands and moaned.

'Come on, it can't be that bad. I can see here the men's names are listed in one column and the women are in another so that's a start.' He peered at the page, running a finger down the list. Emma took a deep breath and did the same, starting at a page entitled January of that year.

Eva kept them supplied with tea and they ate their way through a handful of oatcake biscuits. After an hour's fruitless efforts, Emma leaned back in her chair and stretched her arms above her head.

'This is hopeless.' She looked up the other end of the table where now only one of the older men was seated and appeared to be sketching. 'I've been meaning to ask you something. The landscape paintings which hang on the landing at the hotel. The small ones. Are they a local artist?'

71

Thomas's mouth twitched as he turned another page. 'Might be.'

She leant forward, ignoring the pull on the newly formed skin on her forearms. 'Are they yours?'

His finger followed yet another list to the bottom of the page. He took his time and she was touched by how seriously he was taking her search. 'Yes.'

'They're very good. Do you sell any? I'd like to take one back for Mother when I go.'

Thomas looked up and said nothing for a moment. 'They're not good enough for me to take any money. I can't sell them.'

She looked down at the spidery names blackening the page. 'Of course. I can find her something else, when the time comes.'

'You can take one, Emma. I just won't sell it. A little view of Ireland to remind you of your time here.'

They looked up and smiled at each other, before continuing with the search.

'Now, how are you getting on?' Eva asked as she walked past. The man at the end of the table was attempting to retrieve pencils which had rolled off the table onto the floor.

'Nothing yet.' Emma stood and wrapped her fingers carefully around her right wrist where the itching was becoming once more unbearable.

Eva nodded and moved to where the old man was now standing bent over, supporting himself on the table, and helped him shuffle towards the door. 'It could mean she was at our sister house, which is in the next county.'

'What was that one called?'

'Woodhouse Lodge.'

Emma and Thomas both groaned and Eva continued, 'Oh dear, is that bad news? I think we have their records from when it closed down. Let me just put Alfred to bed and I'll find them for you.'

An hour later, Thomas drove round a final bend before rumbling across the cattle grid Eva warned them they would find. The ruins of Woodhouse Lodge seemed to hug the hillside, its broken windows and ivy-covered facade the result of a decision taken by the Irish council to save only one of two workhouses in close proximity.

He stopped the car near the remains of a place that had once housed over a thousand men, women and children, including Miss Ellen O'Reilly, resident between August 1848 and noted as '*disappeared*' in October 1850.

He turned to look at her. 'Do you want to get closer or is this far enough?'

'I would like to look through those windows, just so I can tell Mother I've seen it. Would you mind waiting just a few minutes?'

There were piles of rubble in every direction.

'I'm coming with you.'

Teeth of glass embedded in broken window frames discouraged them from leaning in to look inside. Instead, they picked their way round the building and found an open door. The wind was enjoying free rein through the building, rattling old fixings and ruffling cobwebs in every corner. The soles of Emma's boots crunched on years of forgotten debris and beetles scurried back to the cover of darkness when Thomas lifted planks of wood. Further into the building, they found themselves in a long room with raised wooden platforms down either side.

'This is where they put the beds, I think,' he said, jumping up onto the higher level and squatting. He pointed to roughly drilled holes in the boards. 'See these holes?'

She nodded and, lifting her skirts to join him, wished she had the same freedom of movement in trousers that he took for granted.

'This is where fresh air would enter from outside, and the stale air escaped through those vents up there.' He pointed to just beneath the ceiling where bricks had been omitted at regular intervals along the full length of the wall. 'Quite ingenious, really, and probably essential if you imagine so many people all sleeping in this one space.'

His voice had changed. He was speaking with an enthusiasm she'd not witnessed before, as if he had a passion for what he was seeing. 'How do you know so much about it?'

'I wanted to be an architect and in the first year of college we studied historical buildings of Ireland.' He ran his hands over the walls and grinned at her. 'It's great to be here, it reminds me of an outing we went on with our tutor. Measuring up and talking about building materials used in the last century.'

'But you're not an architect.'

'No, you're right,' he said. 'I married Alice, who came with a hotel to run.'

He moved towards the wall where ivy had found its way inside, achieving its aim to cover the entire wall in a waterfall of dark green leaves.

'If I'm not mistaken there should be a washroom at this end.'

She followed him through the doorway, relieved he'd moved the subject away from his wife. The conversation was straying into personal territory and Emma wasn't sure she was qualified to comment. Down steps made from bricks once painted white, they entered a small room. Thomas pulled more ivy from something in the corner resembling a giant beehive made of stone.

'They lit fires in these things, to heat water for washing clothes and bed linen,' he said, turning round to check the room's aspect. 'Which must have been a thankless task because disease was rife. Your grandmother did well to escape this hellhole.'

He let the decaying wooden lid fall back into place and a cloud of dust rose into the air, along with two small moths.

'Oh, look!' Emma gasped. 'It's like they're escaping too.'

They watched the moths flitter for a few seconds before landing on ivy leaves. They tucked their wings against their tiny bodies and became, once more, hidden.

'Was she here with her parents?' Thomas asked.

'She was orphaned at twelve and the brooch was the only link to her past.'

'Brooch?'

She'd been thinking aloud; of course he had no idea what she was talking about. Would he think her silly if she told him what she was really hoping to find here? It was a risk she decided to take.

'Nana had a brooch, handed down to her by her mother before she died. Have you heard of a Tara brooch?'

'Of course. It's been a popular symbol in Ireland for a long time.'

Emma leant against the wall. 'Well, her own mother had worn it on a shawl for years apparently. Nana put the shawl in a pillowcase with a few things she planned to take with her when she left in the night. But she couldn't retrieve it when the time came because the guards would have seen her and tried to stop her. So she had to leave it all behind.'

'I see,' Thomas said quietly.

'It's really sad. I only learnt about it recently. It was her final link with her mother. I know it sounds silly, but once I knew I was coming to Ireland, I knew I had to come and look for it.'

'But Emma, it won't be here. Someone will have found it, sold it, melted it. Or it will have rusted away.'

Emma sighed. 'I had to try, I'm sorry. I know it was stupid.'

They left the washroom via a different set of steps, some of which had given up and crumbled away. Thomas paused and reached back his hand for Emma to take. She hesitated. He was married. To touch his skin would be a sin. But the ground was uneven. She accepted the gesture and followed him through a dark corridor which led to the back of the building and outside. Brambles cascaded over broken walls in spiky waves, small pink clusters of blossom promising blackberries later in the year.

Thomas stopped and turned. 'Had enough exploring for one afternoon?'

She stopped next to him. 'Yes, I suppose so. It's been eye-opening.'

They picked their way through fallen trees and more brambles, and back towards the open moss-covered ground in front of the building.

'Hang on, look!' Emma pointed to the remains of a small shed at the edge of some trees and started towards it. 'That was it, I remember now. She said she'd left it in a shed.'

'Careful,' Thomas called after her, but Emma soon reached the door which hung precariously on one hinge. She pushed it and took a step back as it creaked and fell away inside. The top of the door came to rest against the opposite wall amid a plume of dust. In the centre a rudimentary toilet bowl sat gaping, dried out years ago and home only to spiders and twigs.

'Come out, Emma, there's nothing in there.' Thomas stood with his hands on the wall either side of the doorway.

She pulled her skirt round her knees and bent forward while her eyes became accustomed to the dark. There was something grey behind the toilet, and she felt sick with hope. It couldn't possibly be what she hoped it was. The material disintegrated as she pinched at it with her fingertips, but when she reached in further she was able to gain a stronger hold. The lump of heavy material budged and came towards her, bringing with it a mouthful of musty air.

'The pillowcase,' she whispered more to herself than Thomas.

She turned towards his silhouette standing in the doorway. 'The shawl must be inside.'

'Be careful, you don't know what that could be. Mind it's not sharp.'

The outer layer fell apart where she touched it, but beneath the fibres, a different piece of material had hardened. 'My God, it is! This must be my grandmother's shawl, the one she had to leave behind.'

They placed the matter on an exposed rock in the daylight and gently teased the layers apart until the full extent of the shawl was exposed, disturbed from its sixty-year grave. Emma touched its surface carefully all over until at one corner she felt what she was searching for. She turned it over. Rusted into the fabric was the ancient piece of jewellery. A dagger, set in a Celtic circle, lettering long since eaten away.

Emma stared, her fingers shaking.

'Oh, Thomas, I've found it. *We've found it!*' She sank down against the wall, hugging it tightly and let tears of relief flow freely.

He knelt beside her and said nothing.

She sniffed and composed herself. 'Thank you. Thank you so much.'

'What are you thanking me for?'

His modesty was so endearing, she wondered how anyone could want to boss him about.

'I'm happy you were here. I don't know why, and I'm sorry to have taken you from your work.'

He stood. 'Don't be sorry. It's a miracle you've found this today, and if there's one thing we people know all about in Queenstown, it's that miracles can happen. It's that St Colman, you know!'

'The saint?'

'The very same. The cathedral was going to be built further inland but when the famine drew people to the coast, it was decided Queenstown would be a better location, giving folk a place for worship as they waited to sail, or after they'd spent days or weeks at sea and had just arrived.'

The idea that having a faith might have led to this was a new one to Emma, but the warmth which surged through her now left her open to believing. She wrapped the shawl back around the brooch and pulled it free from the remaining threads of the pillowcase.

When he held out his hand once more for her follow through the final pieces of undergrowth which would lead them back to the car, she hesitated again. He'd been so kind, and perhaps it was the euphoria of finding the brooch, but holding the hand of a married man she was drawn to was starting to feel dangerous.

'It's okay, I don't want you falling and landing on those wrists. We need to look after them before your return home or your mother will wonder how you've been spending your recuperation time.'

Still Emma did not take his hand. 'I don't want to go.'

He looked around him. 'Well, there's not much more here. I think we've seen it all.'

'No. I mean I don't want to go back to New York.'

Chapter Twelve

When Thomas and Emma drove home from the workhouse, excited by the day's events and find, neither of them noticed the stationary black Ford a few hundred yards from The Admiral as they turned to park behind the hotel.

As Thomas opened the back door next to the kitchens, a loud and familiar voice stopped them in their tracks.

'Where the *hell* is he?'

Thomas's palms tingled with adrenaline as each terrifying word crashed through the walls. His stomach plummeted and the euphoric mood evaporated.

'You go on up.' He steered Emma past the doorway in the hallway and indicated the stairs.

The dining-room door opened.

Alice looked from her husband to Emma, who was halfway up the stairs.

'*Stop!*'

Emma paused mid-climb.

'Alice,' Thomas ventured, before a gloved hand was thrust a few inches from his face to prevent him speaking further.

'Are *you* the reason my husband is not where he should be?'

Thomas took a step forward. 'I thought you were on tour?'

'Evidently.'

A fire burned in the grate of the hallway, and its flickering flames did little to warm the icy atmosphere.

'I left a list of tasks when I was last home and I see they're not completed. You know I need to rest when I come home.'

Emma started to climb the stairs.

'Thomas? Are you listening to me?' Alice shouted.

He forced his focus back to his wife. 'Of course, dear. Let's talk in the dining room.'

'It's been such a bore rehearsing Cleopatra for the tour. But finally, I can bring you great news as I have landed the best gig. Honestly, I'm exhausted.' Alice went to the bottom of the staircase. 'This career will be the death of me. Have you time to do my shoulders?'

Clive moved forward but was stopped in his tracks. 'No, dear. My husband can sort me out this evening. Come up now, Thomas!'

Thomas felt Alice's finger in the small of his back as they passed Emma on the stairs. She closed their bedroom door with so much force, one of the small watercolours rattled against the wall.

Clive was next to overtake a stunned Emma. 'She's simply exhausted, don't mind her.'

Emma's curiosity won over. 'I don't think we've been introduced.'

'Clive. Alice's agent.' He held out a hand, leaning back down from his two-step height advantage and she immediately regretted agreeing to shake his clammy hand.

She followed at a respectful distance.

'Our next leg of the tour has been brought forward due to exciting news. She wanted to come back to organise the Coronation celebrations, you know, help to make sure Thomas has everything he needs here.'

In her room, Emma placed the brooch on the table then fetched a pot of ink and her pen from a shelf in the hope that continuing a letter home would calm the cloud of butterflies in her belly.

...Today Thomas drove me to the workhouse where Nana lived. It was derelict and in such a sorry state. But I have the best news ever. You'll never guess – we found the pillowcase. Nana's mother's shawl was still tucked away in the little shed, and best of all, the brooch was still there. I am going to get it cleaned at a watch repairer in the town here, and then send it home, where it belongs. With you.

I am praying you are well. Please give my love to Henry. I love you all and will be home...

Emma paused to look through the window at the activity on the quay.

...after the summer. The hotelier here is friends with one of the harbourmasters and they have confirmed I can delay the date of my return ticket. I have decided to stay another couple of months because the air here is doing me the world of good.

I shall soon be able to take the bandages off for good and am getting used to the scars.

Much love.

Em x

A few days later, Emma found Aoife in the hallway.

'Hello, Miss Emma. Excuse me if I don't stop.' The armful of tablecloths she carried were sliding out from her grasp, and she blew strands of hair off her face which had escaped its clip.

'Please let me help, Aoife. I've seen how you do the tables. Just show me where everything is.'

Aoife agreed and Emma, secretly thrilled to have something to do, followed her to the dining room. For ten minutes she folded napkins which she placed beneath cutlery and found herself humming along with the pleasant repetition of the task.

The front door opened and closed with its notorious bang before the dining room was filled with Alice's presence. Clive hovered behind her, half in half out the room.

'Ah, you're still here then?' Alice removed her gloves and slapped them against Clive's chest without looking at him.

'I am, yes.' Emma forced a smile she did not feel like wearing. 'And I'm staying a further month or more.'

'What on earth for?'

Emma checked the spacing between the cutlery and ignored the contempt which Alice had made no attempt to hide. 'I'm recuperating and am finding the town – and your hotel – very agreeable.'

'I've noticed the bandages. Had a rough time of it, have you?'

Clive pulled a chair out and Alice sat down, pushing the cutlery set for dinner roughly to one side. She glanced at Emma, a challenging look in her eyes. 'I've seen women like you, failing at life. Failing even at an attempt to *take* their own life.'

Emma tensed. 'What did you say?'

'Oh, don't act all innocent. You probably didn't slice deep enough. Anyway, what are *you* doing in here? Where's Aoife?'

'I'm here.' Aoife appeared from behind the bar.

'I offered this waif work when her mother told me no-one would give her a job because she's a thief.' Alice left a suitable pause to allow the announcement time to settle, then spoke in a quieter tone. 'But you're getting there, aren't you? And I don't think you'd consider stealing again, would you?'

'No, Ma'am.' Aoife clasped her hands together in front of her apron. 'Emma only offered, and I was busy in the kitchen, so I didn't think it would do any harm. I'm sorry.'

'Really, I was just helping for something to do. There's no need to be harsh with Aoife.'

'Are you now telling me how to run my business?' Alice stood up and in her heels was taller than Emma, and slimmer. In the past these differences would not have worried Emma in the slightest; she was used to beautiful women swanning around New York. But this particular contrast felt strangely unsettling. She took a step back.

'Of course not. I simply—'

'Well, don't simply anything. Leave my staff, *and* my husband, alone!' She turned to Aoife. 'Can you bring my usual nightcap to my room – the air down here is tainted.'

'Yes, of course.'

'And bring your notebook, Aoife. I want to make sure you have the new list before I go away tomorrow.'

Chapter Thirteen

The postmaster licked a considerable quantity of stamps, each printed with the face of the new king, and pressed them on the parcel destined for New York.

'This will take some time, Miss.'

'That's okay.' Emma smiled, then hesitated before leaving the post room.

'Anything else I can help you with?'

'Could you tell me, please, whether women have meetings in the town?'

He looked confused. 'Women?'

'I was thinking women who might meet to fight for the cause?'

'What cause?' Confusion had turned to suspicion.

'Women's right to vote?'

He rolled his eyes. 'There's none of that rubbish around here.'

She stiffened with indignation. 'I'm sorry you think equal rights is rubbish.'

He raised one eyebrow. 'Don't get me wrong, I support women wanting to work – my wife does Tuesday mornings here – but voting? That's a step too far.'

As the door opened and two young boys came in to beg

for sweets, Emma swallowed the words she'd been on the verge of hurling at him and instead told him that she would go and see Mrs O'Connor.

He nodded. 'You do that.'

'Ah, Emma! Just in time for my lemon cake, and Marj is back, so we've got plenty of milk.' Mary was bustling about in her lean-to, moving trays and clanging pots.

'Marj?'

'The blessed goat.'

'Ah.' Emma looked round for such a beast but could see no animal. 'Can I help?'

'Now then, how nice is that? You can slice the cake.'

Emma cut the cake into squares and arranged them onto the greaseproof paper Mary had laid on a tray. 'The spire's growing, I see.'

'It is that, yes.' Mary pushed the stopper back in the bottle of milk and paused. 'That's not what you came to talk about, though, is it?'

Emma glanced up, the knife paused. 'How can you tell?'

'My Harold's just the same, doesn't look me in the eye when he's nervous.'

'Well, you're right.' Emma grinned. 'I came to ask if you knew where women meet around here, women who want suffrage.'

Mary said nothing for a moment before sitting down. 'I know this sort of thing goes on in the big cities, but it will soon peter out.'

'Why do you say that?'

Mary looked at her sadly. 'A few women here and there with big ideas is one thing, but there are so many more men who will shut them up, shut them down. Why waste your energy fighting for something that you'll never win?'

Emma bit her tongue. She glanced up at a finished gargoyle. Was it any wonder the worldview would never change, with attitudes that were as old as the stone being shaped and carved on the cathedral walls? Perhaps the gargoyle mocked her modern views. A stonemason walked past, looked her up and down, then winked. She spun round to face Mary once more.

'You know, for someone as entrepreneurial as you, I'm disappointed.'

'Entre-what?' Mary said. 'I make cakes and pour tea, dear. Something I've done all my life, and something I'm good at.'

'All the more reason to run a business using your skill and earn money for yourself and Harold. Don't you want to be able to walk into a shop and buy a pair of shoes that might have caught your eye for days or weeks?'

Mary stood tall. 'I did alright with the housekeeping my husband gave me.'

'I'm sorry.'

'What are you sorry for?'

'I keep offending people when I talk about hopes for the future.'

'Well, maybe that's because these hopes are for *your* future and us old folk are happy with our own.'

'It's never too late to strive for change, for a better way to live, surely?'

'Hey, no tears in my shed. Now you sit down and eat one of those neatly cut squares, young lady.'

Crumbs rolled down her hand and onto the dry earth floor of the shed as Emma bit into the delicious sponge.

'The thing is, they'd think it unnecessary.' Mary smiled sadly. 'And I'm quite happy in me shed with the tilting roof.'

'Who's "they"?'

'Well, those men who run the town, and meet with the bishop monthly.' Mary licked her finger and retrieved her own crumbs from the cotton apron laying across her lap.

'But they'd have to listen, if you had a vote. That's the point.'

'I admire your enthusiasm. It's a little infectious to be honest. My Bert will have to watch it if I'm going to spend time with you!'

Emma took advantage of Mary's admission. 'In New York last month, thousands of women attended the biggest march yet. I had been going to attend, had I not… had I not come away. You would do me the greatest honour if you would stand by me now if I try and start a group here in Queenstown. Maybe it can be something you continue with once I've gone home?'

'Oh, I don't know. I mean, how would you go about it?' Mary's hand clutched her chest and shook her head. 'Oh, goodness, you'd be upsetting some folk and I don't know if I ought to be part of that.'

'It'll be fun, Mary! Why not help me raise interest? All the women selling fish on the quay have to wait for the men to have made *their* sales before they can set up at later in the morning. I'm sure they would fight for the right to sell early in the morning, alongside the men?'

'Oh, I don't know,' Mary repeated, torn, fanning her face with a tea cloth. 'Perhaps Harold should stay? Perhaps this American dream is overrated? After all, we've recovered from the famine just fine. Yes, he should find a nice local girl who wants a family.'

Emma's heart sank. Another loving mother with great intentions. 'But what if he wants a girl who wants more than a family?'

'He's an old-fashioned boy, my Harold.'

Emma persevered, 'Some women are trying for part-time work so they can enjoy some independence *and* still run a home.'

'I hope he doesn't end up with one of those actresses. I hear America is full of them.'

'Like Alice, you mean?'

'And how is our Thomas?' Mary returned to the sink to wash cups. 'She's a one.'

'A one? What do you mean?' Emma joined her and dried each cup as Mary placed them to drain.

'Well, always gallivanting about when she should be home here with her husband having babies.'

'I've heard she's quite a famous actress,' Emma said.

'Scarlet more like!' Mary's eyes widened, shocked at her outburst. She leaned forward and attempted to whisper, 'Forgive me, dear. I'm a little old-fashioned, I admit, but we've noticed she's away most of the year with that horrid little bald man, when she has a perfectly good husband at home. We don't know what's got into her.'

'We?'

'My friends. They come for tea here, to get away from their husbands, on Thursdays.'

Emma ignored the irony because her heart had skipped a beat. 'How many of you meet?'

Mary squeezed a dishcloth over the stones outside the shed. 'Usually eight or nine.' She pegged the cloth on a piece of string that ran from the corner of her shed to a gatepost leaning in the ground a few feet away.

Emma felt boosted by the possibilities unravelling before her, and even Alice's reputation couldn't dampen the moment. 'I think the acting profession is probably quite lucrative. With men running the film industry and acting dominated by men, I think it's good that women are being recognised as actors who deserve roles. In fact, it's necessary, wouldn't you say? I mean, if films are going to portray realistic stories?'

'Perhaps,' Mary conceded.

'I'd really like to start a Queenstown Suffrage group and I need a right-hand woman like you, Mary. We need to explain the opportunities that are out there for them.'

'You mean women trying to do men's jobs?'

'I mean fighting for the right to vote.'

Mary thought for a moment. 'You mean, if women did get to vote then even my ideas – and you're right, I do have some – might be taken seriously?'

'That's exactly what I mean. You could write a letter and have people sign it, like a list of supporters. Your government leaders would have to take you seriously because its success would affect the whole town, and when a large group speaks together, the message is far louder than one voice on its own.'

'I'll think about it.' Mary stood and organised a fresh tray. 'Help me get the bishop's tea tray ready. He'll be in shortly, and I can show you the mosaic floors which are nearly finished. Oh, the patience those boys needed to lay those pieces!'

Inside the cathedral, the air was cool. Their footsteps echoed, the sound fading away into the vaulted ceiling as high as the sky. Emma stared up into the wooden structure, an inverted rib cage of some enormous mammal. The arched supports flowed back down into stone pillars, each one decorated with the head of a different saint. Marble from Italy, oak from Austria. The construction was a mass European project which had begun forty years earlier. She was sad that her nana wouldn't have known it because building had started after she'd arrived in New York.

Masons worked on wooden platforms hammering tools which chinked at the stone, carving details of faces and clothing, a signature for future generations to admire. Other workers on their hands and knees laid tiny mosaic squares into patterns resembling climbers and vines, tiny purple tiles placed together depicting intricate bunches of grapes. Emma had never seen anything so clever.

'They're so talented,' she whispered.

'Aren't they just? My Harold, he helped with the side doors only last year.' Mary beamed, then leaned in close. 'And you see young Mark up there?'

Silhouetted against a stained-glass window, high on another wooden platform, worked a solitary figure.

'He's painting the details, like the shading, direct on to the glass pieces.'

Emma shook her head in wonder.

'When I tell you he was thrown out the army a few months ago, then slept rough for weeks, you wouldn't believe me, would you? He spent a few weeks going to the Soldiers' Home daily and his anger soon left him. He came up to the cathedral sometimes to help out and was soon offered an apprenticeship with a stained-glass artist from Cork.'

'That's amazing.'

They left the tray of refreshments on a table for the bishop, who was engaged in a meeting, then spent time admiring other ongoing work before stepping back outside.

High on the hill, the wind pulled at their coats. They linked arms and walked along the side of the cathedral that faced the sea.

'You're a real people's person, Mary.'

'Am I?'

'Yes, you are. You want to make a difference to people's lives, but you're loyal to your beliefs. I just need to show you that you could believe in better.'

Chapter Fourteen

It was the end of May when Emma opened her bedroom door and almost tripped over a copy of the *Irish Independent* that had been left on the carpet. She recognised Thomas's writing above the headline. *I thought page five would be of interest.*

Emma took it down to read in the garden behind the hotel. She poured herself a cup of coffee from the dining room on her way through, then settled herself on an old bench, the sounds of the harbour muffled by the hotel garden's high walls. Two fruit trees had made the best of a sunny patch next to the brickwork, their gnarled trunks and forgotten branches providing a stage for chattering songbirds.

The sun felt warm on Emma's face and she lay the newspaper out on the rickety table. She rolled up the sleeves of her blouse to give her wrists another opportunity in the open air, something she would never do in company. She was touched that Thomas had guessed she'd want to read about the New York march. She had shared more than once how sorry she was to have missed it, how special it would have been to march in Martina's honour.

'Oh, I'm sorry, I didn't mean to disturb you.' The voice was Aoife's.

'You didn't, not really. I'm reading about the big march back home earlier this month, look…' Immediately Emma realised her error. 'Sorry, I'll read it to you if you like. Do you have time?'

'I've come out to collect logs, but Thomas won't mind if I'm a few minutes. He always says, as long as the jobs are done he doesn't mind how I manage my day.'

'So, it's Alice who's tougher on you?'

'She's kind in her own way. She's been good to me.' Aoife sat on another chair. 'I'd love to hear the piece in the paper.'

The article appeared in the middle pages, reproduced from the *Harper's Weekly* report, and Emma cleared her throat before beginning, '"*Marching on to Suffrage*", there's a photograph showing the front rows of the congregation. And the report says, "*The women marched against the wishes of so many while banners hung from buildings along the five-mile route. There was a musical accompaniment, including Scottish bagpipes, which turned the event into a vibrant festival as the slow-moving crowd walked from 57th Street to Union Square. Even the Men's League had two hundred members marching at the rear of the procession who received huge applause and cheers when they arrived in Union Square. The youngest attendee was just a year old in a perambulator, and the eldest, a great-grandmother of ninety-one.*"'

'That's so many people in one place.' Aoife stood, her eyes wide.

Emma smiled and closed the paper. 'And there were some men who supported them. I find that even more surprising.'

'In a good way, though.'

'Completely good. More than good.' Emma smiled. 'I'm beginning to wonder if not all men are as barbaric as those I've met in my short life.'

Aoife giggled and moved towards the woodpile. 'John the butcher. He's alright, always laughing and giving out extra bits if he can. And then, of course, there's Thomas here. I don't think he's barbaric.'

The sun moved a little in the sky and Emma's coffee cooled.

'My friend, Martina, would have been right near the front.' Emma concluded and watched a millipede pause its progress across the table's cliff edge. 'She's the reason I became involved with the Women's League. I know my parents think that while I'm here, I'll forget about it, but I can't. I won't.'

'Will you find a group to join?'

'I don't know, I'm thinking of creating one of my own, here in the town.' She gave the millipede a helping hand and flicked it onto the grass. 'Why don't you join up with me?'

'What would we do?'

'We'd count.'

'Count?'

'They need numbers, Aoife. The more women join, the louder the message and the more effective the effort will become,' she said, and pointed to another report from Liverpool, England, where suffragettes had put small explosive devices into post boxes on street corners. 'The English suffragettes are doing things differently while in New York we are still only marching and holding a few speeches.'

'What's the difference?'

'The difference is no-one responds to words alone. Women have been speaking up about wanting to vote for a very long time, but governments in lots of countries don't want to change the old ways.'

Aoife leaned in to look more closely. 'Is that a prison cell?'

'Yes, she's been arrested.' The grainy black and white photo showed a woman gripping bars with both hands, sneering defiantly at the photographer. 'I think she broke some windows of a government building and has been issued now with a public disorder offence.'

'She doesn't look like she's worried,' Aoife said.

'She's not. It's probably what she set out to achieve that day, because the publicity in the papers reaches more people because the papers get sent all over the world. So, you see, the message is spreading. I mean, look what this says: this woman was arrested last Thursday and we already know about it, only four days later!'

Aoife sighed, walked over to the woodpile and started to fill a basket. As she bent down, folded paper fell from her pocket. Emma watched as Aoife hurriedly pushed it back into the folds of her skirt. After a beat, Aoife continued, 'What would the benefits actually be, though? If we won the vote, I mean?'

'You'd have a say in things, your working life, for a start.'

'Are we trying to take over from men?'

'Not so much take over. Most women I've spoken to simply want to work alongside men – good men – and be respected and treated like equals. Many want to be mothers, too, and have the chance to work a day here and there after they've had their children.'

Aoife thought for a moment. 'Or perhaps if they want to work longer hours, or get better jobs?'

'Exactly! It's so exciting, Aoife, I feel we are living on the cusp of a revolution.'

Aoife lifted the basket onto her hip. 'You make it sound like war.'

'It is war. Women against old-fashioned rules written by men.' Emma turned her face up to the sun. 'I want my time here to mean something. Something other than just getting better. So I'm thinking a group here in Queenstown is perfect. Will you help me recruit members?'

Aoife's eyes widened. 'I don't want to get arrested, but I'd like to help you.'

Emma shielded her eyes from the sun. 'Don't worry, you don't have to do anything you don't feel comfortable doing. I'm going to start looking for somewhere we can hold meetings. All I'm asking is for your help to try and change the views of the women you know around the town. Show them there's a different way to the only one they think they know.'

'Imagine the women of Queenstown, marching and speaking up in public.' Aoife giggled. 'Actually, maybe this could be fun.'

Emma nodded. 'The town's very name reflects a woman who had to survive in a man's world. She reigned for over sixty years, Aoife. Her son, Edward, did ten and this year, George will be crowned at the age of forty-six, so he won't beat his grandma. I tell you, Victoria set a record that will never be broken. What better icon do we have?'

Aoife went inside leaving Emma to read through the rest of the paper. There was a double-page spread about the Royal visit to Dublin planned for July. The people of Ireland were separating into those who no longer wanted to be under English rule and those loyalists who still stood for the Monarchy and being part of a United Kingdom. Emma hoped the divide would not affect the female population's desire to win the vote, irrespective of their political standing.

Later that afternoon, Emma arrived at the Soldiers' Home, where she had started to spend a couple of afternoons a week with the soldiers, some of whom seemed so quiet she couldn't actually believe they had it in them to fight. She took off her hat and placed the pin in the felt for safety. Michael, who she had seen the previous week, was sitting by the window.

'Shall I read to you?'

Emma selected an armful of books from the shelf in what Mary called the reading room. She laid them out across the table for the young seaman to choose. He'd said nothing since his arrival a few minutes earlier and looked young enough to still be in school.

'Michael, isn't it?' Emma ventured gently.

He stared at the books for a moment.

Emma waited.

His finger pressed down on a blue hardback cover which he pushed slowly away to the other side of the table. Then he placed the same finger on the next book and did the same. He continued until all of the books she'd offered lined the opposite edge of the table.

Mary had told her what to expect with this one so Emma pulled the botanical guide back towards them and sat down next to him.

'I thought it would be nice to look through the illustrations in this and you can tell me if you recognise any from your home in England.'

She turned the pages and wished there were English names printed alongside those in Latin.

Michael was not looking anyway. 'No good.'

Emma was shocked momentarily to hear him speak. 'What's no good, Michael?'

'No good.'

'Oh, look, here's some roses. Did you have roses in your garden at home?'

'No good!' he shouted, and banged the table with his fists, making Emma jump.

Emma closed the book, her heart racing. The door was open and she could hear Mary in the next room.

'What's this one?' she said, and pulled a different book back from the edge. 'Oh, look. It's poetry.'

She moved to the window and sat on a large box – placed there to deter anyone from leaning out – and began to read aloud.

Michael stayed silent and the whites of his knuckles turned pink as he released his fists and the tension drained away. The chinking of crockery in the next room provided homely background noises to Emma's reading.

Neither of them had heard of the poet, an Australian called Henry Kendall, but his lines transported them to the outback, a place neither of them were ever likely to go.

When the poem came to an end, Emma ran her fingers

across the words written nearly a hundred years before and marvelled at the visions they evoked. She almost forgot Michael was in the room as she turned the pages and read on.

'My mother had yellow roses.'

Emma looked up from the pages. 'She did?'

Michael nodded. 'In a big round flowerbed in the middle of the grass.'

'That's nice.'

'I helped my father dig that bed. I was nine.'

Emma smiled and willed him to continue.

'I was fourteen when he died, and sixteen when Mother died.'

'Oh, Michael. I'm so sorry.' She put the book of poems down quietly on the table and poured them each a cup of tea from a pot on the sideboard. She made sure it was cooled with enough milk, in case he spilt it.

'The day after she was buried, my uncle took me to enlist in the army.'

No wonder the boy didn't know whether he was coming or going. He'd had no time to grieve. She'd spent four years grieving for her brother and she still didn't feel she was over the loss of him. Perhaps that feeling would never come.

'There now.' Mary arrived in the doorway, bringing with her an abundance of energy and smiles. 'How're we doing?'

'I'm learning all about his mother's rose-bed back home in England.'

'Oh, I do love a rose.'

Michael yawned. 'Sorry.'

'When did you last sleep, young man?' Mary bustled about him without making eye contact. 'I've prepared the bed in room number seven for you. Go and take yourself off for an hour and put your head down.'

Michael stood and looked at Emma. 'May I take the poetry book with me?'

'Of course,' Emma replied.

She gave it to him and he thanked her. 'My mother was Australian. Father had met her while he'd been in the navy. He brought her back to England and she said she'd never known roses at home, so we gave her the flowerbed.'

'That's a lovely memory, Michael.' Mary touched his arm.

'It's been okay.' He nodded, looking at the floor. 'To remember them today. Thank you.'

Emma leant against the window and listened to their voices as they retreated down the corridor. Some of the men slept like logs when they visited the Home, unable to sleep undisturbed in the shared dormitories at the barracks.

Mary came back. 'You've done well with him, today, Emma. I've not seen him that relaxed for weeks.'

'I can't begin to imagine what he's gone through, being made to join the army so quickly after the death of his surviving parent.'

'I know. It's tough, but what we can do is give him hope. For a brighter future. He's a good sailor. The nightmares stop him sleeping regular and the deprivation leads to exhaustion. Then he can't see the woods for the trees. We have lots like that, come in once a week for an afternoon and they often sleep for much of it.'

Emma sighed. 'Is reading to them really any help at all?'

'A huge help.' Mary assured her and tidied away the teacups. 'Being here is like a home from home. Just a few hours with a change of scene. Back on barracks, there's no-one to talk to if they're feeling low. Just the expectation they'll deliver and go on delivering.'

'I hate the army,' Emma said flatly.

'No, you don't,' Mary said. 'What you hate is what's missing from it.'

Emma looked up at her. 'What do you mean?'

'The scope for men to talk openly about their feelings. They should have someone, alongside them at all times. I don't know, a comrade in uniform, who trains with them, fights alongside them but whose main job it is to be there for them. My wish is for every regiment to have someone like that.'

'Specially trained to understand the mind, you mean?'

'Yes. Exactly that,' Mary agreed. 'Of course, it'll never happen.'

'What they need is someone like you, Mary.' Emma smiled and added her cup to the tray.

'Women in the army? That'll be the day!' Mary giggled. 'Come on, let's see if Frank and Bennie are here yet. They always arrive together. I think they only come for my biscuits.'

Chapter Fifteen

Flags hung lifeless in the heat, strung from lamp posts along the streets of Cork, the Coronation only a few days away. The temperature had been rising steadily for days and it hadn't rained for five weeks.

'Clive has secured Alice an audience at Dublin Castle during the King's visit.'

'You must be very proud, Thomas,' Emma said.

Aoife had begged that they take Emma with them to the city for the weekly supplies and now Aoife was lagging behind, peering into shop windows along the riverbank.

'It's the life Alice wants.'

They crossed a bridge over the river. Skippers on the barges were shouting at each other, tempers flaring in the heat. A tangle of vessels jostled for space along the docks.

'You'll go to watch her, of course?'

'I don't know... perhaps.'

This wasn't a subject he wanted to discuss. Emma did not need to worry about the details of his marriage. It was hardly conventional, he knew that, but the routine they'd fallen into meant the future of the hotel was safe. He'd be forever grateful for the gesture Alice's father had made all those years ago. It had made his mother's final weeks bearable, and he'd always put others before himself.

They separated briefly to allow a group of shrieking small boys to run between them, ducking and diving, whooping with joy and waving little flags on wooden sticks. A man in a brown knee-length coat ran after them, hollering, his delivery cart abandoned outside a shop.

Aoife caught up, then ran ahead and disappeared in through a doorway to a store selling a variety of different teas.

Emma and Thomas waited outside.

'Sorry, it's none of my business,' she said quietly.

'I don't mind the question, Emma. Alice's career is important to her and I've always supported it.'

'But she's so…'

He waited for her to finish. Light reflected off her chin from ripples on the river's surface. 'She's so… what?'

Emma shook her head and looked away.

'I don't think you should worry about Alice,' he said. 'Or me.'

Aoife re-appeared with a paper bag and untwisted the paper to show Emma the contents. 'Lemon sherbets.'

'Lemon what?' Emma peered in and studied the boiled sweets the colour of daffodils.

'Go on, try one!'

Emma popped one on her tongue and Aoife watched intently.

'Mmmm.'

They fell silent for a few moments as the sweets were passed round and enjoyed.

'Is there time for me to go and find King Street?' Emma asked. 'I'd like to visit the Soldiers' Home headquarters.'

'You want me to come with you?' Aoife asked.

'No, you carry on collecting what you need. Shall I meet you back in the Square at the car?'

Aoife looked to Thomas for confirmation. 'That should give us time to get to the butchers and bakers.'

Thomas gave Aoife a list for the bakers; he went in a different direction. He waited to cross the street while a city tram made steady progress, its wheels scraping against curves of old tracks embedded into the road surface.

Perhaps he should not have allowed the conversation to escalate the evening before. It had started with Emma's statement – *She leaves you lists of things to complete as if you were the staff, as if she doesn't trust you to carry out the tasks without her instructions* – which had thrown him, and which he was struggling to shake off today. They'd found themselves alone in the dining room and he'd poured them both a brandy. Aoife had gone home and the guests were all in their rooms. He'd gone on to explain he was happy with his own company, and that with Aoife's help they had a lovely hotel in a busy town with plenty of customers, so what more was there? But Emma hadn't dropped it. *But you have no time for yourself.*

When an hour had passed, Thomas gave the car keys to Aoife and walked to King Street. Emma was in a city she didn't know and there was a knot in his stomach, a feeling of unease. Perhaps he should have insisted Aoife go with her. But it wasn't long before he saw her running towards him, an arm waving to catch his attention. Relief washed through him.

'Sorry! Sorry! I've been learning all about it.' Breathless, Emma fell into step. 'You weren't worried, were you?'

'No, no.'

'Oh, it's amazing, these Sandes Homes. Mrs Sandes, it's all her doing, do you know her?'

'Not personally.' He was happy to listen, her excitement infectious.

'She's set Homes up all over Ireland for soldiers and sailors. Why doesn't America have something like this?'

Thomas couldn't expect her to stay indefinitely, however much the notion appealed. He enjoyed her company. That was all it was. She was still talking ten to the dozen.

'...another genius woman who has made a difference to the lives of so many. If you start looking, there are lots of great females who have done amazing things over the years.'

'So you're going to volunteer regularly?'

'If I've time. If it fits in with my other plans. I know John would want me to.'

Something shifted in his belly. 'Other plans?'

'I think the port needs a suffragette group.'

He despised himself for feeling euphoric at the thought her plans might keep her in Ireland for longer.

'I just need to find somewhere for us to meet regularly.' She looked at him, expecting him to say something.

'Interesting.'

'Cat got your tongue? The women of Queenstown, Thomas, fighting for the vote. Just think!'

A well-dressed lady of mature age approached them on the path. 'Thomas, dear boy! How are you?'

He took off his bowler hat and inclined his head. 'Good morning, Mrs Walsh. I'm well, thank you, and yourself?'

'Yes, we're all in good working order.' The woman tapped her cane against her leg. 'Even the old knee isn't playing up now it's warmed up. Now, who's this charming creature?'

'May I introduce one of our guests, Emma Quinn. She's over from New York for a few weeks.'

'Oh, how wonderful. I hope Thomas is looking after you well, Emma?' Mrs Walsh asked, then turned back to Thomas. 'And Alice? She's to perform in Dublin, I hear?'

'Indeed she is,' Thomas replied. 'And your husband, he's well?'

Three policemen running along the cobbles in pursuit of two men interrupted the exchange. Whistles were blown and crowds scattered. The two men were caught and wrestled to the ground.

Mrs Walsh tutted. 'More nationalists, I shouldn't wonder. Honestly, they need to be stopped or they will ruin the mood of this visit. The King should be shown respect.' She tapped her walking cane against the ground and addressed Emma. 'I know what Thomas's thoughts are, but what do people in America think of it all?'

'I can only speak for myself, but I adore the Royal family. We have nothing to compare to their ceremonies and history.'

'I love them too.' Mrs Walsh beamed. 'But I tell you one thing, if we could have a slice of their wealth injected into politics… oooh, just imagine!'

'You're involved in politics, Mrs Walsh?'

'My husband is mayor of this town, and behind closed doors we talk about everything on his agenda. I'm sure he finds me a burden on occasion' – she winked at them both – 'what with the suffrage group I help run and our recent boycott of the census, but he's a supporter beneath the exterior.'

Thomas noticed Emma's wide, unblinking eyes, fixated on Mrs Walsh's every word.

'I heard about the boycott, from Aoife.'

'We'd been planning it for months, including the slogan "*No Vote; No Count*".' Mrs Walsh put her hand on her hip. 'Until we have the vote, why the hell should we be counted? A resounding success, I'd say, that hundreds of names were not included on the forms this year.'

'Where were you, the night of the count?' Emma asked.

Thomas worried that Emma's personal question, brought about by enthusiasm, might offend Mrs Walsh.

The older woman's eyes sparkled with mischief. 'I went to the park. My husband was mortified, but he knew I'd planned to be out.'

They talked a bit longer until Thomas checked his pocket watch and said they needed to get back to Aoife. 'Do please come and visit the hotel, any time you like.'

'We will, my boy. I very much enjoyed the sea air last time. Oh, and don't forget the club. Robert's told me you've not been for a long time.' Mrs Walsh wagged a finger in his face.

'I saw Patrick a few days ago.'

'Ah, so you'll know we are low on numbers.' Mrs Walsh gathered herself before departing. 'No excuses, Thomas. Make time for it.'

As they drove back to Queenstown, Emma watched the landscape. She had sat in the back, leaving the passenger seat for Aoife. Her thoughts were alive with Elise Sandes and now, Mrs Walsh. Both leaving their mark on society and her conscience. Before the fire, Emma had known very little other than what she'd learned from her parents. But now, for the first time in her life, she'd begun to realise there was a whole world of thoughts and differing opinions on all manner of subjects. She found the prospect liberating and exciting.

The education she'd received in Manhattan until she was fourteen had leant towards old-fashioned habits. Sewing classes for girls, while boys were taught to read and write. Girls learned basic cookery for when they started caring for their husbands. The pattern of women serving men was horrifyingly evident.

After a few miles in silence, Emma took a deep breath and borrowed some courage from the women she'd been thinking about. She moved forward and rested her arms on top of the bench seat.

'So tell me more about Mr and Mrs Walsh, Thomas.'

Aoife turned and spoke first. 'They came to stay for a night last spring, didn't they?'

'They did.'

'She's nice. I really like her,' Emma said, hoping the awkwardness of earlier had passed.

Thomas agreed, 'She reminds me of my mother. Tough but kind.'

Aoife twisted round the face Emma. 'Maybe we could write to Mrs Walsh and offer our services for the cause?'

'Aoife, I was thinking the same thing.'

And just like that, the atmosphere in the car returned to what she'd come to love when the three of them were together. Chats such as they'd had last night would have to be avoided. Alice was Thomas's business and nothing good could come of Emma pointing out his wife's faults. Even if Thomas was blind to them.

'What did Mrs Walsh mean when she mentioned "*the club*"?'

'She and her husband are the patrons of a rowing club here on the River Lee. I made the mistake of telling them I had rowed there in my younger days, and they keep asking me to re-join.'

'When did you last row?' Emma tried not to visualise Thomas in scant clothing, his arms and shoulders working to propel the long, thin boats through water.

'Before I was married.'

'Alice not keen?' Emma bit her lip, the words had slipped out and she hoped there'd been no note of sarcasm.

'She hates the water.'

'No, she doesn't,' Aoife countered. 'She's looking forward to going to America one day, Hollywood or something. Says she can't wait to sail on one of those luxury passenger liners.'

'Really, she said that?' Thomas asked.

Aoife's cheeks turned the colour of Alice's lipstick. 'Just something she said last time she was home. She's hoping one day to act in silent movies.'

Thomas's jaw twitched. The lanes lead them back to Queenstown, and as they reached the top of the hill, the sea came into view. The sight never failed to impress. Emma sat back in her seat as they descended the hill. She looked through the window to her left at the outline of the cathedral, against the sky, reliable and confident, quiet and reassuring. She wondered if people could be the same, or whether their personalities meant you never quite knew what they were thinking.

Chapter Sixteen

The sun shone for the King's Coronation.

Thomas was putting finishing touches to the table settings for lunch when Aoife came rushing through from the kitchen, breathless. 'Mr Thomas, Chef has had an idea, and it's a really good idea.'

'Tell me,' he invited, and continued to place cutlery on the tablecloths.

'He'd like to carve the beef outside, in the garden, the centre piece of a picnic. They can eat it cold, with salads, which I can make. We think it's too hot inside, and we've only the three couples staying.' She barely paused for breath. 'You said you wanted to use the garden more?'

Emma was reading the telegram from her father, which had arrived that morning. It informed her he was happy to pay for her to stay longer. She'd been trying to decide whether to feel offended that he didn't want her home or delighted that she'd be able to continue with her voluntary work. She elected to go for the latter and finished her second cup of tea. 'Oh, go on, Thomas. It sounds fun.'

'Alright then.' Thomas looked at the settings he'd spent the last few minutes perfecting. 'If you're sure we can take everything we need outside. What about tables?'

'We don't need tables. It's all the rage to stand around with a plate and pick,' Aoife said.

'Pick?' Thomas didn't look convinced, but Aoife persevered, describing how she'd already worked it all out with Chef.

Thomas watched her return to the kitchen, then turned to Emma. 'So, you're staying around to listen to the Coronation?'

'I'd love to,' she said. 'Alice not about?'

'Ah, I forgot to update you.' He felt more relaxed than he had in days. 'She sent a telegram yesterday. She's celebrating in London with friends and travelling direct to Dublin next week for her reception with the King.'

'I see.'

Thomas stood at the window, staring out to sea. 'She's invited me to travel to meet her in Dublin.'

'That'll be nice.'

He turned back to Emma. 'I'm still thinking about whether to go. But right now, I'm intrigued as to Aoife and Chef's plan for this buffet lunch in the garden.'

Emma followed him through to the drawing room. Thomas lifted a green velvet cloth from a small sideboard against the wall, revealing its true identity – a wireless, bought by Victor some years earlier.

Guests were invited to gather round to listen to the commentary from Westminster Abbey. In clipped English tones, the reporter narrated the scene. *'The King has walked through the entrance now, into the Abbey, wearing his crown, and the crowds outside are barely able to contain themselves. It's a sight to behold.'*

Emma fanned air against her face with the suffragette leaflet she'd designed and had printed. The sluggish air which entered through the open window was no cooler than the air it met inside. The scientists were calling it a heatwave and it was getting worse. Emma wondered if the King was hot in his robes. Thomas knocked out his pipe against the side of the fireplace. She'd come to love the smell of his pipe, more than the cigars guests smoked after dinner.

The buffet was a success, and the makeshift canopy Thomas erected from the back wall of the hotel to the higher branches of the apple tree provided welcome relief from the sun. During the afternoon, Emma dried dishes in the kitchen while Aoife washed pots at the sink. Thomas let the kitchen staff have the evening off once their work was done, to go and celebrate with locals in the harbour.

Emma found him in his office.

'Here you are.'

'Guilty.' He sat back in his chair, small grey swirls of smoke obscuring his face for a moment.

'A good day.' Emma sat down in the chair before noticing the painting and getting up again. 'I didn't know you'd started another painting?'

'Just checking to see if the tubes had dried out.'

'I can see already it's the back garden, with the little chair and table I like to sit at. It's good, Thomas. Really good!'

'If you say so.'

She sat back down, sighed and looked at him. She'd noticed he'd seemed happy this morning.

'Thank you,' he said.

'Whatever for?'

'For helping out here so much, when your days are full of your volunteer work.'

There was a faint note of whiskey in the air.

'That's alright, Mary had the Home covered but didn't expect many visitors today. The outside celebrations would have drawn the soldiers for sure, their readings and prayers forgotten for a day.'

Thomas nodded. 'How long do you think you'll stay?'

The unrelated question caught Emma on the hop. She was enjoying her routine, her return date had no limit and she hadn't thought about it for days. 'I don't know.'

Thomas pointed to a front-page article. He turned the paper round and held it up so she could see the grainy black and white photograph. 'If you'd wanted to travel back to America in style, you could have sailed on this new ship which left Liverpool last month. It's so fast, the crossing only took six days.'

'Six days? You're joking, let me see that.' The White Star vessel with its four huge funnels certainly looked impressive, and Emma repeated the name beneath the photograph, '*Olympic*. I suppose it's the future. Bigger boats, bigger cars. There's even talk of people flying in passenger aeroplanes soon.'

'Give me a boat any day, even a small one.' Thomas chuckled. 'I know what I'm doing with oars.'

She laughed with him and then Thomas put the paper to one side.

'Am I in the way?' She didn't know where the question had come from. She certainly hadn't planned it. The heat made her uncomfortable and she wriggled in her seat to disperse the itching her clothing was delivering.

'No, you're not. Far from it. I think you're becoming a valuable member of the community.' He smiled and leaned forward on his elbows. 'And I wanted to ask whether Mrs Walsh has replied to your letter yet?'

'She has. There's a big suffrage committee in Cork who meet above a tea shop. She's invited me to attend their next meeting and was delighted by my suggestion that I start a group in Queenstown.'

'And you're quite sure you want to get involved? It could delay your return home.'

Having said she wasn't in the way, why would he make it sound like he wanted to get rid of her? 'You know how important this is to me. I feel stronger here. I want to do this thing and go home having achieved something.'

He appeared to consider his response for some time. 'There are a great many men based in the harbour who may not like it, and who could make trouble for you.'

'Like who?'

'Most of the husbands of the women you'd be enlisting, for a start.'

'That's the whole point, Thomas.' Emma struggled to contain her irritation. He didn't deserve a raised voice in his office, but she couldn't help it. One minute in full support, the next apparently wanting to write the whole thing off as a waste of time. 'It's that very prejudice we have to stand against, don't you see? Nothing will change until they question the very men who don't want them to have their say.'

Thomas held up his hands in mock defeat. 'I'm not trying to stop you, Emma. I simply think you should be aware of possible consequences.'

'Well, let me worry about that, will you?' She stood, pushed her chair away from the desk, knocking over a glass of water. 'Just because you take the easy path in life, doesn't mean we all have to.'

'What's that supposed to mean?'

She leaned on the desk, fury driving her mood. 'Never standing up for yourself, letting your wife walk all over you.'

He glared back at her. 'You'd do best to keep your nose out of other people's business.'

She covered her face with her hands, horrified she'd been shouting, and started to gasp.

'Sit down a minute,' Thomas said, before wiping the spill on the desk.

'I'm sorry,' she said. 'I had no right.'

He made no attempt to argue but nodded slowly and then, as if he'd reached a decision, 'I do know how important this is to you, and I will back you all I can. God, you can even use the dining room for meetings if you want.'

'Really?'

'I've never met a woman like you, Emma. You're a risk-taker... it's true, don't shake your head at me. You wouldn't be here today if you hadn't been willing to take an enormous risk.' He paused. 'There are things about me you don't understand, but I do support the suffrage movement.'

'It was rude of me to shout, though, inexcusable.' She stared up to the ceiling. 'It wasn't ladylike.'

Thomas flapped his hand, as if the matter was already forgotten. 'You see, Emma, I have a problem. I seem to be riddled with a need to protect you. It's ridiculous, I know, and definitely inappropriate, but there's something about you that I've never seen in another woman, and certainly not my wife. I'm not saying you're vulnerable. You ooze self-confidence and I know you could hold your own in any debate.'

'But?'

'There's something else.' He looked at her. 'Something missing. A supporting role, a soulmate. I suppose your friend Martina was that for you.'

Emma rolled a crumb across the leather desktop. Perhaps Thomas had eaten a piece of toast late last night. 'She was my best friend, but I'd not known her long. My soulmate was someone even more important.'

'Your brother.'

She nodded and silence filled the room.

Eventually Thomas changed the subject. 'You don't seem to think about your wrists much these days.'

He was right, but now he'd brought them to her attention, she slid her hands back onto her lap.

'Sorry,' he mumbled.

'Don't be.' She breathed in deeply. 'It's true. I don't think about them as much, and I also don't find them quite so revolting to look at.'

She turned her hand over and stared at the purple line which ran from the base of her thumb and disappeared beneath her sleeve but which travelled diagonally towards her elbow. The stitch scars were neat purple dots, like the splashes created by oars either side of a rowing boat viewed by the birds which flew over the river. She ran her index finger along her skin, imagining Thomas laughing with his friends and having fun.

'How's the other one?' Thomas asked.

'Ugly.' Twisted skin stretched across the whole of her left wrist. Recently, she'd been allowing herself more time without a bandage but only when in the hotel.

'Hey, hey, what's wrong?' Thomas reached his own hand across the table, leaving his empty palm facing up to the ceiling.

'It's nothing.' She wiped away a tear. 'I'm being silly.'

'Emma, talk to me.'

She shook her head.

'How can I begin to help if you won't share what's troubling you?'

How could she say out loud what had been worrying her for weeks? She looked at his hand still resting on the desk.

He waited.

Her heart beat a little faster.

'I'm worried any children I have in the future will be scared of my scars, and therefore scared of me.' There. She'd said it.

'Whoah, slow down. You didn't mention being worried about a man being scared by them.'

'Oh, I'm not.' She straightened in the seat. 'I will marry a man because he loves me for my mind and my heart, not what I look like.' Men she could cope with. It was the thought of a young child, who would rely on her for support and safety, growing up and noticing the scars for the first time, and then being repulsed, which had caused her sleepless nights.

'Any children you have will think the scars are just part of you, and won't judge you.'

'You don't know that.'

119

He said nothing for a moment, and then, 'My mother had a terrible scar which crossed her cheek from her ear to the corner of her mouth which she'd acquired while I was baby. When I was old enough to realise she looked different from my friends' mothers, I saw only the love she had for me.'

'Oh, Thomas.'

'It intrigued me at first, like she might have been some sort of adventurous pirate. But later, when she told me why my father was no longer around, I understood. I understood her nightmares, her fear of other people, especially men. I understood her need to teach me to put others' feelings before my own. She'd only known selfish men, you see.'

Emma stared, her heart pounding.

'I was seven when I learnt what my father inflicted on her, and the scar only made her more special in my eyes. He had wanted to put the knife into my sleeping body, to remove the thing which took her attention away from him. She was prepared to sacrifice herself that day she moved, guarding me from his rage and his knife.'

'Oh, that's horrible.'

'She was a survivor and I vowed to always protect her until the day she died. And protect her, I did.'

'Thomas. I don't know what to say.'

'You don't have to say a word. But promise me one thing.'

'What's that?' she whispered, as she located something to wipe her tears.

'Don't settle for a husband who is anything less than kind.'

She looked at him, fresh tears sliding down her cheeks. 'I promise.'

Chapter Seventeen

The newspapers in July were declaring the heatwave now affected the whole of the northern hemisphere. North America had been hit hardest, '*158 People and 600 Horses Dead*'.

'I should be at home,' Emma cried. 'What if it's a punishment for my staying?'

'This can't be blamed on anything other than science,' Thomas said, turning the page.

'I can't leave Mom to cope with everything on her own, I should be there.' She gripped his arm, eyes wide with fear. 'She doesn't do well in the heat.'

'I'm sure she'll be fine; she sounds a tough one, your mother.'

He opened the window which made no difference, their clothes sticking to their limbs.

The harbour was quiet. Fish sellers packed away by nine each morning, before the sun baked the little silver bodies in their wicker coffins.

'Shall I see if I can get you on a ship departing this week?'

She nodded. 'Please.'

Was he really about to send home the best thing that had happened to him in years?

'Thank you,' she whispered.

He nodded and hoped she couldn't detect the sadness he knew he had no right to feel.

It was the letter from America, arriving later that morning, which released Thomas from needing to book the ticket.

Aoife had taken the letter up to Emma's room and returned an hour later when she was worried she'd not come down. She'd crept in and found the tear-streaked letter had fallen to the carpet.

'Mom thinks I should stay. To do it for Nana. That my being here – she actually wrote the word *adventure* – is a once-in-a-lifetime opportunity. I've never known Mom to think like this.' Emma wiped her face and sighed. 'She even said she was proud of me, and that I should finish what I've started, and that I'm a role model for Henry, where poor John could no longer be.'

'Wow.'

'Exactly.' Emma turned back round. 'I don't know what's happened to her.'

For days, the heatwave continued to grip the country. The decision to stay had left her torn. She yearned for home, to curl up with her young brother and read him a book. But each time she read the words from her mother, she felt a little stronger. To know her mother was proud gave Emma a renewed sense of purpose.

If she left now, she would be turning her back on the men at the Soldiers' Home who had come to enjoy her readings. There was no doubt being with them had eased, just a little, the guilt she carried about not helping John. Then there was the Queenstown suffrage group which was garnering more interest than she'd at first dared to hope.

Aoife stepped out from the hotel's back door into the garden. On her tray was a jug of iced water, a glass and a currant bun, knife and butter.

'You read my mind,' Emma told her gratefully.

'You're in the best place, out here. It's stifling inside.' She put the jug on a table. The tree's branches, laden with fruit punctured by wasps, provided a mottled tent big enough to offer some shade.

Aoife batted one away. 'I see Thomas's Samhain bonfire is growing.'

'Samhain?'

She nodded to a pile of old crates at the back of the garden. 'We're going to have a gathering at the end of October. Mother says you'll be calling it Halloween in America.'

Emma's mouth fell open. 'Yes! We New Yorkers have been celebrating Halloween for a few years. It's crazy but fun.'

Aoife twisted an apple from a branch, one the wasps had yet to start devouring. 'Mother says you got it from us originally. From when the immigrants travelled there. The festival is an ancient one.'

Emma sat back. 'I didn't know that.'

Aoife continued, 'It's to mark the end of the summer and the start of the dark season apparently. The townsfolk have really scary masks. You wait and see.'

'We've got a lot to thank you guys for, all in all.' Emma laughed and poured herself some water. The ice chinked against the glass.

'There's apple bobbing and nut roasting and games like the peel which tells you the name of your future love.'

'How does that work?'

'You take the peel off in one long strip… I'll show you.' She picked up the knife from the tray and carefully worked the apple round in her hands until a length of red peel hung down in front of her. 'And then… you tear it off and toss it over your shoulder and see what shape it falls in.'

Both girls moved to stand over the peel, which had formed a circle with one end trailing.

'And then what?' Emma asked.

Aoife laughed. 'This is my initial. Oh, well. I suppose it only works on Samhain night, but it's meant to spell the starting letter of your future spouse or special person.'

Emma sat back down and smiled properly for the first time in days. 'Aoife, I'll look forward to that night. We can do another of your outdoor buffets, but this time in the dark, although there'll be the light of the bonfire.'

'Yes!' Aoife clasped her hands together, then jumped as two wasps flew close. 'I must collect this fallen fruit and make apple cakes. The little ones will love those on the night.'

'I'll help you do it now if you like, do you have a basket?'

They'd finished clearing the fruit when Mrs Walsh appeared in the doorway and called out a friendly greeting.

'Come through, Mrs Walsh, don't mind us.' Emma indicated the chair in the shade.

'I hope you don't mind me calling unannounced, but Robert's meeting with the harbourmaster about some boat business.' She flapped a hand as if dismissing trivia. 'It pleased me when I realised I could travel with him and have the chance to call on you.'

'Well, it's lovely to see you. Can we get you something? It's so hot.'

'I'd kill for a tea. Call me mad, plenty do, but I must have tea midmorning.'

'I'll get it.' Aoife went inside with the full basket.

There was something motherly yet faintly mischievous about Mrs Walsh which Emma rather liked.

'I must start by saying how very sorry I was to hear of the heatwave in New York. Thomas mentioned you were worried about your mother.'

'I was, yes. Still am, really.'

'But you decided to stay a while longer?'

'Well, there wasn't a ship to New York for three weeks and the more I thought about it, the more I wanted to finish what I've started. I know if Nana was still alive, she would want me to do what's right – my mother said as much in her last letter. I feel at home here and I'm making friends, so another couple of months, perhaps.'

Mrs Walsh sat back in her chair and smiled. 'Well, my dear, I think it's a fine decision and one your grandmother would be very proud of.'

Emma swallowed. 'Thank you.'

'Now, I wanted to talk to you. To ask you something.'

Aoife arrived briefly with the tray, then went back inside.

'Please, do,' Emma invited, stirring the Darjeeling tea leaves in the pot and the silver ribbons of steam smelt of both fruit and smoke.

'Have you heard of Isabella Tod?'

'No, I haven't.'

'No reason why you should. She was an amazing women's rights campaigner who came from Edinburgh to Belfast just after the famine was coming to an end. She founded the North of Ireland Women's Suffrage Society, although we've managed to change the name.'

'Change it?'

'Indeed. It needed to encompass the whole country and from next month will be known as the Irish Women's Suffrage Society.' Mrs Walsh accepted a cup from Emma and added milk. 'After you and I met in Cork, I spoke with some of my superiors and informed them that I had a potential new contact in Queenstown willing to wear the sash.'

Emma's heart jumped. Martina would be jumping on the spot with excitement. 'I'd be honoured, Mrs Walsh.'

'Call me Margaret, please.' She bent down to pull from her bag a green and purple silk sash and a handful of leaflets. 'I've had copies made for you to hand out, but feel free to add any wording and have more copies made up. I'm sure Thomas has good relations with a printer in the town.'

Emma took a leaflet.

'Sadly, Isabella passed away some years ago, but her work goes on and if she knew we were on our way to securing votes across the *whole* of Ireland, I know she would thank us. I spent many an afternoon with her over tea and cake when we travelled to Belfast.'

'These are great.' Emma pointed to the information. 'And I see you're having a procession in Cork soon.'

'Yes. In her honour. We've organised a small gathering next month starting by the river. We'll walk along the High Street and end in Grand Parade. I thought it might be an opportunity for you to come and see what we're all about, and if there's time for you to enlist ladies from the harbour, so much the better.' Mrs Walsh picked up her china cup and blew ripples across the tea's surface to cool it down.

Emma spread the sash across her knee. 'This is so exciting. I can't tell you how happy it's made me. I did march once, last year, back home.'

'Yes, I know that too. It makes you the perfect candidate as many of the women in the villages and smaller towns are, shall we say…' she leant closer, 'a little timid. But I know damn well they want equality just as much as those of us who are more forthright.'

'Probably more so?' Emma ventured.

'Quite. However, we do have one issue to deal with that dear Isabella never worried about.'

'Oh?'

'Some women want Home Rule and others oppose it, yet they all want to vote. That divide is gathering momentum and it's my aim to see suffrage secured before the men of this country slice us in two.'

'May I now ask something?'

'Go ahead.' Mrs Walsh returned her cup to its saucer, a ting on bone china.

'Is there a reason you've not asked Alice to become involved? I'm not the woman of this house and I know you're great friends with Thomas.' Emma paused. 'He thinks very highly of you, of both you and Robert, and I would hate to step on anyone's toes.'

'There are reasons, Emma. In fact, there are two. Alice is never here, for one, and secondly, she is… how can I put this without disrespecting either of them… a little self-indulgent.'

Emma let the words linger in the air and found she couldn't disagree.

'If there's one thing a suffragette cannot be, it's selfish. We stand together, for *all* women, and must work as a team. I'm afraid Alice Murphy is only out for herself.'

Emma said nothing.

Margaret glanced towards the hotel. 'It's my belief she carries on behind Thomas's back. Now while their private life is none of my business, that boy has *always* been my business, ever since his mother and I met in the same hospital ward to have our boys.'

'Oh.'

'Gossip is rife in high society, and Robert and I attend lunches with some very powerful people. It is said Alice keeps her agent on a tight rein. That they benefit, if you get my meaning, from each other. Hence her career is guaranteed, irrespective of ability.'

Emma gasped. 'I assume Thomas doesn't know.'

'We're not sure, but he's a good Catholic man and he chose to marry her for better or worse. I suspect he may be the sort to turn a blind eye, which makes my blood boil. Is he with her now, in Dublin?'

Emma's head was spinning, but she managed to nod, and Margaret continued, 'Hmmm, he's a loyal man, although I fear his loyalty may be misplaced. Anyway, let's talk about this march.'

Emma tried to concentrate on the details Margaret was giving her – the location of the tea shop in Cork above which monthly meetings were held – but visions of Alice taking advantage of Thomas interrupted her thoughts on a repeating cycle.

Mrs Walsh stood and dabbed at her forehead with a folded handkerchief. 'Emma, listen to me. What I've told you must be kept to yourself in the strictest confidence. Do you understand? You asked me a question and I answered it truthfully because I'm confident I can trust you.'

'You can rely on me, Margaret.' Emma walked her to the hotel's back door. 'And I will sweep Queenstown daily until I have the support of every woman I can find.' *Apart from one*, she thought to herself.

'Good. Right. Robert told me I had half an hour before I was to wander down to join them for a light lunch.'

'That sounds lovely.'

'The food will be, but they'll not stop talking business, my dear, it will be positively dreary. There's some new ocean liner due to dock here next spring and it's bigger than any they've had before, so it's all rather complicated and plans need to be made for it to anchor out in the bay. Nothing we need bother ourselves with – as far as I can tell, there seems to be a new ship launching every time I look up these days!'

Chapter Eighteen

Early August found the hotel filled once more with Alice's daily commands, if not to her husband, then Clive, who spent most of his time gripping a cigar between his teeth and sweating profusely. He was rotund and could move nowhere at speed. Frequently Emma found herself squeezing past his bulk in one of the hotel corridors. He would nod a greeting, having come to recognise her.

Alice breezed in and out at unpredictable times of day, waving scripts in Clive's face and very often insisting he accompany her upstairs at that very moment to go through important scenes. Aoife ran around tending to Alice's every whim, and there were many. Not enough lemon slices for her tea, the bedroom window needing to be opened more frequently as the stale air was damaging her vocal cords.

She had recently returned from the Royal event, but the experience had not softened her. She continued to treat everyone with as much disdain as she could muster. One morning just before lunch, Emma was returning from the printers and, as she neared the bandstand, saw Alice coming towards her on the path.

'So, you're still here then,' Alice said, Clive in tow.

'I am, and I'm having a wonderful time, thank you for asking.'

'I didn't.'

'I know.' Emma risked a smile before regretting her quip. 'How was the King?'

'Oh my goodness, what a treat that was!' Animosity averted, Alice basked in the memory. 'He asked us how long we'd been acting as a cast. Not all the members were able to be there – but those who were gave him a shortened version of one of our favourite scenes.'

'So he likes plays?'

'He *loves* them! And he's such a sweetie. He winked at me, didn't he, Clive? He said afterwards I was the best Cleopatra he'd ever seen.'

'Congratulations.' Emma found she meant it. 'Not everyone can say they've met the King.'

They returned to the hotel together but sat at separate tables in the dining room. Emma smelt the tantalising scents of fresh baking coming from the kitchens.

Thomas brought in a tray of refreshments for a couple who were waiting to board a ship to Canada the next morning. Emma watched him exchange a few pleasantries before turning to Alice. 'Are you hungry?'

'I really don't know.' She blew cigarette smoke into Clive's face and asked him, 'Did you not say earlier you'd be taking me to Cork this evening to dine with that new orchestra maestro?'

Clive took his half-moon glasses from his red nose and spent a moment wiping them. 'Did I?'

The look Alice gave him was not lost on Emma.

Clive pushed his glasses back up the bridge of his nose

and met Alice's stare. 'Oh yes, so I did.'

Alice turned to Thomas. 'I have another arrangement so won't eat now and ruin my appetite.'

Thomas turned and offered Emma the potato and leek soup which Chef had made that morning.

'Sounds perfect, I'd love some.'

A few minutes later Alice and Clive left the room, and met Aoife in the doorway.

Aoife stepped back. 'Sorry, after you.'

'Are these yours?' Alice talked quietly as she picked up one of the rolls from the plate in Aoife's hand.

'Yes.'

Alice took a bite. 'They're good, Aoife. You have many talents. I've left you another list on my bedside table. Be sure to retrieve it soon.'

Aoife blushed and nodded, then put the bowl of soup down in front of Emma. 'There were two rolls, sorry, I'll just get you another.'

Emma smiled and touched Aoife's hand. 'Please don't, one will be fine. The soup will fill me. It all smells gorgeous.'

'I've been practising making bread for weeks now, with help from Chef. Thomas said I could, as long as he got to eat them too.' Aoife grinned and looked out the window at Alice and Clive walking away across the road. Emma wondered if Aoife was scared of Alice, or simply desperate to please. 'I've always dreamed of running a bakery of my own, but that obviously won't happen.'

'Why won't it?' Emma tore the roll apart and released steam from the still-hot dough.

'I can't see the likes of me being able to rent a shop. I'd be happy just to do the baking part.'

'You are more than capable. I'll help you put a plan together.'

'Oh, Miss Emma, I couldn't expect that of you.'

'Say no more.' Emma put up her hand. 'It'll be a pleasure. It's a way I can thank you for the help I know you're going to be at our first committee meeting.'

'Are we having one?'

'Indeed we are. Mrs Walsh has given the go-ahead. I've some papers to sign in Cork but Queenstown will officially have a branch of the IWSS, that's the Irish Women's Suffrage Society.'

When at last the clock ticked its way past ten and the remaining guests had filtered back to their rooms, Emma found Thomas in his office. She leant against the edge of the door, watched him filing papers.

'How was Dublin?'

'It's a beautiful city,' he said. 'I didn't get to meet the King – only Alice and her company were allowed audience with him. The performance was good, though. There's no denying it: the company has some fine actors.'

'You must have been proud.'

'I don't think I felt anything, other than perhaps injustice.'

'Injustice?'

'From a distance, I saw the King and Mary in their finery, their bodyguards waiting outside the theatre. Carriages, horses and uniformed soldiers parading; days of ceremonies. Yet not two streets away from the theatre was a group of beggars, some no older than ten. They've been wasting away in this heatwave, discouraged from gaining

133

access down to the river to cool off because the authorities were worried their presence would put be off-putting for tourists arriving to see the King.'

'Oh, that's awful.'

Thomas poured them each a drop of brandy from a hip flask. 'Just a small one. It's been a long week and I could do with it, and you're celebrating.'

She laughed and took the tiny glass he held out to her.

'I gave some of the youngest a shilling or two. It's the government who should do more.'

Emma sipped the brandy and let it warm her. 'Alice must have hated those backstreets.'

'She wasn't with me.' Thomas downed the liquor in one and poured another. 'The company all ate together. I wasn't invited.'

'Oh,' she said again.

'I wasn't bothered.' He sighed and flexed his fingers. 'I just wanted to come home if I'm being honest.'

She looked at him over the rim of the glass and found him looking at her with an intensity she'd not seen before.

Chapter Nineteen

Emma was filled with a sense of déjà vu as a breeze snapped at the banner she and Mrs Walsh held aloft.

VOTES FOR WOMEN

The material rippled in time with the surface of the River Lee. Cooler weather and skies filled with clouds had arrived at last, chasing away the heatwave. But even the threat of rain could do nothing to dampen the enthusiasm that buzzed through the crowd gathered in Cork.

Many of the women present had travelled a long way to take part and their collective voices brought the streets in the city alive like blood pumping through veins of someone ready to fight. On the main street, a blocked artery in the form of policemen, their arms locked in unity, marked the boundary past which they believed the protestors would not be marching.

Emma glanced round, enjoying the noise and excitement in the atmosphere, and noted a number of men in doorways and on balconies who clapped and hollered their support. Men who were not in unity with the police, or the majority of the male population, but who supported what the women were trying to achieve. *I hope you can see this, Martina.*

Mrs Walsh checked her sash to ensure the lettering was not obscured, then scanned the crowd. 'Oh, look, Emma – there's Rosie Hackett. Did you see her in the newspapers last week?'

Emma saw only a sea of faces.

'She works at the Jacob's biscuit factory in Dublin and encouraged all her female colleagues to stop work and join the male workers outside who were striking for better working conditions. Her actions helped secure those rights and she's become a bit of an icon.'

'It's wonderful what you can achieve when you've got the guts to stick your head above the parapet.' Mrs Walsh stood on tiptoes. 'Oooh, she's coming this way.'

Emma watched the girl no older than herself, laughing and shaking hands with everyone who reached out to touch her. The calls and screams of adulation grew louder as she drew closer. The girl paused briefly to look up at Emma's banner – 'Perfect, ladies. Enjoy your day' – and then walked on through the crowd.

An older woman climbed makeshift steps on to a raised platform and held up her hand for silence.

'Here's Delia,' Mrs Walsh whispered as the hubbub faded like songbirds at dusk.

'Welcome! You have come from near and far to stand up for the right to be heard.' She turned to take in the crowds. 'The vote was invented to give people the right to have their say. Are women not people?'

A roar of concurrence filled the air.

'Did you know that the Irish Transport and General

Workers Union aims to help only male workers? Naturally the committee is made up of only men.'

The women heckled and booed.

'It is my goal to represent the many thousands of women in factories, working as many hours as men, and see to it they are treated fairly. This goes hand in hand with our fight for the right to vote. So, today we march to show the solidarity of our sex.'

The speaker calmed the cheering with another request for silence, but a man's voice interrupted her preparation. 'Get on with it!'

A smattering of laughter from a handful of his supporters followed, but Delia responded, 'We take our time, young man, to think things through, rather than diving in head-first which often results in a need to mop up damage.'

The cheer which met her words drowned out any further protest the man may have been considering. Emma looked behind her and spotted Mary O'Connor, and they exchanged a wave.

'We are more than wives, mothers, sisters and aunts. Yes, we want to work, but let's also start providing better education for our little girls. We want them to have greater opportunities on the job market. One day I hope women will apply for roles in Government, because how can men know what it is we wish for? Don't you agree that we need a few of our own at the top, helping to set the rules?'

The women cheered again and stamped their feet on the ground, and Emma was sure the ground was shaking.

Two days later, Emma was still buzzing when she held her first Queenstown meeting in the drawing room of The

Admiral. She welcomed the twelve women into the room in which a semi-circle of chairs had been prepared. She was sorry not to see Mary among them. Emma handed out leaflets as the women filtered into the hotel. Once settled, she began by reading out an article in the *Irish Citizen* reporting on the peaceful demonstration in Cork.

A woman whose proportions were trying to burst free from a dress too small put up her hand.

Emma paused. 'Yes?'

'My husband says he's happy for me to join the marching, but he doesn't think it will change Parliament's view. That Asquith fella won't have it, will he?'

'Well, you have a valid point… it's Sue, isn't it?'

'Yeah, Suzannah, really, but my bairn couldn't say that, so we taught him Sue and it's stuck. He's eighteen now.' She laughed and the others laughed with her.

Emma smiled. 'The marches may have to become more active before Parliament will listen. In England, women are taking a more militant approach and we have to consider doing the same.'

'What's militant mean?' Sue frowned.

To Sue's left, a girl with red ringlets said, 'That would be those windows getting broke and stuff, like when the King was in Dublin.'

Sue twisted her generous frame on the seat to look at her neighbour. 'I never heard that. Mind you, I never read the papers. My husband says he'll tell me if there's anything in it I need to know about.'

Emma put her hands up. 'Ladies, I'm afraid the time for words alone is coming to an end. If the Government won't listen to reason, taking action will be our next plan.

I know none of us want to vandalise property, but a few broken windows in carefully selected buildings will mean we make the front pages of the papers, and if enough of us get involved, they'll have to take us seriously.'

Another lady looked horrified. 'But they'll arrest us!'

'That's what I want to talk about. When we are next invited to join a Cork city march, or a gathering outside the ministerial building, we must *all* go if we can. Be prepared to get caught up in scuffles and yes, there may be a possibility of arrest, but they'll only keep us a day or two. They don't have room in the gaols for petty crimes.'

'I don't know where you get your ideas from, gel, but they're strict round here. My sister's in the city gaol in Sunday Wells, so she is, for stealing some apples from the fruit cart three months back, and they've still got her.' Sue crossed her arms. 'I've got her kids. I can't risk ending up in there too.'

'Well, let's hope it doesn't come to arrests.' Emma tried to sound positive, but the prison angle hadn't been an aspect she'd discussed in depth with Mrs Walsh and she was starting to wish she had.

At the end of the meeting, the women jostled for space around the table and Emma handed out forms. 'Can you each fill one of these out, please, and also we need to think of the best day for our first march through the harbour, just to show our presence.'

'Friday's good, how 'bout walking from the White Star building and ending up at the bakery?' Sue called from the other side of the room.

'Can you help me?' Aoife whispered, holding her form under Emma's nose.

'Of course, let's get this lot away first.'

By the time she closed the front door, Emma knew it was imperative they find bigger premises but was grateful to Thomas for letting them use the drawing room tonight. The few who'd made it were each keen to go in search of more members.

'Sit down, Miss Emma, and I'll fetch you some tea. You'd make a wonderful teacher,' Aoife said.

Taking the weight off her feet in one of the wing-arm chairs, Emma closed her eyes for a moment.

She knew Thomas had arrived in the room when the smell of his pipe reached her nostrils and Oliver's tail rubbed on the carpet as he wagged it back and forth. She opened an eye. Thomas's old tweed jacket made her smile, he looked comfortable in it and it suited him. He flopped down in a matching chair on the other side of the unlit fireplace.

'You look like you could do with your bed.'

'It's been an exciting few days,' she said, and yawned.

He laughed and lit a match, working the tobacco deeper into the bowl with a fingertip.

'How was the room?'

'It was lovely, thank you. But if we get more members next time, it's going to be a squeeze.'

'I've heard the assembly rooms is empty most evenings. I bumped into Mrs O'Connor this morning – she was outside chatting with the mayor. Quite taken it upon herself to find you ladies somewhere else to meet.'

'She wasn't here tonight.'

'Harold's a bit under the weather, so she probably didn't want to leave him alone.' Smoke billowed in front of him and for a moment, she could only see his crossed legs and shoes.

'Poor Harold,' she said.

'Mary thinks he's been working too hard, saving for that ticket to America.'

'I'm not convinced she really wants him to leave.'

Thomas nodded and sucked on the pipe. Tiny crackles filled the space between them.

Chapter Twenty

'Alice is gone until Christmas, Aoife is taking a holiday, and Chef and I have talked at length. It's all arranged. I'm closing the hotel for two days.'

'What? Can you do that?'

'Already done it. September is our only quiet month. I'm going fishing with Patrick along the coast at Ringaskiddy. It's something I've wanted to do for ages and September is always great for mackerel.' Thomas was sat at his desk.

She smiled as she pictured the two of them messing about with fishing lines, knowing he was taking advantage of Alice's absence. Emma would miss him, but she couldn't deny it was precisely what she'd pictured for him.

She stood in the doorway to his office, leaning against the lintel, which was becoming a habit. 'I'm pleased you've decided to do this.'

He sat back in his chair. 'Why are you grinning? Do you want to get rid of me?'

She laughed. 'Far from it. No, I'm happy for you. This is the first time I've seen you doing something for yourself and it'll do you the world of good.'

'Well, actually…' He pushed a lid onto his pen until it clicked. 'I was thinking about asking if you'd like to come with us.'

'Me?'

'It's a chance for you to see a bit of the coastline out on the estuary. It's really beautiful. But there's no obligation if you'd rather stay here.'

Emma pressed her lips together to keep from allowing her smile to take over her face. 'I have a Federation meeting Friday, but nothing until then.'

'I've a delivery of coal Thursday, so we'll be back in plenty of time for your meeting.'

She tilted her head slightly. 'Are you sure, though? Wouldn't you rather talk men stuff while you fish?'

He tapped the pen against a page of figures.

'I would like to show you somewhere different, and you'd have your own cabin for the night.'

The mention of a night away from the hotel – in his company – sent a ripple of nerves racing across her tummy.

'I'd love to then, thank you.'

His imperceptible nod was backed up by a twitch of his moustache. 'That's settled then.'

She turned to leave him to his papers. 'You won't expect me to fish, will you?'

He chuckled. 'Not unless you want to.'

'What time do we leave?'

'We need to be on the boat by eight o'clock tomorrow morning.'

Patrick's fishing boat was far bigger than Emma had imagined.

As she stepped on deck the next morning amongst the coiled ropes that smelt of sea salt, she spotted a set of narrow, wooden steps down into what Patrick had called the galley.

The men were still on the gangplank engaged in quiet, but animated, discussion, so she left them to it and went down inside the boat. She opened tiny wooden cupboards with brass handles and found homes for the food items they'd brought from the hotel. The tiny kitchen was well kept and smelt pleasantly of beeswax.

'It's tiny but perfect,' she called over to them when she went back up. 'I love it.'

Patrick looked up and grinned. 'I've collected everything in miniature over the years; there's no meal I can't make down there. And the best thing: I never have to move from one spot to reach it all.'

Patrick jumped easily aboard. 'Look, sorry, Emma, but something's come up and I can't go. But you're in good hands with Thomas.'

'Oh.' Emma looked from one to the other. 'Perhaps we should leave it until another time when you can make it?'

'Rubbish!' Patrick reversed down to the gangplank and started to unwind some ropes that held the boat to its mooring. 'The boat's ready and you're both looking forward to it. Don't let my date with the court stop you going.'

Thomas had gone the colour of ash as he climbed into the boat beside her.

'I'll be honest with you, this isn't what I'd planned. He received a telegram from the solicitors in Cork where he's doing articles and has to attend a case they thought wouldn't come up for a while.'

'I'm not sure this would look good, Thomas. What will Alice say, or anyone else, come to that?' The words were out before she realised they'd labelled what had been an innocent trip into something else.

'I can't reschedule as the hotel is already closed.' Thomas moved past her and coiled the rope Patrick had released.

The little motor at the back of the boat was chugging quietly to itself from where Patrick had started it before updating Thomas a few minutes earlier. Emma, deep in thought, watched the water bubbling on the surface.

'Take care of her.' She heard Patrick's words and wasn't sure if he meant the boat or her. He waved, then turned around and started walking back to the harbour.

'Why does this trip now feel wrong?' Emma chewed the side of her nail.

'If you'd rather stay back, I would totally respect your choice.'

Emma was torn. She'd been excited about the trip, but now her stomach churned with worry.

'Let's put our cards on the table,' Thomas said. 'What are you worried about?'

'You're a married man.' She took a step back, as if a little space between them would calm the butterflies in her belly.

'What's that got to do with a fishing trip with private sleeping quarters? Treat it like a fairground ride, at sea.'

'With an overnight,' Emma added.

'I have no intention of—'

'Of course! I'm not suggesting you had. Ohhh…' Emma put her head in her hands. 'If only Aoife was here.'

Thomas was getting into the swing of activity on the boat and untying different ropes near the boom. 'You think you need a chaperone?'

She looked back at him and realised how ridiculous she was sounding. 'I'm sorry. You've never given me any reason to doubt you. It's fine. Let's go and see these fish.'

'Right you are, Captain.'

They spent the next half hour negotiating the harbour and began to head into the mouth of the river where there were fewer boats. The sun was warm and Emma slipped out of her fitted jacket, which she folded neatly and placed on a bench towards the stern of the boat. The breeze cooled her skin through the cotton of her blouse. After they'd gone a little way along the coast, Thomas threw the anchor over the side. She heard the metal chain clanking against the hull.

He had disappeared a few minutes earlier but now stood in front of her wearing only a bathing suit. 'Coming in?'

Mortified, she didn't know where to look. 'Er... no, no, I'm fine sitting here.'

She'd never seen a man's bare legs before, nor a set of arms and shoulders as shapely as those which flexed as he moved things to locate the set of rope steps Patrick had shown him.

The stripy material of his suit followed the contours of his body, leaving very little to the imagination, and she caught her breath as he stepped up onto the side of the boat before diving in head-first.

She gripped the bench with knuckles which turned white and waited for him to resurface, which he did within seconds, releasing a *Whoop!* of delight. Drips from his hair sparkled in the sun as he trod water.

'You should come in – it's refreshing,' he said, panting. She laughed. 'You mean freezing.'

The idea of feeling the weight of the sea against her limbs she found both terrifying and exhilarating, but there was no way she could take any more clothes off in front of him. She looked away, back out to sea and the way they had come. She listened to the regular splashes of his swimming strokes and soon, from the corner of her eye, saw him swim his way around the boat.

Seeing Thomas playing like a child, watching him relax and have fun, was having a strange effect on her. She'd assumed going out on the boat with him would simply be a change of location, that she would be watching the man who ran the hotel do his thing but on a boat. But this wasn't the hotel Thomas she'd been getting to know. She sat and watched him in the water, one minute diving below the surface, then turning to float on his back. This was a different man completely, and one she found intensely attractive. Her tummy fluttered again as she tried to focus on the gentle sway of the boat. She lay down on the bench and looked up at the sky. A seagull balanced on the top of the mast. Its surprisingly large body jolted in time with its high-pitched *yack yack yack* as it called to its entourage circling overhead. They must be hoping for fish scraps, although they'd have to wait until Thomas had finished swimming.

'Now, that was good.' Thomas re-appeared over the side of the boat. 'Can't remember the last time I did that.'

She pushed herself upright, surprised by the heat her skin had absorbed. The view of the coastline from the water was one of rugged inaccessibility. Rocks jutted through the surface near the water's edge at peculiar angles like a baby's first teeth. Coastal birds soared out from the land mass, flew in circles before landing on ledges in the hillside, camouflaged and out of sight.

Her blouse was stuck to her skin and had become transparent. She looked around, but the only place to hide was below deck.

Thomas rubbed his wet hair with a towel and seemed not to notice her discomfort. 'Shall we have a lemonade to cool down?'

'Do we have any?'

'Patrick always buys it for his fishing trips. There's a cooler in one of the benches below, I'll go and look.'

Within half an hour her blouse had dried and they'd eaten the crabmeat sandwiches he'd prepared in the hotel kitchen that morning. There was no shelter from the sun, neither in the sky nor from reflections which sparkled on the water. Eventually she dared to discard her skirt to sit cross-legged in cotton drawers. Her mother would be horrified, but she'd never know. It wasn't like she had to include these details in her next letter and it wasn't as if the seagulls could fly across the Atlantic and betray her.

Thomas even persuaded her into the water at one point and helped keep her afloat, his hand supporting her belly while her hands grabbed at handfuls of water. Her legs turned to jelly with the effort of kicking and she was grateful that he couldn't possibly know what effect he was having on her. Mouthfuls of salty water each time she laughed resulted in Thomas ditching the swimming lesson. He helped her back to the rope ladder at the side of the boat.

'Remind me not to let you on the rowing team.

Swimming is a big part of the training.' He laughed as they stood dripping in close proximity on the deck.

The sun moved round the sky and later in the afternoon the shadows lengthened. The skin across her cheeks was tight where the sun had dried away the sea, leaving a salty residue. Thomas caught three mackerel and showed her how to boil seawater and collect the distilled droplets to drink. He cooked the fish, turning them over in a blackened pan sizzling with butter, and they ate the flaky meat with their fingers. Emma had never eaten such fresh fish.

When the sun dropped even lower, Emma leaned over the side to watch undulations in the water's surface. Mini waves slapped against the wooden planks of the hull, painted the same blue as the sky had been before it darkened to the wool of policemen's uniforms. As the boat turned slowly in the breeze, and out of the glare, she could see the fishing line disappear through the surface a few yards across the water and heard Thomas mumbling to himself, 'Here we go... yes.'

He wound in the reel and soon a wriggling silver body hung above them in the evening light, its individual scales glittering like jewels. He swung it towards him and held it, taking the hook from its mouth and dispatching it swiftly before holding up his prize.

'Well done – that's breakfast sorted,' she said.

When darkness finally crept silently upon them, they went down into the galley and Thomas lit the paraffin lamps.

'You've gone red.' Thomas pointed at her exposed shoulders in the warm glow of the light. The oily smell of paraffin was not unpleasant. *Rather fitting*, she thought as Thomas sat on the portside bench across from her. His

149

arms were smudged with the efforts of the day, but she'd never seem him so relaxed and happy.

Their feet were only inches apart.

She turned her head to put her lips on the hot skin of one shoulder. 'They do feel a bit prickly.'

But she found she didn't care. Nothing could ruin the day.

Thomas dunked a cloth into a bowl of cold water and laid it across Emma's left shoulder.

'Oooosh.' She winced before appreciating the sensation. She sat back and closed her eyes. 'That's really nice.'

Although her cotton bloomers and corset had dried fully, and it was warm inside the boat's galley, goosebumps grew on her skin as trickles of cold water ran down her upper arm and dripped from her elbow onto her thigh.

She started to shiver.

Thomas retrieved a blanket and wrapped it round her. She wondered, not for the first time, where she was expected to sleep, and asked him about it.

'There's a berth at the front there which you can have and I'll…' he indicated the floor and smiled, 'roll that blanket into some sort of mattress.'

'Now I feel awful,' Emma protested.

'You don't need to. Honestly, I'll be fine.'

There was nothing more she could say so instead elected to enjoy the gentle movement of the boat and the close proximity of Thomas's knees against her own. It was easy to pretend they were the only people alive. For those first few months, he'd been no more than a guide and the owner of the hotel where she was staying. But since the summer, he'd become a friend and someone who really cared about what she was doing.

There was something magical about being out on the water, away from reality. She could pretend things were different here, and as he moved around the galley, bending and stretching to reach cupboards, the desire to pretend grew stronger. She squeezed her hands together in her lap, fighting the overwhelming desire to touch his face, his shoulders, his chest, to feel the shape of his arms on the palms of her hands. She wondered what kissing him might feel like, whether his moustache would tickle her and whether she would search out his tongue like Martina had told her she should do one day.

'Want to share this beer?'

They looked at the bottle Patrick had left on a shelf.

'I don't think I should,' she said.

'Why's that?'

She didn't answer.

'I'm sorry to have put you in a difficult position. I know it was selfish of me to want you to come, but I thought you would enjoy it. And you have.'

She watched his hand splayed over his thigh and resisted the urge to place her own hand on top.

'I've loved it,' she whispered.

He opened the beer and took a swig.

She pulled the blanket more tightly around her, stood and walked to the doorway that led to the cabin, hoping he couldn't hear her heart hammering inside her chest. 'Right. Well, I'll turn in for the night and leave you your space.'

'Goodnight, Emma,' Thomas said, and she looked back.

Her shoulders were burning again. 'Could you do the cold-water thing one more time, please?'

She was shocked to find herself walking towards him and not away to the privacy of the cramped room in the bow of the boat.

Thomas obliged and she waited once more for the water to trickle down her arm. She shivered, but not from the cold, and stared into his eyes. His return gaze didn't falter.

This was trouble and she'd caused it. She should turn around and walk away.

He lowered his head a little and paused. Instinct found her reaching round the back of his head to pull his face closer. She inhaled before his lips met her own. They were warm and when he pulled away, she kept her eyes closed in the hope it hadn't simply been her imagination. He kissed her again.

She let him tilt her head back and gave in to the passion which surged through her. Her tongue knew what to do and as her body responded, she wasn't sure whose moan of pleasure passed between them.

'This is wrong of me, so very wrong. We should stop,' he whispered into her ear.

'But how can something so wrong, feel so right?' She pulled him closer still.

Chapter Twenty-One

The onset of autumn brought with it storms which battered the harbour for days. The locals were used to such conditions and kept rickety shutters closed against fierce gales which forced their way into nooks and crannies of ageing buildings.

Emma wrote to her mother and glossed over the details about working hard to enlist more volunteers. Not quite lying but hoping her mother would think she meant for the Soldiers' Home. Penning this deceit sat more comfortably than the reality Emma was struggling to comes to terms with.

The shame of what she'd done cloaked every waking moment with worry. In private moments she would curl up in a tight ball on her bed and berate herself. There was no denying she'd had physical relations. And worse, they'd been with a married man. There was simply no other way to describe the event. What terrified her most was how willingly her body had responded.

Thomas had spent the morning after apologising and raking his hands through his wonderful curls. Curls that she knew felt glorious between her fingers. They'd cut the second fishing day short and returned to the harbour in silence.

Since then, he'd become obsessed he'd ruined things for them both, disrespecting her in the process. *Good married men just don't allow that to happen, for God's sake. I'm no better than the scum I hate. What must you think of me?*

Emma had been hoping to regain some of the atmosphere from before, but it remained elusive, and instead, when she thought back to the boat trip, all she could think of was his wife. Emma was well acquainted with guilt and she'd known sadness, but never had she experienced the feeling of self-loathing that had become her daily shadow. She cried into her pillow most nights but knew she deserved to feel the anguish. She no longer felt relaxed at the hotel, but the thought of leaving Thomas behind and returning to New York broke her heart in two. Was this what falling in love was meant to feel like?

When Martina's older sister, Anna, had met the man she wanted to marry, they had courted for a few weeks and Martina had spied on them. *They behave more like business associates*, she'd told Emma one morning, and gone on to admit she'd followed the couple as they walked through Central Park. *They didn't hold hands once!* Yet Anna had married the man three months later.

But this was different. Every time Emma saw Thomas in the dining room, her heart squeezed tight, restricting her breathing and rendering her unable to utter a word. Sometimes she managed a smile before having to leave the room again.

If they passed on the stairs or in a corridor, her eyes focused on parts of him previously unnoticed, like the mole on his neck and the way the top of his right ear kinked slightly and didn't match the other.

The knowledge of what she'd become woke her most nights. She would lay in the dark feeling desolate, a prison sentence forcing her to face her wrongs. But when light filtered through the curtains, and the now-familiar items came into view, relief that she was still near Thomas would temporarily wash away her regret.

Leaning close to the mirrored wardrobe door, she touched her rosy cheeks, no longer seeing a young innocent girl. He'd kissed every inch of her face, sending sparks through her body. His warm breath on her eyelids had left her clinging to him for more. Each day now passed with huge chunks of time lost to dreaming, recalling a fantasy that could never be repeated.

She opened the wardrobe door and searched for something to wear.

On the chair next to the bed lay the mask she and Aoife had made ready for Samhain. She picked up the donkey, its hardened papier-mâché rough between her fingertips, the long ears cleverly created with wire, then built up with layers of newspaper soaked in a mix of flour and milk. They'd covered it with scraps of brown material Aoife had brought from home and it looked more than good. It looked lifelike and terrifying, like some possessed animal.

'Yes, that's right. An ass. How appropriate,' Emma mumbled to herself.

The donkey's teeth were big and it seemed to be laughing at her. She threw a shawl over it.

They'd spent a week making all the farmyard animals; Aoife planned to wear the sheep and Chef a cow. Thomas would not wear his mask while they tended the fire, but she'd seen the fine horse's head he'd worn for years. It had been his mother's.

A mask was just what she needed, something to hide behind while she focused on her work.

Matters of the heart had taken precedence and she was fighting it with everything she had. The fact her IWSS work was no longer the first thing she thought about on waking was something she needed to change.

They'd managed to hide their return to the harbour from all, and Thomas had assured Emma that his friend would be telling no-one they'd been out unaccompanied. They'd even agreed not to inform Aoife that Patrick had missed the trip.

She had a few weeks, including Christmas, to patch up her heart and put Queenstown behind her. Nobody knew she was falling in love, and if she could keep it that way, she could depart and leave behind no damage.

The last day of October arrived, and by early evening, the hotel garden was filled with excited men, women and children, all dressed in ghostly costumes. Emma had thought the masks she'd seen people wear in New York were spooky, but they were nothing compared to those which filled the garden. Paint effects had been skilfully used to depict bleeding animals and great horned mythical creatures with glass eyes queued at the table for drinks.

'The false faces represent death, mostly,' Aoife explained.

Emma poured cider into cups and small jugs people had brought with them. A permanent line of outstretched arms holding cups for refilling. Ribbons tied to horns caught in the breeze. Emma recognised no-one but smiled politely as she used the tin ladle.

'That's it, girl. Fill her up,' said a particularly short pig with horrible teeth painted halfway up each side of its head. The man inside laughed at her discomfort. 'Took me four months to make this!'

'It's…' She hesitated.

'Bloody heavy!' called a woman's voice next to the pig, its owner hidden behind a wrinkly grey face with cut-out holes where eyes should be. 'She don't recognise me… you don't recognise me, do you? It's Sue!'

'Oh, Sue.' Emma's hand flew to her chest. 'It's very good. Horrible, in fact.'

'Looks like her bloody mother, if you ask me,' said the pig, who walked off with his second cup of cider.

'The cheek of it.' Sue lifted her mask to take a sip. 'Oooh, that's lovely, that is. Aoife, you make a mean tipple. You should serve this at meetings.'

Flames from the bonfire flickered behind the silhouettes of bodies gathered near it for the heat. Emma could feel the warmth even twenty yards away. But she couldn't see Thomas. Thankfully, they'd been so busy preparing, their paths had barely crossed in the last few days. Patrick handed long sticks – their ends alight with small flames – to the children so they could poke the ground and watch the sparks fly.

Chef and Aoife brought out plates of muffins, tin trays of sticky toffee apples with stick handles wedged at jaunty angles. The murmur of the crowd filled her head like the hum of bees, or was it the cider that had altered her hearing? Emma drank another cup and found it soothing.

The old wooden furniture donated by the townsfolk was being consumed by hungry flames. The noise of crackles and snaps from the fire were getting louder.

'Can we have some?'

Eager faces of children had gathered at the table, drawn in by the sugary scents as chef delivered a second urn of spiced cider to the table.

'I don't think so,' said Emma.

'Spoilsport!' one cried, and then ran off laughing.

'You're a cruel donkey!' said another, and ran off after the first, pumping the air with a fist and laughing.

'Ignore them.' Aoife picked up a hard brown nut and a grater.

'What's that?' Emma asked.

'It's a nutmeg, and if you grate some on to the top, it floats and smells like Christmas.' She started to grate the nut and a fine dust settled on the surface of the hot cider.

'Won't it burn their tongues?'

'Don't worry, we let it cool before we serve it,' Aoife said.

Movement at the side of the garden caught Emma's attention. Thomas was trying to drag the little rowing boat towards the fire. Patrick intervened and stopped him. A discussion was taking place which she couldn't hear and then Thomas returned to tend the fire while Patrick placed the boat back beneath its cover.

She'd been sorry for the atmosphere between them, but there was no-one to blame but herself. She was supposed to be a modern woman and should have seen the danger of allowing herself to get close to him. Her life was shaping up to be a pattern of punishment for stupid mistakes.

Within a few days, she'd known there was little point in daydreaming about a future that couldn't be. Thomas was a good Catholic who would stand by his wife. And maybe God would allow good Catholics to make one error of judgement.

Thomas had whispered in her ear on the boat that he'd not lain with anyone for over eight years. His slate had been clean until she had presented herself to him like easy pickings. She shook her head. He'd barely spoken to her for days. He must hate her.

Patrick appeared at the table. 'Can we have two ciders, please? It's thirsty work keeping this fire in check.'

Emma handed him two tankards. 'Was he going to burn it?'

'The rowing boat? Yes, he was. I couldn't let him. Bertha has belonged to the club since it started. He took it to restore. Just because Alice hates it, and he thinks it's taking up space, he wanted to get rid of it, but I know he'd regret it.'

'Why does Alice hate it?'

He took a sip. 'I don't know. Some people just don't like being out on open water. Or maybe the project took his attention away from her.'

'Maybe.'

'I've said too much. I can save the boat but not his personal life. Thanks for this.' He held up the tankards before disappearing into the crowd.

Emma waited for a quiet moment and then walked across the garden and lifted the corner of the cover. A tin of dried-up paint had fallen on its side, the contents hardened. A hint that Thomas had once been working on it. *How sad,* she thought. Alice was a lucky woman, yet she took him for granted, and Emma still couldn't understand why.

Emma missed chatting to Thomas, spending those moments leaning against his office door. As much as their being together on the boat had been incredible, she could not be sure it had been worth the loss of friendship.

The night wore on and the flames ate their way through chairs, tables and planks, reaching high into the sky, energised by the dry fuel. Flickering light danced yellow on the masks of those standing closer to the fire, their laughter creating an eerie sense of customs past.

Some of the townsfolk had moved on, leaving the hotel to go out into the harbour to meet up with friends.

Emma felt a little giddy but swilled back her fourth cider before pulling her donkey head back down to cover her face. She sat on the grass and watched more people leave. Through the eyeholes, she found she could conceal her study of Thomas perfectly as he went about throwing partially burnt pieces of wood back into the centre of the fire. A painted table leg sent green flames skywards as paint melted and sizzled. She watched a piece of something alight fluttering on the breeze and followed its progress high into the night sky, her breathing loud inside the papier-mâché helmet. Her breathing increased as she strained to follow it, laying back on the grass. The head was tight and seemed to be closing in around her. She tried to twist it off. The blackened sky was sprinkled with orange sparkles and she watched those instead, mesmerised, unable to escape.

A shadow came into her vision, a devil's head with horns; voices spoke in ghostly whispers over the top of her. Were they laughing at her? More heads appeared. Did the townsfolk know now that she'd tricked them and had been no more than a whore all along?

She was drowning beneath their laughter, teeth and eyes. Death had come to find her. Death in the form of another fire. Of course. That would make sense, and this time, she wouldn't fight it. She would let her body succumb to the heat, to shrivel away to embers. At least she could be with Martina and never again have to face the reality of not being with the man she had fallen so helplessly in love with.

She squeezed her eyes tightly shut and waited for the pain. When it didn't come, she sat up and let the hands guide her up from the grass. Colours blurred through tears and the black shape of what was left of the crowd morphed into a hunched black monster, pushing and shoving, roaring at her. She screamed and pulled again at the mask. Pieces came away in her hands, and once she was free of it, she bolted for the hotel's back door. Running away was something at which she'd become expert. She slammed her bedroom door closed, slumped onto the bed and pushed her face into her pillow.

'Forgive me,' she moaned for her best friend, pulling her knees to her chest. For an age she lay still and listened to the sound of voices outside and was almost asleep when she heard footsteps.

Aoife's voice was getting louder. 'I don't know. Haven't seen her for nearly an hour.'

'Have you checked upstairs?' Thomas's voice was still faint. He was downstairs.

It was too late to do anything about preparing herself. The footsteps came closer and her door opened. 'Oh,

Emma, you're here. She's here!' Aoife added loudly for Thomas's benefit. She came to sit on the edge of the bed.

Thomas appeared in the doorway, then hesitated. 'Shall I leave you two alone?'

Aoife spoke first. 'Or why don't I go and make us all a nice cocoa and you stay and talk to her?'

No, don't go, Aoife, Emma willed her from behind her hands. Emma was in no fit state to have a serious chat with Thomas.

Emma felt the bed dip as he sat down. She didn't have the strength to fight her body's tilt towards him.

She turned away from him, her hair lying in tangles over her face. Silent tears squeezed out from her eyes and slid down her cheeks as she stared at the window.

He moved closer and found her hand. 'Was it the fire?'

'I think so,' she whispered.

'Come here.'

Pushing herself up, she let his arms surround her and breathed in the smell of woodsmoke on his clothes. Nothing in the world mattered at that moment, other than being in his arms.

'Why didn't I think of that?' He squeezed her closer to him. 'I shouldn't have put you through that. I'm an idiot.'

'Don't say that.' She sniffed and pulled back a little. 'I can see how everyone loves this festival and the hotel is the perfect place to hold it. It's me. I shouldn't be here, that's all.'

He wiped her cheek with his thumb. 'And don't you start down that track. You're welcome here for as long as you like, you know that.'

'I've missed you since...'

Thomas stared at her for a moment. 'I bet I've missed you more.'

Maybe it was the cider, but the tears came again and there was nothing she could do to stop them.

'I've been so selfish. I honestly don't know what to do to help you. I had no right to expect anything from you,' he continued.

'I wanted you, Thomas. I've never felt that way before. It was me that took advantage of you. You've been celibate for eight years, what's that if it's not a good man? You respect your marriage vows and I respect you for doing so. But you're human, and I made it easy for you.'

'But I'm the man, I should have taken the lead and… not let anything happen on that boat.'

'Excuse me, with your high and mighty speech.' She sniffed again and wiped her nose with the back of her hand. 'I'm fighting for the vote, for equal rights, and if I want to take responsibility for what happened, I implore you let me.'

His smile was the first he'd given her in days. 'Well, maybe a part then.'

They heard Aoife's approach on the landing and Thomas moved to sit nearer the end of the bed. Aoife brought in cups of hot chocolate and Emma was once again wrapped in their kindness. They talked and laughed about the masks and how well the refreshments had been received and consumed.

'All your guests are downstairs and we're up here,' Emma said.

'There aren't many left now, and those who are will be fine, I've left Patrick in charge.'

'You're fine. I'll go check on them.' Aoife closed the door gently behind her.

'She's such a good girl,' Emma said, and breathed out with a sigh.

'She is.'

Thomas sat closer, took Emma's hand and kissed it. 'Tell me what you're thinking.'

'The flames... it was like it happened yesterday. I felt so guilty all over again. Guilty for having a life, for having feelings.' She looked at him.

'You've come a long way, Emma, but the memory will rear its ugly head from time to time.' The warmth of his hand radiated through her.

She giggled at his pun, and he joined in. Something tight had been released and a sense of the old atmosphere they'd always shared was returning.

She smiled. 'Martina wouldn't want me to feel guilty forever, would she? She'd want me to fight. And this guilt is simply another thing I have to fight. She wanted to travel, and I think she'd be proud that I've come over here.'

Thomas stood up with a start. 'You've given me an idea.'

'What?'

'It's a secret...' He turned and kissed her forehead. 'For now. I should go back down. Come back out if you feel up to it.'

She allowed herself the luxury of accepting the kiss without feeling guilty. A friend's gesture.

'Oh, I almost forgot.' He reached into a back pocket and pulled out a crumpled envelope. 'This letter came for you this morning.'

She took it and turned it over. 'An Irish postmark.'

Emma slid her finger behind the flap on the envelope and pulled out a folded piece of paper.

She read the short letter.

'It's from Eva. Remember, from the workhouse?'

'I remember.'

Emma read the words once more before saying them out loud. 'She's saying she thinks she's found what Nana left behind.'

Thomas frowned and took the pipe from his mouth. 'I thought the brooch was the thing she'd left behind.'

'So did I.'

Chapter Twenty-Two

Eva opened the door and ushered Emma and Aoife inside. Snowflakes followed them in on the wind and settled in wet dots on the flagstones. Thomas had driven them to the outskirts of Cork, where Eva lived in a first-floor apartment of a Victorian townhouse, and then driven on, having agreed to let the girls visit Eva alone.

'Come in, come in. So glad you could come.' Eva invited them inside. 'I'm just sorry it's taken so long.'

Emma accepted the offer to take a seat and Aoife leant against the kitchen sink while Eva popped a kettle on the stove and busied herself making tea.

'It was something you said in your thank-you letter. I was so touched to receive it and delighted – well, amazed, if I'm honest – that you even found your grandmother's brooch, but it was when you said she'd called it the most "precious thing she'd left behind" that I started to think.' She reached for three cups on a shelf and turned around.

'Which was?' Emma prompted.

'My father still tends the graves at some of the workhouse sites. He's been doing the job over forty years.'

Emma held her breath.

'I went over to Father's for supper a couple of weeks back

and he was talking about the grave-diggers running out of room at St Mary's of Kilworth. That's a few miles north of here. We were reminiscing about the time he'd taken me as a child to that church for a day and I'd played all over the gravestones, as children do. May the Lord forgive me.' Eva raised her eyes to heaven and crossed her chest. 'And it was then I remembered the tiny headstone near the wall. Under a big fir tree, it was, and Dad always said that tree kept the bairn warm.'

'Eva. What are you talking about?'

'Sorry, sorry, yes. Well, this one tiny grave I was drawn to because it had a rough carving – not professional, like, but amateur – of one of them Tara brooch shapes, with the sword and all. And the name of the baby scratched on the stone was Peter O'Reilly.'

'I don't understand,' Emma said.

'Well, the people who died in the workhouses were not always buried on site but in allocated sister church yards – especially if someone came forward offering to cover the cost. Different houses had links to different churches. It seems your grandmother's workhouse had a link with St Mary's.'

'Go on.'

'It's my belief that…' She paused and swallowed. 'Emma, I think your grandmother may have had a child while at the workhouse.'

The room began to spin. *A baby? A baby* before *she met Grandpapa, Peter? How could that be? Yet, the baby was called Peter?* Emma's chest tightened and her mind raced.

'How can you be so sure this grave is linked to my grandmother?'

'Because my father arranged for me to see the historical

log of burials in the churchyard. It goes back eighty-four years and I read it with my own eyes last Monday, Emma.'

'I saw it clear as day. Baby Peter O'Connor, two months old. Father Peter O'Reilly and mother Ellen McCarthy. The plot was paid for by the O'Reilly family of Cork. They were a family who ran a butchers.'

The room fell silent. Emma heard only her breathing while she tried to make sense of what she'd been told.

'I'm really sorry, Emma.'

Emma's head was throbbing. 'So, she must have met Grandpapa long before they sailed over to America. Their chance meeting by the bins next to the boarding house was a lie.' Emma pushed the chair back and the legs scraped harshly against the floor. 'How dare she lie to me. Why would she do that?'

'You don't know if it's a lie, Emma,' Aoife soothed.

'It's got to be. How can it not be if they'd been together all those months before? What, a year, two years before, perhaps? Why would she have been in a workhouse if they were together and his family had a butchers? It doesn't make sense.'

'Perhaps the business was failing? A lot of couples came to the workhouse together, Emma,' Eva said, pouring more tea. 'Perhaps Peter had no choice but to be separate from her, to continue his trade? Maybe he'd gone in there to be with your grandmother? Perhaps because she was pregnant at the time and they didn't realise they would be separated?'

'Oh, God.' Aoife looked stunned. 'That's terrible.'

'It's sad but true. All the women were housed in one side and the men in the other. Healthy men were taken out to build roads and bridges, all sorts of manual jobs. The women worked in the laundry and cooking and gardening, but they were never allowed to mix. She may never have known he'd gone.'

Aoife banged the table with defiance. 'I think your grandfather knew that if he left the workhouse and went back to Cork, even though it broke his heart to leave you and the baby, he knew he had a better chance of securing your future if he could stay in the business and keep it going.'

'But why would he then bother to leave the country?' Emma said.

'We checked the records and O'Reilly butchers stopped trading in 1849 and Father says that times were pretty tough in the meat trade. After the potatoes were wiped out, it wasn't long before all the animals had been eaten too.'

'So. Somehow…' Aoife stared at the ceiling. 'Peter and Ellen knew their only chance of a life together was to emigrate and they met up in the port.'

'And somewhere along the line, the baby didn't survive and they had to bury him before they left.' Emma's hand pressed against her chest, the pain of the truth tearing her already broken heart into ever-smaller pieces.

'And he must have found enough funds to pay for the burial because they had no choice but to leave Peter behind,' Eva concluded.

'I want to see the grave.'

'Are you sure, Emma?' Aoife asked.

'I'm sure.'

The cedar tree smelt of pine and earth. Eva lifted the lower branches and bent low to crawl beneath its skirts.

Emma gripped Aoife's hand while they waited. Perhaps Eva had forgotten which tree, which wall, which church.

What had seemed like a good idea an hour ago in Eva's kitchen now filled Emma with anxiety. Here was another member of their family who should have lived, should have grown up and been her mother's elder brother. But he had wilted and died, probably from starvation like millions of others at the time, and Nana would have been so young and helpless, not knowing what to do, how to look after the baby. They would have been an unmarried couple and perhaps that was why Peter had ended up at the workhouse too. His family perhaps disowned him, or paid for the burial, buried the evidence and sent Peter on his way. Yes, that would make more sense as to why they'd both had to start afresh.

'It's here. It's still here.' Eva's voice came from the thick fir. 'Come and see.'

Aoife lifted the same branches and beckoned for Emma to go through. Eva had pulled ivy from around the old headstone which had sunk into the soil at an angle. Its green mossy surface was damp to the touch, but Emma could make out the small lettering which spelt out her uncle's name. The uncle who never was.

'I don't think Mom knows about him,' Emma whispered. 'Because she's never said anything. Not a word.'

She ran her fingers along the lines of the dagger engraved as part of the brooch. No wonder she'd wanted to take the brooch with her when she left and been so heartbroken when she'd had to leave it behind.

'At least Mom has laid the brooch on Nana's grave. She wrote and told me,' Emma said quietly.

Eva nodded and laid a hand on Emma's shoulder. 'Yes, you gave her back her baby.'

Chapter Twenty-Three

Emma's head was fit to explode and the pills Aoife had found in the cupboard had done nothing to help. Squinting at the daylight pouring in through the window, Emma felt wobbly whenever she tried to step away from the bed, and sitting on the edge with her head in her hands was as far as she'd managed all morning.

'Emma?'

Thomas called from the landing. She winced at a sharp pain slicing through the side of her head. She prayed when she opened her eyes again that the floor might have stopped spinning. When it hadn't, she groaned and laid back against the pillows.

His voice came again. 'Emma, are you okay?'

She mumbled incoherently and covered her eyes with an arm to darken her world. The door opened.

'Hey.'

She felt the bed sag, as it had the night of the fire. She moved her arm just enough to peek at him. He touched her forehead gently with the back of his ice-cold fingers. 'God, you're burning up. I'm getting the doctor.'

Within minutes, Aoife had laid a cold cloth on her head. 'Doctor's on his way.'

'I… feel… sick.' Emma groaned, her belly knotting in spasm.

Aoife ran for a bucket and was back just in time. Emma retched, leaning off the edge of the bed. When it was over, the pain behind her eyes renewed its hold on her senses and she whispered an apology.

'Don't be daft. I've dealt with far worse with my little brothers and sisters.'

She stared at her favourite watercolour hanging from the picture rail – the cathedral with the sea behind it. Everyone knew Thomas as the businessman but not as the artist. She closed her eyes and pictured him standing at an easel, the strokes of the paintbrush on the paper like rice moving across an oven tin. As the moments passed, the pain released its grip a little. The spinning had stopped.

Later, the doctor snapped his bag closed.

'I'll need to do further tests at the clinic, but I think it is safe to say you are with child and experiencing a violent bout of morning sickness.'

She couldn't be pregnant. That was ridiculous. Their boat trip had been almost four months earlier.

'I thought morning sickness was experienced in the first few weeks,' she said, feeling at once numb and horrified.

The doctor turned to look at her. 'It is my experience that ladies suffer the traditional symptoms at different times during their trimesters, and for different reasons. The human body is an incredible thing and right now, my dear, yours is nurturing a new life. I take it your husband will be along to join you?'

She knew that to reply would shatter his assumption. She could hardly lie, pretend she had a husband and then none appear.

'I'm not married.'

He lifted the bag from the end of the bed and failed to hide his disproval.

'I see.' He looked about him a moment. 'What are you doing, precisely, staying in Mr Murphy's hotel? I assumed you had a husband who had a contract of work somewhere in the area.'

Emma reminded herself that while the doctor's statement was impertinent, predictable and utterly unwanted, he was a friend to Thomas and she may need him again.

She lifted her chin and answered, 'I was sent here by my family to recuperate from a fire in New York.'

'Well, it looks like you rather enjoy playing with fire.' He reached the door and turned back to offer his advice. 'I've got details of somewhere you can go – to sort out your predicament. We won't blacken the hotel with this news. I shall tell Mr Murphy you have influenza and that I shall be offering you some time in a private hospital, to free this room up for paying guests.'

Emma stiffened. 'I am a paying guest.'

'I doubt you will be much longer. Once you start to show, you'll be thrown out. Like I say, let's save the good hotelier any embarrassment and get you sorted soon. Good day.'

She stared at the door long after he had closed it quietly behind him, her fist against her mouth, and prayed he would keep his word and not tell Thomas. Not because she wanted to save him the embarrassment but because she needed time to think. Time to work out how to tell him herself.

Rolling the edge of the sheet between shaking fingers and willing time backward, she remembered how they were before the boat trip. What would she give to not be pregnant, and to have only the worries she'd thought enormous before. She was meant to find a husband before children became part of the agenda, and she hadn't planned to worry about that until she'd made her name in the suffrage movement – preferably on both sides of the Atlantic. How could life be going so wrong?

Emma pulled the sheet over her face and breathed in the scent of lavender from Aoife's cotton sachets of dried flowers which hung in the airing cupboard.

Emma groaned, not this time from pain. The dread of what must surely now be coming her way. Alice had been away for weeks and, since the Halloween festival, things had been calm and relaxed in the hotel. Emma had a terrible feeling that all that was about to change.

'The flu is serious, Emma,' Thomas reasoned from the end of the bed an hour later. 'He says he will send for you within a few days and take you to somewhere where he is better able to monitor you.'

'I don't want to move anywhere.'

Seagulls went about their untroubled business outside. If Emma let them take the baby from her body, she'd be going against everything she was fighting for. How could she possibly stall their arrangements without telling him the truth? Within minutes of the doctor leaving the room she knew she wanted to fight for this baby's chance of survival; in fact, she'd never been so sure of anything.

Thomas smiled. 'But I want you to get better and he's a great physician. Let him treat you and soon you'll be right as rain again and strong enough to march in January and chant and shout to your heart's content.'

Emma's heart ached for him and these final moments of ignorance. He was referring to the biggest meeting Mrs Walsh had organised to date, and one Emma had been helping to organise. The women of Cork were due to host groups from all over Ireland. They were expecting over a thousand women to stand protest outside the Parliament buildings by the river in the city. The idea of missing the march filled Emma with devastation.

'You have to do what he says, Emma.'

She looked away when he sat on the bed. 'I refuse to be ordered about, by him or you.'

'I'm worried about you.'

'I'm going to be just fine, I can promise you that.'

'How can you be so sure, I'm known of people who've—'

'Died from influenza?' The sarcasm sounded horrible, even to her.

He nodded.

'I haven't got flu, Thomas.'

He stared at her and waited.

A nervous laugh escaped her mouth as adrenalin surged through her veins.

She took a deep breath. 'Thomas, I'm pregnant.'

She'd never seem him move so fast. 'But—'

She put up her hand. 'You don't have to worry about a thing.'

'How can you be sure?'

'There are many unmarried mothers in New York. I know what I'm doing,' she continued, not hearing him.

'Emma! How can you be sure you're pregnant?'

She picked at threads on the bedspread. 'Your doctor is pretty sure. He wants to do a blood test at his clinic to confirm, but – as you said yourself – he's a great physician and knows what he's talking about.'

He sat back down, his face white as the sheet which covered her. 'But it was only the once, and I thought we'd been careful.'

'How do you mean?'

He looked at her and shook his head. 'I was careful, or thought I'd been careful.'

'But I thought we…'

'Not completely…' He was struggling with words and she had no idea where he was going. How could he mean they had not been united when she had felt him?

She tried not to focus back to the moment that had caused the situation they now found themselves in. 'Well, it seems it was enough for you to leave your mark, as it were.'

Any embarrassment was soon replaced by frustration.

'And, unlike the assumption made by your doctor friend, I would like time to adjust to the possibility that this might actually be something positive.'

Thomas started pacing the room. 'I've put you in an awful situation, Emma. Hell, this will ruin your life.'

The heat of anger now burned in her belly. 'How can you say that? A child is a beautiful thing, Thomas.'

'Yes, a child is the perfect addition to any family unit, but—'

'I know. You're married. You don't need to remind me.'
She got out of bed and yanked the gown from the back of
the door, wrapping herself away from his sight and praying
the headache from hell wouldn't return. 'Look, we've been
through this – I don't hold you wholly responsible for what
happened. We're both to blame, if you want to use the
word—'

'I'd rather we didn't.'

'I wanted to be close to you, more than anything in the
world. But I realised in the days that followed, that having
a relationship with you was a silly dream.'

He hung his head in shame. 'This is not how I thought
it would be.'

'How *what* would be!' Emma spat words back at him,
terrified he was referring to their sleeping together.

'Finding out I was to become a father.'

'It's too late for that sentiment. I'll leave before I start to
show, don't worry. And Alice must never know. It wouldn't
be fair on her.' She looked away, aware it was not only her
life being torn apart.

'I will not let this baby die, Thomas. I shall bring him
into the world, love him and nurture him well enough for
the both of us. You need not worry about us and I don't
expect a thing from you.'

When he came to stand in front of her, his cheeks were
wet with tears.

'I've made terrible decisions my whole life. It's pathetic,
Alice's father was right when he told me I'd amount to
nothing.'

She took steps towards him and they held each other for
a long time. It was Emma's tears that stopped falling first.

'You haven't ruined anything. Don't you see? You've added clarity to it. There have been too many deaths in my life. There's no way I'm adding to them.'

He took her hands in his and kissed each palm, then whispered against her ear, 'The baby may not be a him.'

'Oh, I think it is.' She kissed his cheek and smelt the scent that was him.

He gently pushed her away so he could look at her. 'You're proving again how brave you are, while I feel helpless, hopeless and selfish.'

'Thomas, I chose to go with you on the trip because *I* was selfish and knew I wanted time with you away from the hotel. And as those hours passed, it was my choice to respond to feelings in your presence.'

Perhaps it was a lifelong belief he wasn't worthy that found him nodding.

'I'm fighting for the vote, yes, but also women's rights, so they can start to make their own decisions. The decisions I made that day on the boat have had consequences I will now stand by.'

'But I've been more selfish because you are single and I am not, and if you choose to have this child, I can't be part of its life.'

'That night was down to both of us. Never forget that. I'm not angry. I don't regret it. In fact...' She turned his face so she could look him in the eyes. 'The more time that passes, the more I believe it was meant to be. With you, I've discovered what real love should feel like. And now, it seems, you've given me a part of you. The most precious part of you that a woman could ever have. You're married to Alice, and we can never be together – that's true – but

I'll never forget our time together. I came to find my grandmother's past and I'll be going home having found my future.'

The next morning, Emma lay back in the bath and placed her hands on her flat belly. So what if she was pregnant at the march? She recalled her mother's physician advising Maggie to take a daily walk well into the seventh month of her pregnancy with Henry, before she followed his advice to rest during those final weeks.

Bringing up Thomas's baby up without him by her side was a way of life she was not yet willing to contemplate. She knew fatherhood was something he'd hoped for but had he truthfully wanted children with Alice – a woman who treated him with disdain – or simply assumed they would become part of his marriage?

After drying her body on soft towels, Emma released the plug and the water gurgled its departure from the iron bathtub on clawed feet. She was thankful the doctor's new Midol pain pills seemed to have done the trick for what he called a migraine, leaving her feeling human once more, albeit exhausted.

So engrossed was she in her thoughts that when she walked back in her room, she didn't at first notice Aoife sitting on the edge of the bed.

'Aoife!'

'Sorry to startle you, I had to see how you were doing.'

'Thank you, that's kind, and I'm fine, really I am.'

'The doctor asked to see me earlier, before he left. Thomas has had to pop out so he doesn't know I'm in here.'

Their eyes met and Emma wondered if Aoife knew. 'What did he tell you?'

Aoife looked down at her hands in her lap. 'He just looked at me with sad eyes and whispered that you'd probably be needing a friendly female ear as you didn't have a husband to attend to your emotional needs. I didn't have the faintest idea what he meant at first, but after he'd gone, something clicked with the sickness thing and him saying about a husband. I mean, what would a husband have to do with a woman's wellbeing?'

Emma flopped down beside her.

'And then it hit me. You're pregnant, aren't you?' Aoife said.

'It looks that way, yes.'

Aoife took Emma's hands. 'It's Thomas, isn't it?'

Emma gulped back tears and nodded.

'What are you going to do?'

'Why, keep it, of course.'

Aoife's eyes widened. 'Will you stay here?'

'I think I'll have to leave, but I don't want to go.' She bit her lip. 'I don't want to leave here. Or him. Or you, come to that.'

Aoife managed a smile. 'I've seen the way he looks at you. He thinks I don't, but I do. I know him. I've watched him change these last few months. Seriously! I have – don't look surprised. It's sad, but Alice only drains him, whereas you breathe life into him.'

Emma slumped back against the pillow. 'Has it been that obvious?'

Chapter Twenty-Four

Thomas drove up the hill and out of Queenstown. He'd rehearsed the conversation he was about to have with the doctor and it wasn't going to be pleasant.

The headlights glowed yellow on the stone wall outside the large house on the edge of town and he brought the car to a stop.

'Come in, Thomas, what a lovely surprise.' Julia, the doctor's wife, welcomed him in. The smell of pine needles mixed with fresh washing on a wooden horse in front of a range was comforting as they walked through the house and into a drawing room. 'Thomas here to see you, dear.'

The doctor stood from behind his immaculate desk and checked his pocket watch. 'Is everything alright? A strange hour for you to be out of the hotel, but always lovely to see you.'

Thomas smiled at the wife, who nodded and left them to it, closing the door behind her.

'Sorry to turn up announced, but I had no choice.'

'Sit down, please.'

'It's the American, Emma.'

'I thought it might be. I've made some enquiries and have a bed waiting for her in Cork infirmary.'

'I'd really rather we treat her flu at the hotel.' Thomas focused on coloured swirls in the middle of a paperweight. 'If you could just give me any medication you think she'll need.'

'Thomas. I think her case is quite severe. It's far better she's in good medical hands. Then she can return to the hotel when it's all over.'

'No!'

Thomas had never shouted at his doctor, nor anyone he respected. Possibly no-one. But since the map of his life had shifted, an overwhelming sense of protection had begun to steer his every thought and move.

The doctor sat back and narrowed his eyes. 'Look, Thomas. I admire your ambition to look after her, but she's too ill for you to be making these judgement calls.'

They were dancing around the truth. Thomas sent a prayer of forgiveness to the ceiling rose, illuminated by a smart chandelier. 'She's not ill, and we both know it.'

The doctor sighed. 'What the hell are you protecting her for? She'll have slept with God knows who in the town and the silly girl now needs sorting out. What are you asking me to do? Ignore my role as the town physician? I have a reputation to uphold and this... predicament is not what you and Alice need at the hotel. Just imagine what Victor would think. He'd be turning in his grave.'

Thomas squeezed his hands into fists. Thirty years his senior, the doctor had looked after his mother and him all his life, and to hear him side, albeit ignorantly, with his wife's family angered him even more. 'Victor isn't here. I'm thinking about Emma, who wants to go home to New York in a few weeks. It's her life and her decision.'

'You've gone soft.' The doctor narrowed his eyes.

'Maybe so. If it helps, remove me from your records and I'll find myself another doctor.'

Thomas's heart thumped against his ribs. He was aware of his body rising from the chair, the foreign rush of fury splitting him in two, the original version retreating to the corner of the room.

'I'm sorry to say you will have to.' The doctor rose to meet Thomas's gaze. 'Although I shall be extremely sorry to be terminating our alliance. You realise I shall be unable to make visits to the hotel in future, to treat your guests – something, may I remind you, that Victor arranged with me years before your mother's boarding house was incorporated—'

'Leave my mother out of this.'

The doctor walked to the door. 'I treated your father, you know, just before he died. He begged for my help.'

Thomas ground his teeth together, nipping his tongue in the process. The metallic taste of blood in his mouth was abhorrent. 'That man was an animal.'

'What happened was unfortunate, I grant you, but perhaps your mother had driven him to—'

The Thomas in the corner watched in horror as the devil in him marched to the door and swung a right arm through the air, his fist making contact with the bone of the doctor's cheek.

Both men, upstanding citizens in the local community, breathed hard and faced each other, unsure what came next.

'My mother saved my life, and I hers with my ridiculous marriage arrangement. I've done my duty these years and would ask you to remain impartial.'

Thomas looked into the grey eyes of a man he'd called a friend. A reflection from the oil lamp on the desk dulled a little and the doctor nodded. 'I'm sorry. Your mother was a good woman. I shall cancel the booking at the infirmary, but it may be too late to stop the gossip there which tends to accompany such arrangements.'

'Let me worry about that.'

It was a different Thomas who left the doctor's house, his head low and his heart heavy.

Chapter Twenty-Five

'You've all done Christmas before, what's wrong with you people?' Alice hated having to re-do the decorations due to incompetence, yet it happened each festive season.

The Canadians were arriving soon and the hotel was far from shipshape. She'd sent Clive home to London for a week. He hadn't wanted to go but she couldn't help that. She needed this time away from him, away from the stage, the auditions, the hopes and dreams which seemed ever on the horizon.

Well-to-do couples, businessmen and their wives, over for their annual pilgrimage, would soon be filling the hotel for the weekend before Christmas. Their Irish relatives – or those who could afford to travel to the port – would arrive from inland counties to spend a day with their descendants. Alice always made sure to be home for the festive period and liked to personally oversee the needs of the Canadians. She found them generous with their time, and particularly generous with their money.

The clock in the hallway had just struck three when the first guests began to arrive.

'So lovely of you to host us again, Alice.'

'You're so welcome, Frederick. How's that pretty wife? Have you left her behind?' Alice kissed both his cheeks, cold from the snow flurries which had been falling on and off all day. She guided him through to the drawing room where Aoife was serving a punch, some obscure mix of tastes she'd insisted would go down well. Alice was still rattled from their conversation the night before.

Once Frederick had consumed two glasses and retreated to his room for a rest, Alice walked over and pulled Aoife to one side. 'Christmas Day is important to me.'

'I told you, my mother needs me to help at home, Miss Alice.'

'But I need you here. I'm due to sail to Liverpool the twenty-eighth for the start of the New Year tour. Tell your mother she can postpone her Christmas for when I've gone.' She was being too harsh on the girl, but she had to maintain her reputation or she might just unravel.

'I'm not sure.' Aoife hesitated.

'Look, Thomas does his bit, but really, it's you who keeps this place going in my absence, you who Chef can rely on, you who the regulars come to see. My father would be proud of you, Aoife.'

'He would?'

'He would, yes. As am I.' Alice sat down. Her fingertips tingled and the edges of the furniture began to spin.

'Are you okay, Miss Alice?' Aoife rushed over and knelt on the carpet.

The spinning slowed. 'I'm fine. I've not been sleeping, that's all.'

'You go up, and I'll bring you a warm drink.'

'You're a good girl.' Alice placed a hand on Aoife's shoulder and left it there. The girl had matured in the last year. She was no longer the shy and timid child who had arrived as pot-washer. She'd be a pretty woman one day, with the right guidance. Alice sighed and took her hand away.

In the hallway, Emma was on the stairs, reaching over the banisters to add final decorations to a huge fir tree placed, as always, against the curve of the staircase.

Alice coughed to gain her attention, noting the terrible choice of clothing Emma seemed to have adopted these days. 'Thomas tells me you've been a little under the weather, which has delayed your return home?'

'I'm better now and I'm sure in the New Year, I'll be fine to travel.'

'Oh, that's good.' Alice leant against the newel post at the bottom of the stairs. 'Forgive me for asking, but what exactly is it you've been doing with Margaret Walsh?'

'Suffragette work.'

Alice rolled her eyes and sauntered over to the mirror. Their eyes met through it.

'You do realise, biology is biology and we'll never be the same as men, don't you?'

Emma was getting tired of having to defend the right to fight and the benefits winning the vote would bring. 'I'd have thought an independent woman like you would be at the front of the queue to fight for the right to vote.'

Alice laughed, lit one of her thin cigarettes and placed it in a carved jade holder. 'I'm far too busy fighting my own battles, dear.'

'I admire you.'

'Now, why would you do that, when you know nothing about me?'

'You're an actress who has performed in some of the

biggest cities in the world, and in front of the King.'

'Pah!'

'But isn't that what you've always wanted to do? Aren't you living the life you've always dreamed of having?'

Alice stared hard at Emma and drew in another lungful of smoke. 'Appearances can be deceptive.'

Emma said nothing.

Aoife came through from the dining room. 'Chef said I'd made too many. These were left over, and did we want to share?'

Alice considered the contents of the tray. 'What are they?'

'They smell delicious,' Emma said, walking down the stairs. She picked one from the tray and popped it in her mouth.

Alice waved Aoife away. 'No, thank you, I can't afford to lose my figure.'

'Can I get you something else, Miss Alice?'

'Actually, you can.' Alice thought for a moment. 'Have a bottle of champagne sent up to my bedroom in twenty minutes. And please send my husband to see me.'

For three consecutive days, Alice relished her role as front-of-house, regaling the guests with stories from her city adventures and providing live renditions of songs she'd performed on the stage.

She changed her outfit twice a day before lunch and dinner and played up to her audience, many of whom clamoured for her attention. Finely dressed men congregated in the drawing room, leaving their wives gossiping in the dining room.

'If I may say so, Mrs Horinger, you look incredibly

well.' Emma helped the eldest guest upstairs at the end of the night. Betty was hugging the banister as she went.

'Thank you dear. It's the whiskey.'

'I'm sorry?'

'Whiskey. I have a tipple every night before bed.' She giggled.

'Oh! Shall I get you one from the bar?'

Mrs Horinger winked at her. 'No need. I have a small bottle in my room.'

Aoife had turned down the beds, lit the oil lamps and refreshed the jugs of water in the bedrooms.

Mrs Horinger patted Emma on the hand. 'I've had a lovely couple of days here, Emma. This could be my final visit, so I'm delighted to be here enjoying the company of my son and daughter-in-law, Sally. Dear Jack passed away last year, so they brought me along so I wouldn't be alone.'

'That's nice of them,' Emma said.

'Yes.'

Betty's shallow breath rattled.

'Is there anything else I can get you before I go down?' Emma felt faint. She'd been on her feet all day.

'No, no. I think Sally will be up shortly and she'll see to me.'

Emma gently closed the bedroom door and hesitated at the top of the stairs. She'd had enough of watching the men drooling over Alice, who made no attempt to discourage them, but she had one more table to lay before retiring for the night so made her way back down the stairs. She hated that Thomas didn't seem to notice his wife's inappropriate behaviour. Perhaps Aoife had been close to the truth, and theirs was a marriage of convenience.

Back in the dining room, Thomas was serving liqueurs to the more boisterous characters who had no intention of retiring to their rooms. Alice was sitting on the knee of a rotund man who wore a three-piece suit. Emma sat and polished some cutlery.

'Oh, Frederick, if you insist.' Alice slid from the man's knee and lifted the lid on the box on the sideboard. 'Clive acquired the gramophone for us last year, boys. You just wait.'

She removed the black disc from a waxy sleeve and set it on the turntable before moving the cumbersome arm over the edge and winding the handle. As crackles of sound gave way to instrumental orchestra notes, Alice sat back on Frederick's knee and cleared her throat. Her chest heaved above the lace frill of her boned bodice as she began to sing. Cigar smoke circled above them. The men were in rapture.

'Careful, Fred, you'll not be able to stand up with dignity soon!'

Thomas dried glasses in silence, stacking them on glazed shelves behind the bar.

When the song came to an end, the men asked for more.

Emma shook out a clean tablecloth and let it settle.

'Come over here, little missy.' A man with a curly yellowing moustache patted his knee. 'Come and keep old Walter company for a few minutes.'

'Yes, come on, Emma,' Alice said. 'Show us what you're made of.'

Emma glanced over. 'That's kind, but I'm fine. I'm a bit tired.'

'Don't let the side down – we girls need to stick together when there's ruffians around like this lot.'

'Ruffians, hey?' Yellow moustache leant forward to speak in Alice's ear, but the alcohol he'd consumed had stolen his ability to whisper. 'I'll show you rough.'

Alice laughed loudly. 'Honestly, the cheek of it!'

'We need after-dinner entertainment and you two beauties are perfect.' Walter's agility belied his age and in two strides was at Emma's side. He lifted her swiftly off her feet and carried her back to his stool. She wriggled and squirmed while his surprisingly strong arms positioned her on his lap, arranging her weight where it pleased him.

Alice threw her head back and laughed, her cleavage straining. 'She looks terrified, Walter, do be gentle.'

Emma made a grab for Walter's shoulder to save herself slipping to the floor and he misread the movement. 'That's it, hold on tight!'

With one large hand against her back, he placed the other in the folds of her skirt.

Emma screamed. 'Stop it!'

There was a smash, as Thomas dropped a bottle.

'Oh, *do* be careful, Thomas!' Alice said.

Thomas came round from behind the bar, his face red. 'Emma, I think—'

'I think *you* need to leave Walter to his fun,' Alice interrupted.

But Emma had managed to pull away from the man who had white spittle in the corners of his lips. She made her excuses and escaped behind the bar and went into the kitchen.

'Oh, how very disappointing,' moaned Walter.

'You've lost your charm, old man.' The others roared with laughter, but Walter hadn't given up hope and called through the empty doorway, 'Come see me later – in room thirty-two!' Walter tickled Alice under the chin like he might do a child. 'Or how about sending me that pretty little housekeeper you have here?'

'No!'

For a moment, there was silence in the dining room. Alice's defiant reaction had stolen the heat of the moment and the only sound to fill the bar was Walter's wheezing lungs.

'What's wrong, Alice? You look like you've seen a ghost.'

'I'm fine.' Alice took a deep breath and fixed her smile.

Emma found Aoife standing at the butler's sink, elbow-deep in water.

'Evening, Miss Emma. Sounds like a real party out there, you don't have to leave it if you want to carry on, I'll have this done in no time.'

'I'd rather be here. Those men are pigs.' Emma perched on the stool she'd seen Chef use when he chopped vegetables, and took some time to steady her breathing.

Aoife turned and dried her hands. 'Actually, pigs are nicer.'

Emma giggled and reached for another tea towel.

Aoife pointed in Emma's face and quickly altered her stern look for a smile. 'No, you don't. You relax.'

'Thank you, Aoife. You're good to me.'

Alice had started to shout.

Emma froze.

'Are you soft on that girl, Thomas?'

The men were trying to regain Alice's attention; Emma

could hear their mumbling, over which Alice and Thomas were in heated discussion.

'Answer me, and pour me another brandy!'

'Alice, please calm down, and don't you think you've had enough to drink?'

'How dare you tell me what to do in my own home? I knew something was amiss when you refused to share my champagne.'

'Another song, Alice. We want another!'

'Can we discuss this later? We have guests,' Thomas said.

'I think you like her. Let's ask her… Emma?' Alice shouted.

Aoife shook her head and put out her hand to stop Emma going anywhere.

Suddenly, Alice was standing in the doorway. 'I'm asking you a question. Are you sleeping with my husband?'

Chapter Twenty-Six

The new doctor finished his examination. He was no older than thirty with fair hair that refused to stay in a parting.

'My name's Sean Forbes. Don't call me doctor. It makes me sound ancient.' His manner was kind and he'd said it with a smile.

Whatever he may have thought of her pregnancy, he'd not openly judged her and Emma was grateful. The blot on the landscape was that he was advising she postpone her return voyage until late February, declaring high blood pressure as the reason.

'You're not doing anything that you can't do sitting down,' Aoife told her while the doctor put his jacket back on.

He made a vague effort to flatten his hair. 'That's it. You keep an eye on her, Aoife.'

'Thank you,' Emma said.

The days passed and she became bored. Writing copy for newspapers on the activities of the IWSS was all well and good. What she wanted more than anything was to join in with the march in Cork.

Her belly had become taut, and it fascinated her that while her clothes still fit, when she pressed her belly, it no longer felt soft. The doctor had assured her many first-time mothers did not start to show until fourth or even fifth month. As she hemmed new curtains made for the bedrooms by Aoife's mother, Emma felt sure she could march and no-one would suspect a thing.

In her bedroom, she sat at the table in the window and reached for a new piece of paper. Below her the front door banged, and through the window, she saw Thomas walk across the road towards the market stalls.

She'd yet to declare the pregnancy to her parents. Turning up heavily pregnant might be a bigger shock than informing them now, which would at least give them a few weeks to get used to the idea.

Dear Mom,

Something about the New Year has compelled me to share some news which I admit I've been avoiding telling you. Father will disown me, but I hope that eventually you might forgive me. I fell in love, but it's complicated, and I'll not be coming home on my own. I am expecting a baby at the beginning of June.

I refused the suggestion to get rid of it, and have made an enemy of the local doctor here, but I told you once before, I don't care what the doctors say!

I have a lovely new doctor now who will visit regularly. He informs me that the baby will be taking nutrients from me, irrespective of how I'm feeling. Some days I feel like I can conquer the world and others, I feel like sleeping for a week. It seems babies make themselves a priority in a mother's life long before they are born. He says I am well but should not travel for a while.

I have a friend in Aoife, here at the hotel, who looks after me well, so please don't worry. My only regret is that Nana is no longer with us to meet her great grandchild...

She looked out of her bedroom window, pen in hand. Thomas had long since disappeared into the crowds and her stomach clenched at how out of reach he was. Just as he always would be.

She reached across the little table and touched the window glass with her fingers, its chilled surface causing condensation to appear around her fingertips.

She planned to keep the pregnancy a secret in Queenstown for as long as she could, although Mary had asked twice how Emma was feeling the day before when she'd burst into the hotel with news. *He's only gone and done it!* Mary had rushed into the dining room, and Emma had lowered the *Irish Citizen* as Thomas led Mary to a table near the window.

'What's he done?' Thomas asked.

'Harold's saved enough to buy a third-class ticket on that new ship... oh, what the hell's its name... New York was always a dream for that boy, but I never thought for a minute he'd really go.'

'You mean the *Titanic* sailing in April?' said Thomas.

'I'll be so proud to wave him off.' Mary blew her nose on a handkerchief.

'I think that will be a bit difficult.'

'What?' Mary looked up. 'Why?'

'She'll be anchored out at Roche's Point. The passengers will get to her by tender.'

Mary's face fell. 'Oh, damn. I wanted to see him go up the gangplank and all.'

Thomas scratched the back of his head. 'Well, I'll put a good word in for you, Mary. Perhaps there'll be room for you to hop on the tender with him. I know the lace vendors will go out to spend a few minutes on deck, so there's no reason if we give you something to sell, you can't—'

'My buns?' Aoife blurted from the bar.

'Perfect,' Thomas said, pointing in her direction. 'There'll be passengers on the ship who won't be getting off and would appreciate one of your pastries. I'll get a licence arranged for you and no-one can say a word.'

Mary clapped her hands together. 'You always were the nicest man.'

'And you tell him to look me up once he arrives in New York,' Emma added from near the fireplace. 'He'd be very welcome to come visit.'

Mary fanned her face. 'You don't know what that means to me, Emma.'

Emma smiled. 'I'll leave you my address so he knows where to find me. I should be going home in the next couple of weeks.'

'I'll be sorry to see you go, dear.' Mary finished her tea. 'We all will, won't we, Thomas?'

There was a beat before he replied, 'Yes, we will.'

'Well, there's not many weeks I can spend with that boy now, so I must be getting back and ensure he's remembered how to brush down that tweed suit of his father's.' Mary stood up and then sat back down. 'It is safe over there, Emma? I mean, one minute I'm fine with him going, the next I think he's going to disappear into a huge hole and never find his way out. It's such a big place, he'll get lost, so he will. Oh, dear… perhaps I should never have encouraged him?'

'He'll be one of hundreds of young men travelling,' Thomas said. 'They'll all look after each other.'

Emma slowly released a breath she wasn't aware she'd been holding. Who would look after Thomas when she'd gone? He had a wife who didn't notice him and now Emma was nurturing an unborn baby who would never know its father. Could life be more unfair?

'Well, I'll be off.' Mary slipped on her gloves and gathered the leaflets she'd agreed to deliver. 'Are you sure you're alright, dear? You look peaky to me.'

'I'm fine. Never better.'

'Tell Aoife she's to bring leftover buns and cakes up anytime – the spire's growing and the workers are always ravenous. You never know, one of those nice young fellas might even ask her out.'

'We will, Mary.' Emma walked her back to the front door. A gust of wind billowed dust into swirls as Mary turned for home.

Thomas placed another log onto the fire.

Emma tucked her skirt beneath her and sat down next to the fire watching the sparks fly and settle as the existing logs welcomed the newcomer.

'Mrs Walsh has sent a telegram.'

'Oh?'

Emma looked at Thomas, dressed in his usual comfy clothing, and found herself picturing what lay beneath the cotton, wool and tweed. She fought the urge to talk about her feelings. 'Yes, she wants to give some of the poorer women a few of the lower leadership roles in the Society and has asked me to consider who in the locality that might be. She believes if we are fighting for *all* women, we have to prove that all classes of women are valued. We're going to talk more about it at next week's meeting.'

'Are you sure you've got enough energy to be attending meetings?'

'Oh, I'm fine. It's what's keeping me going.'

Thomas sat in the chair opposite and leant forward with his elbows on his knees. 'I didn't think for a minute I'd be able to talk you out of it.'

She risked a smile and he returned one, making her heart pull. She looked down into her lap, both adoring and hating the love which ran through her veins with abandon.

As had become habit, Aoife ate supper in Emma's bedroom and chatted about bread-making, clothes or anything else which came to mind. Aoife had moved into the hotel before Christmas when Emma suggested it would save her having to travel in freezing weather. Alice was away until early April.

'What's this?' Aoife picked up a sketch. 'Is it yours?'

'That was Nana's brooch. The one Thomas helped me find last summer. I sketched it before I sent the original home.'

'It's beautiful.'

Emma looked at the pencil sketch. 'It's one of the best things about my visit here.'

'Lots of good things have happened since you've been here,' Aoife said.

'My friendship with you.'

'Your friendship with Thomas,' Aoife added with a smile, and looked over at the table. 'You're writing another letter?'

Emma pulled the unfinished letter towards her.

'Yes, it's time I warned Mother it won't only be me returning next month.'

'How do you think she'll take it?'

'It's not her I'm worried about.'

'Your pa?'

Emma nodded and sighed. 'What I feel is so hard to explain. I'm guilty I've done wrong, but the baby itself and his chance at life feels so right. All my life I've been taught that women who have children out of wedlock are less wholesome than a married woman who has a family.'

'What will he say, do you think?'

'He'll be furious. Worried what others will think, perhaps even disown me.'

'What others, who are these *others*?'

'All his friends, business contacts and so on.'

'What does their opinion matter?'

'Sadly, Aoife, these things really do matter to some people. I will have let the family down as far as he's concerned.'

'I think this is where my mother would say something rude about those other people's opinions.'

Emma laughed. 'Over here, with you and Thomas, I feel like I can be the person I want to be. And my view of what it means to be a woman is changing. I've learnt the world doesn't stop turning if I do something unexpected. So that's why I know it's time to write home and say that I'm proud of my impending motherhood.'

Emma stood and took in a deep breath. 'What Pa does with that information is anybody's guess, but if he wants to keep a daughter, he's going to have to accept a grandchild.'

Chapter Twenty-Seven

Emma refused to listen to Thomas's attempts to persuade her not to join him shopping in Cork. Doctor Forbes had agreed she could purchase a ticket to travel home at the end of February and she'd been grumpy ever since.

'I'd like to come, it'll be a change of scene.'

'I was thinking of the baby.' Thomas stood by the car, blocking her route to the passenger door. 'The only way I'll agree to take you is if you stay *in* the car when we get there.'

'Oh, great. Now you're treating me like the family pet. Well, fine.' She left her coat undone as it was more comfortable.

Thomas pulled out into the road behind two horse-drawn carts carrying blocks of stone for the cathedral. The roof of the car had been up since the autumn, but Emma noticed small white dots of mould had formed on the corners of the hood where moisture had seeped through over winter and not yet dried out in the sun.

'I'm still not happy about this,' Thomas said.

Emma shuffled in her seat. 'I've noticed something.'

'What?'

'You stand up to me. You argue with me.'

He glanced in her direction before negotiating a tight bend.

'Yet you don't say a word to contradict Alice, even when she is totally unreasonable.'

He groaned. 'I've learned it's fruitless to try because there's no such thing as a two-way discussion with Alice. It's her way, or no way.'

'Isn't that rather defeatist?'

He offered no further comment as he changed gears up the hill out of town. The engine whined with the effort of climbing before the road levelled out again.

Emma turned her attention to the newspaper which she'd taken from the hall table. 'It says here that trouble is expected this week because some politician called Churchill is coming over from London. He's due to speak in Celtic Park tomorrow… look.' She angled the paper towards Thomas, but he didn't take his eyes from the road.

'I bet they didn't dare send Asquith,' he said. 'Churchill's just some expendable young cog in the wheel of politics. They're probably testing the water before Asquith pays a visit, either that or Churchill has put himself forward because he's got desires for his own for promotion.'

Emma followed the article with her finger as the car lumped through undulations in the road.

'It goes on to say the Unionists are planning to disrupt proceedings, and more police have been called in. Even the infantry have been put on alert.'

'So you can see now why I wanted you to stay away?'

'Cork city will be fine, Thomas. Stop worrying,' she said.

'Don't you believe it. Protestors sniff out trouble and a small gathering can escalate into full-scale strife within minutes,' Thomas said.

Emma turned the page. 'Oh, dear.'

'Now what?'

'Shipyard workers were planning to overturn Churchill's car yesterday when he arrived in Belfast, but because his wife was in the car, they refrained at the final moment.' She let the paper drop to her knee.

'Leaving you in the car then is the best plan. Your presence should preserve it, if any errant shipyard workers should be in the vicinity—'

'Hey!' She nudged him with her elbow, relieved that recent animosity had been replaced by a renewed sense of their old friendship. They were both trying to ignore her impending departure.

Thomas parked in front of a row of shops that included a butchers they'd been to before. 'Right. I'm going to into O'Grady's to pick up this week's meat and order the hog for the street party.'

He opened the driver's door then hesitated.

'Go on. I'll be fine. I've got reading material and a letter to draft – a response to an article by someone who thinks suffragettes undermine her womanhood. She thinks suffragettes all walk around wearing men's clothes, swilling beer and smoking.'

'Good luck with that.' He grinned and stepped out before she could take another swipe at him with the paper.

She wound down the passenger window as he walked round the front of the car, pausing to allow people going about their business to pass, and called out, 'Don't be long.'

He waved. 'I won't.'

She wound the window back up as the winter air was cold. The street party which he'd been planning for weeks was something she'd be sad to miss. In less than six weeks, the scheduled docking in April of White Star's latest and largest, most luxurious ship off the production line was already causing a stir. The *Titanic* would be calling at the port of Queenstown, her final stop before heading over to New York. The Admiral was fully booked, and the event was a welcome contrast to the political troubles on everybody's minds. Emma placated herself by knowing that, having gone home to New York, she would at least be able to watch the ship come in to dock in Manhattan – and could look out for Harold and then write to Mary that he'd arrived safely.

Next to the butchers was the bank. Large doors were propped open and men in smart suits and bowler hats passed in and out of the building in a continual stream like ants on a mission.

She cupped the gentle curve of her belly, a movement which had become instinctive. The area was harder still, as if the baby had built a fortress around itself, safe from the harsh world outside. When she was alone she talked to her bump and did so now, giving her son a running commentary on the world outside the car. It helped her to picture him as a real person growing inside her, and she'd given him a cute little face, a first outfit and even saw herself pushing him in a perambulator along the sidewalks back home. She owed him that vision, in case he'd heard those early voices who had rather his life had been snuffed out.

The windows of the bank turning opaque did not fully register until the sound of it smashing reached her ears, along with screams from passers-by who had witnessed the man throwing the brick.

The shop window shattered, smothering the display behind it. A toy car parked next to a three-storey wooden dollhouse, examples of what the bank might help purchase – set up to tempt bystanders to request a loan – sat glistening beneath a covering of sparkling shards.

Injured people littered the pavement and she wrestled with a desire to get out and help but remembered her promise to Thomas about staying in the car.

A man appeared near the driver's window, one arm raised, and Emma held her breath. He hadn't seen her. He hurled another brick over the car and through the window of the shop on the other side of the bank and then ran away shouting.

She had to get out. Before she had a chance to reach for the door handle, the car rocked like a small boat caught in the wake of a larger ship. A group of three, perhaps four, men were pushing against it, chanting something she couldn't hear. Their attention was drawn to a brawl in the road and they moved away.

She gripped the edge of the seat.

Twisting to look through the back window, she saw a young newspaper delivery boy being pulled from his bike and beaten.

Stones were hurled into the crowds, the shops no longer the sole target, and innocent bystanders scattered for shelter in every direction.

Police blew whistles and tried to break up the riot, but the protestors were seeping from the crowd, previously camouflaged, and now outnumbered the authorities.

For the second time in her life, Emma was trapped and petrified.

Through the passenger window she watched a man spray words onto the butcher's window with a brush covered in red paint – '*HOME RULE ENDS NOW*'.

He finished his masterpiece and glanced behind him. That's when he saw her.

She gasped when he lurched towards the car, the glass of the passenger window the only barrier between his breath and hers.

Yellow twisted teeth were the last thing she saw before he filled her view with red horizontal stripes. The lines of overlapping paint dripped like rivers of blood. Someone else pounded the bonnet with a rock, then climbed up onto it and knelt down, his hands flat on the windscreen, and leered at her.

He opened his mouth like an animal about to howl and licked the windscreen. Then leant back and took aim.

'Thomas!' she cried to no-one, as a loud crack filled the car with noise and shattered glass. The heavy stone that hit her chest stole her breath just before everything went black.

Chapter Twenty-Eight

Emma listened to the pitter-patter of rain against the window and tried to turn over. She had only seconds to discover the window was in the wrong place before pain shot through her body.

'Emma, it's alright. Stay still.' The voice was female but not Aoife's.

'Where am I?' Emma whimpered.

'Is she okay?' a new voice asked.

'She's fine.' The kind voice again. 'You're in hospital, Emma.'

There was an urge to retch.

'Try not to move. We suspect you've broken some ribs.'

'So tired.'

The nurse leant over and shone a light in her eyes.

'Ouch.' And then, 'My God – my baby!'

'Your baby's fine,' a nurse reassured her.

Emma grabbed the nurse's hand. 'Thomas?'

'I'm here.'

He came into view.

'Why am I here?'

The nurse fussed around her. 'You were caught in the riots.'

'You've been asleep for sixteen hours,' Thomas said as he dragged a chair from next to the wall. 'God, I've never been so worried.'

She reached out her hand and whispered, 'What happened?'

'Sinn Fein.'

'There was a man… he covered the window.'

'Don't worry about that, now.' Thomas took her hand in his.

'I don't remember much.'

'That's normal,' the nurse said while taking Emma's pulse.

'I'm so sorry.'

Thomas said nothing.

'The baby's alright?' she asked again.

He nodded.

'Oh, no… the car!'

'It can be repaired, although it's going to take some time.'

'Thomas, I should have listened to you and stayed at home. I would never forgive myself if I'd lost him.' Emma winced with the effort of breathing.

The nurse's eyes were fixed on the watch pinned to her uniform. 'Still feel sick?'

'A little.'

'That'll be the pain relief. It should pass.' She was satisfied with Emma's progress and left the room.

Emma looked back at Thomas. 'Why are you smiling?'

'You still think the baby's a boy.' He laughed but didn't finish the sentence. Instead he stood up to lean closer and moved Emma's hair away from her eyes, then kissed her cheek before sitting back down.

That short moment, in a strange hospital bed, was the closest they would ever feel to a family. She tried to imprint the feeling to her long-term memory.

'I'll call him Thomas.'

Thomas looked away.

'He'll grow up to be kind and thoughtful, he'll respect women and be conscientious,' Emma continued, 'just like you.'

Silence filled the air.

Her heart was shattering into a thousand pieces, exactly like the windscreen, but thankfully he wouldn't be able to see that part of her. She closed her eyes. Eventually sleep pulled her to a distant place, although later, when he slowly removed his hand from hers, she felt the warmth of its departure.

'Sorry, Mr Murphy, but she needs to rest now.' The nurse spoke quietly through the open doorway.

'I'll see you tomorrow,' Thomas whispered close to her ear. 'Sleep well, my love.'

She felt the kiss on her forehead, heard his footsteps retreating and treasured his words. She wished she could call him back, to tell the whole hospital that his wife didn't deserve him, to explain he was a fool to stay with her and to tell them that she – Emma – would love him forever.

Dear Thomas,

I'm still in Paris but have the most amazing news, and simply had to write and tell you.

I have secured the lead role in a new film to be recorded in Hollywood. Clive has worked so hard for me these past months I've already signed the contract and we leave in April. He's bought first-class tickets on that luxury ship sailing to New York. Aren't we lucky she's docking at our little town? We will then travel by train across America to the west coast, where I am told California has guaranteed sunshine. I could be gone for up to six months!

We must stay strong because I may soon command the big bucks, as they say in America. Talking of America, I trust Emma has now finally departed? I'm not at all sure she was good company for you, or Aoife. I think you've taken your eye off the ball since she's been around and I'm worried she may have influenced dear Aoife to expect more from life than is realistic for someone like her.

We plan to be back in Queenstown from 9th April and I hear a party is planned in the harbour the night before we sail. Can you arrange for me to sing in the bandstand? I'm sure the locals would enjoy a chance to witness my talent. Be there to watch me, darling, like you used to when we were first together? Things may have been strained between us these last few years, but I cannot deny your loyalty.

I will have to leave overseeing the redecoration of the drawing room this spring to you. Can you manage?

Anyway, must dash. We're attending a dinner this evening in an exclusive club on the Champs-Élysées.

Alice x

Thomas laid the letter on the desk and covered it with a book. His wife was going away for half a year. While he waited for a feeling of devastation to arrive, he pulled open the drawer and retrieved the hip flask.

He'd made a real mess of things. He was evidently a useless husband, or his wife wouldn't be sleeping with her agent. And one glorious, if frivolous, night with Emma had resulted in a child he would never see. Years before, when Alice had suggested they have a more open marriage, he'd immediately rejected such a notion. He put the ridiculous idea down to the company she'd been keeping at the time, and in turn had hoped she might respect him enough to do the right thing by him, as he had by her.

He had never questioned his Catholic way of life before, believing that while he walked this earth, he would never separate from Alice, however harshly she treated him.

Aoife's distinctive footsteps were coming his way and he put the hip flask back into the drawer as she came into the room.

'I've prepared her room, Mr Thomas, is there anything else before I go? Just, there's painting today at the Soldiers' Home and I promised Emma I'd be there on her behalf if ever she couldn't make it.'

'That's fine. You go, and thank you for staying longer.'

She struggled with the arms of her coat. 'Can't wait to have her back, Mr Thomas, can you? Damn these sleeves.'

'It's been a bit quiet, without her. Can I help with that?'

'S'okay, I'm in. Bit tight, but I was practising with mother's sewing machine last night. This coat was my sister's and she's… well, she's taller than me so it drowned me before I started.'

'Okay then, well goodnight.'

He sat back and slid the lid onto his ink pen and held it between each hand, twisting it back and forth while he considered the number of days Emma would spend in the hotel before she departed for home. The violent snap made him jump and stung his fingers. Black ink spread across his palms and dripped onto his trousers. Jagged edges ensured there was no way the two halves could ever be re-joined.

Chapter Twenty-Nine

Emma glared at the elderly surgeon with thick white hair which matched his white hospital coat. 'I can't do that. I need to have this baby at home. I mean, my home in New York.'

Ten days had passed since the riot and being marooned in hospital was wasting valuable time.

'Well, I'm sorry. You can travel to the hotel, but the ribs will take at least six weeks to mend and that takes you to over seven months. I would suggest at that stage in your pregnancy you'd find a week's voyage most uncomfortable and would advise against risking it.'

He scribbled something before clipping the board over the rail at the bottom of the bed, then peered at her over the top of his glasses. 'It's best for baby.'

'I suspect I shall be *uncomfortable* wherever I am.'

She hated petulance but couldn't stop herself. She laid back and sighed.

'I think you're doing a wonderful job.' He glanced down the ward. 'I'm aware the father is not around and you'll no doubt have received much unpleasantness from people who do not approve.'

She looked back at him, speechless.

He smiled and moved to the side of her bed so he could speak more quietly. 'But I have to say, I admire you. Your escape from the fire and now your work for suffrage. My wife's a suffragette.'

Her heart skipped a beat. 'Who told you about me?'

'My wife is a friend of Margaret Walsh.' He smiled. 'Good luck, Emma.'

He walked away towards another patient whose leg was wrapped in thick plaster, elevated by a complex system of pulleys.

Three days later Emma was back in the hotel, with strict instructions to take it easy.

But she had a plan.

She made it her mission to endure the agony, to get dressed and move around anyway in the hope she could pretend she was more advanced in her recovery.

On the fourth evening, during supper in Emma's room, she took Aoife into her confidence. 'You must help me, I simply have to get well enough to travel or this baby will be born in Ireland. And... without Thomas, I need my mother.'

'This isn't right, Emma.' Aoife wrapped a skirt around Emma's curved belly, all the time shaking her head. 'Shouldn't you be resting?'

'I can rest when I get home, I can rest on the voyage. I don't want to be here when Alice comes back next month. Now, let's concentrate. I've been wanting to show you this.' Emma gave Aoife a sketchpad and hoped it would take their focus off her broken ribs. 'Open it.'

Aoife lifted the cover and gasped at the detailed painting. 'Emma, it's amazing!'

IRISH WOMEN'S SUFFRAGE SOCIETY
QUEENSTOWN BRANCH

'Thomas let me borrow his watercolours and showed me how to mix the colours. So this shows what I'd like the banner's design to look like. I'd like us to make it together, from scraps of material. It will hang in the assembly rooms which Mary has managed to book for Tuesday evenings. Queenstown is now on the map and I know you're going to be a big part of it, Aoife.'

Aoife dropped the book to her knees, still open at the page.

'But you're our leader,' she said quietly.

'I'm not going to be here much longer, am I?' She looked away. 'So, I need you to start to take over while I'm still here. I'm getting on a boat and soon, Aoife. The baby may not be due until June, but I want to be home before then. Between now and then, with Mrs Walsh behind us, Mary and Eva joining the ranks, we have an amazing team and *you* will continue to have a great team when I'm gone.'

Aoife looked again at the sketch and sat on the edge of the bed. 'Mother will have lots of leftovers, and green is a popular colour this year.'

'Green is your country's colour.' Emma's hand went to her belly. She looked through the window at the sea. 'What better view is there than this for me to take home?'

'I wish you didn't have to go.'

'Come now. Let's not get all sentimental.' Emma undid buttons on her jacket and reached for a hanger from the wardrobe.

Aoife jumped up. 'That reminds me. Look, I altered one of your blouses too. I hope you don't mind?'

She pulled the blouse from its paper cover and pointed at the extra panels of material she'd sewn between the seams down either side.

'You're so clever,' Emma said, and meant it.

'It was easy. I unstitched the seam under the arm and added the triangle piece to give you more room, but the front still looks the same. Oh, I've upset you. I didn't mean to.'

'You haven't. Crying seems to be a regular side effect to being pregnant.' Emma managed a laugh. 'What you've done for me is beyond amazing. I will be honoured to wear it.'

'It's been a pleasure. You're like a big sister, teaching me to read and helping around the hotel.' She pulled the blankets down on the bed. 'I'll be very sorry to see you go when the time comes.'

'So will I, Aoife. So will I.'

Two weeks later, Emma waited in the hallway for Mrs Walsh to collect her. Another member of the English Parliament was due at the Town Hall. Mrs Walsh thought it was the perfect opportunity for a quiet demonstration outside the building to keep the suffrage discussion high on the agenda. Emma hadn't wanted to miss it and Margaret had offered to collect her.

'This is ridiculous. Surely, this time, you're going to see reason?' Thomas said.

He was right, but she had put herself and the baby first. 'Stop worrying, I won't be at the protest. Margaret wants me based back at the office. She thinks there'll be new members turning up on the doorstep if they see the procession today, so I'm going to be sat behind a desk, perfectly safe. You see?'

Thomas ran his hands through his hair. 'You'd better be right.'

She pulled on a pair of gloves. 'Here she is!'

Emma opened the door and sunshine lit up a rectangle of floor tiles as Mrs Walsh came up the steps.

'Oh, good, you're ready. Ah, morning, Thomas, how are you? You look flustered.'

Emma stepped outside to meet her. 'Shall we go?'

Thomas was still stood in the open doorway when the car turned the corner and disappeared from view.

Mrs Walsh's driver pulled up outside the council offices to let her get out.

'Thank you, Gerald. When you've delivered Emma to the office, can you please park down Angel Street so I know where to run if the tearaways appear?' She laughed and patted Emma's hand. 'The forms are all on the desk when they start arriving. Just get them to fill one in and file it where I showed you, that's a good girl. Are you sure you're up to some office work?'

'Quite sure, it was driving me nuts wandering around the hotel.'

'That's the spirit.'

Then she was out of the car and gone.

Gerald drove away from the small gathering of women who had commandeered the steps outside the Town Hall. After a minute or so, Emma leant forward on the leather bench seat.

'Gerald?'

He turned his head a little to show he'd heard her.

'Would you mind dropping me here?'

He looked in the rear-view mirror, his eyebrows knotted together. 'It's quite a walk to the offices on Grand Parade from here, Miss.'

'I know, but I'd like the fresh air.'

'If you're sure.' He pulled over and she thanked him, then waited for the car to pull away and become absorbed in a line of traffic.

She turned to walk back the way they'd come.

This was her final opportunity to demonstrate. She checked the hem of the blouse was hanging loose and not tucked in. She was starting to show, but with the winter still upon them and layers of coats and scarves expected, it was easy to disguise.

She neared the Town Hall and noticed the crowd had already doubled in number. Margaret was visible in her straw hat at the top of the steps, and Emma pulled her felt hat further down her forehead and slipped in amongst the women at the back.

A long black car with huge headlamps turned into the road. Two of the women ran towards it, shouting and yelling. They banged on the car windows with stones, causing one to shatter as the driver slowed. The terrified faces of the occupants threw Emma back to the day in Cork. Was she no better than the man with the spray can? Did a desire to fight for what was right turn you into a criminal intent on damage?

By the time the car stopped at the bottom of the steps, it was surrounded and the passengers had a job getting out from the back seat.

Emma's heart raced with adrenaline and excitement as the chanting gained momentum. The politician's face was as pale as the grey skies above. He pulled a document bag into his chest and tried to keep his head down as he made a dash for the door. But the tide of women was too strong to swim against. Emma had to stop herself from rushing to join those who tugged at his suit. Someone swiped the bowler hat from his head and threw it across the road, where it travelled some distance before landing in the River Lee.

The women were getting their message across.

They were united in wanting to be taken seriously.

The politician discarded any notion of reclaiming his hat and continued his struggle up the stairs, losing his footing twice but eventually making it through the tall doors of the building.

A few yards further down the pavement, a reporter stood behind the wooden legs of a camera tripod. Emma watched, expecting him to pack away his camera now the visitor had gone inside. Instead, he stayed beneath his black shroud, evidently recording the gathering, exactly as Margaret had hoped. Emma stepped further into the crowd in the hope her identity would not be spotted if his photographs made the next day's newspapers.

'Which room is his meeting in?' the distinctive voice of Sue called over the heads of the others.

'That one,' said another, pointing to a first-floor window.

'How the hell do you know that?'

'I just saw him behind the glass.'

Sue drew her arm back as if she was about to bowl a cricket ball. 'I'll give him something to discuss!'

The half brick made a perfect arc and smashed two

windowpanes, and the wooden strut which had held them in place.

Others followed and soon a shower of stones cracked against the stonework and smashed further panes of glass. Officials began to appear at the front door and from the side of the building, grabbing the women who were nearest to them. But still, the protestors would not be silenced. 'We want justice. We want the vote!' they called in unison.

Within seconds the air was filled with the sound of whistles.

Emma crossed the road, away from the gathering, and started walking along the path next to the river, hoping to give the impression she had simply been walking past the commotion.

'Oh, no you don't, missy! I saw you throwing bricks.' A policeman had her arm and twisted it behind her back. Pain sliced through her shoulder.

She was forced towards a parked van with oval windows in the back doors and was unceremoniously pushed inside with three other women, including Sue.

'Didn't see you in the crowd.' Sue grinned.

Emma's first thought was to beg Sue to stay quiet, but instead fear stole her ability to form any words at all. She looked out through the back of the van and shivered, the weight of her world firmly on her shoulders. If she was lucky, the police would only interview them and let her go with a warning. She might even make it back to the office above the tea shop before Mrs Walsh got back.

Chapter Thirty

Emma sat on a thin layer of straw which smelt of mould and other undesirable qualities. The damp from the bricks soaked through the smock they'd forced her to wear, and her hair was still matted from the de-lousing powder which buckets of cold water had failed to rinse two days earlier.

The guard hauled his whip back and released its length with a flick of his wrist. The boy, not yet a teenager, screamed when it made contact with his back. Emma covered her ears and brought her knees up to her chin.

She'd been hauled from her cell for two hours in every six, all day and all night long. Pulling threads from tar-covered ropes, she'd soon discovered the painful task of oakum picking. Now as she sat a few feet from the boy with the bony legs, she watched him struggle to take the big steps necessary to work the wooden slats of the treadwheel. His grime-streaked thighs glistened where he had wet himself.

The guard was a man close to her in age. He wore dirty brown trousers too short for his legs and a collarless shirt with stained armpits. He drew back his arm and wrinkled his nose in concentration. As he took aim, his tongue poked out from between rotten teeth. He paused and looked over at Emma. 'What you lookin' at? You'll be next if you don't mind your own, and I won't worry about only hitting your back. That bastard inside yers will get it too.'

The boy yelped and his body lurched to one side in a futile effort to evade the whip's sting. His snivelling was drowned out by a second box of ropes being dragged along the flagstones of the corridor. The older of two warders on duty pointed at her measly collection of gathered threads. 'Keep going 'til I say.'

Working the ropes had already taken its toll on her fingers which were bleeding and sore. There were four pickers in the room, one in each corner, not close enough to engage in chat. A raging thirst had seized her tongue. The first guard paused in his whipping to sip from a tankard which he kept in a space in the wall where bricks had fallen out. She licked her lips and tasted the salt of hard work and no bathing. The boy slipped off the treadwheel again and was trying to clamber back up when the guard hurled the contents of his cup over the child's back.

Emma felt sorry for the little one in front of her. She'd learned from standing in the queue for the tiny breakfast that boys up to fourteen shared the otherwise women-only prison. He was somebody's son. She wondered what heartbreak his mother must be feeling.

'Maybe you'll stop your thieving soon, you little smut. Speed up!' The guard whipped the boy's heels. 'Fourth time inside – has that orphanage taught you nothing?'

Later that day, she lay on the stinking mattress in her cell and faced the wall. She watched a centipede negotiate the undulations of the bricks, their surfaces gouged with letters from names carved by previous inmates. It disappeared through a gap left by lost mortar.

Cradling her tummy through the smock, she thought about the policemen back at the station. They'd not been interested in her explanation, and when she'd raised her voice in panic, one had slapped her face. Not even Mrs Walsh's arrival the next morning at the goal's entrance had made a difference to their plan to imprison her. From the first-floor window at the end of the wing Emma had seen Margaret leaving.

More humiliating than the slap had been her five-month pregnant belly on full display. Six of them had been arrested and taken to the gaol, then ordered to strip for the de-lousing. Emma knew her secret was the talk of the guards – the lewd comments hurled in through the bars as they passed her cell were testament. She doubted Thomas would ever speak to her again, her having put his child in danger for a second time.

The gaol doctor was doing his daily rounds, and while she lay on the damp mattress she listened to the door bolts clanking open and closed as he made his way along the row towards her. To pass the minutes until she would have to endure his examination, she scratched her own name into a soft brick with a splinter of wood.

Cold air crept like mist through a gap at floor level. She'd tried to cover it with the mattress in the night but had been beaten by a guard who patrolled the small hours, his sole task to keep the airways clear. 'Keeps the air clean, or you'll get dysentery,' he'd said after delivering the blow to her shoulder when at first she'd refused to remove the mattress.

On the third day, a woman behind her whispered as they shuffled along the corridor for an afternoon oakum-picking session, 'Psst. Is it your first?' She was older than Emma, although it was hard to tell by how many years in the dim light.

'Yes. I'm over halfway.' Emma looked back but kept moving.

'Small baby then. I was a balloon by five months.'

'You're a mother, then,' Emma said, needlessly.

The woman chuckled. 'That I am, got six of 'em. Big babies, every one of 'em, not that it saved the first two from catchin' typhoid and dyin'.'

'I'm so sorry.'

'That's life, girl. It's why we went on and had more. Anyway, you in from that demonstration?'

'I didn't break any windows, I was only observing.' Emma knew how pathetic she sounded.

'They wouldn't have cared if you'd been at the front wielding a machete, or at the back reading a novel – they see us all as one. The same movement, same problem. One which needs wiping out before it gets a grip.'

'I'm Emma, by the way.'

'Josie.'

There was no hand-shaking, just the simple nod of being welcomed to the fold.

Lunch arrived on a dented tin plate and Emma eyed the stale-looking bread.

'Eat and work at the same time,' the guard instructed as he carelessly dropped plates in all four corners of the room. He returned to his tankard in the wall and found it to be empty and blasphemed.

'I'll be only a minute, don't you lot get up to anything while I'm gone.'

Emma watched his shadow follow him down the corridor and caught Josie's eye.

'Are you a suffragette?' Emma asked her.

'I'm a suffragist, yes.'

'Is there a difference?'

'We're all suffragists. It was a newspaper reporter a few years back who coined the word suffragette, believing it would be demeaning to our movement by adding a pretty ending to the word.' The woman stretched out her legs with a moan. 'Idiot. Didn't work. The more militant groups happily adopted the new word and went on to prove the more feminine name would not result in a softer approach.'

'That's funny.' Emma smiled and rubbed her cold feet.

'They'll never have the last laugh, those pompous politicians, mark my words.' Josie rubbed her own generous belly. 'Now, you gonna have my soda bread? I can't stand the stuff, and your bairn needs it more 'an me.'

The doctor was the best-dressed man she'd seen inside the gaol. His knee-length black jacket displayed pale marks where he'd had to kneel on grit-covered ground. An assortment of silver instruments tinkled as he unrolled a leather pouch.

He shone a torch in her eyes and ears, forced her tongue flat with a miniature paddle so he could study the back of her throat, placed his stethoscope roughly against her shoulder blades for a few seconds and completely ignored her belly, much to Emma's surprise and relief.

'I'm only interested in whether you're bringing in disease, which would add to my workload.' He rolled his pouch back up. 'Got yourself into some mischief by the looks of things. Keep yourself to yourself and you'll be out of here in a day or two.'

She found the piece of bread in her pocket which Josie had thrown over in the workroom. A small amount of water sat at the bottom of a wooden cup from a previous meal. She took a sip and made it last while she consumed the hardened dough bite by bite.

On the fourth day, Emma and Josie found themselves together during enforced exercise. They walked around the perimeter and out of shadow cast by the west wing into the orange glow of an evening sun. A separate building made of the same grey stone sat to one side of the grounds. There were bars at its windows too.

'What's that place?'

'Sanatorium for the worst cases of typhoid and cholera. Hold your breath,' Josie warned.

'How do you know so much?' Emma said from behind her hand.

'I bin 'ere a few times.'

Emma covered her belly with her other hand as if to protect her baby from the groans and wailing as they walked past. 'Everywhere looks so run-down, there are so many broken windows, and look at the weeds.'

'What do you expect? Been here over a hundred years. There are much bigger prisons in other cities and the government ain't bothered with a small place like this. It's why they made it a women-only gaol and left only a handful of guards to keep us in check. We're not important.'

Josie laughed. 'Mind you, I think after the famine, people committed crimes so they could actually get *in!*'

'No, really?'

Josie coughed and spat before nodding. 'It was considered better living than the workhouses.'

'I'd heard they were bad.' Emma ignored the blisters forming on her heels from wearing her boots with no stockings. Young green nettles reached out from unkempt lawns to sting their ankles at the edge of the stony path. The sun dropped out of sight and the air's temperature plummeted.

The governor was in his office as they walked past the window at the front of the prison. He was bent over paperwork on his desk, and the flame in his oil lamp cast flickering shadows on the wall behind him. Another new inmate stood before him, as Emma had done only a few days before. It felt as though a lifetime had passed and perhaps this was where she deserved to be.

They had filed into the main hall when the governor's assistant walked out of another office.

She held a piece of paper above her head. 'Release paper for Emma Quinn.'

Emma looked at Josie. 'What does she mean?'

'You're getting outta here, girl, that's what that means.' Josie grasped her hand. 'And you take good care of yourself.'

'Is one of you Emma Quinn?' the woman repeated, searching the line.

'Me.'

'Anything you want from your cell?'

Emma shook her head. 'How will I get back to Queenstown?'

'Don't ask me. We've just been told you're being collected at six. Governor wants to sign you out, so come on, let's not keep him waiting. Looks like he's got me a new one to de-louse.'

The governor slid a page of writing towards her on the desk. 'You need to read this and sign it. Seems someone must think a lot of you. Your freedom comes at a price.'

She read the statement and scribbled her name at the bottom. The form stated that for the sum of two hundred pounds – money to be used for the renovation of the gaol's fabric – the release of Emma Quinn would be granted and charges dropped. It stipulated on no account was the claimant at liberty to request knowledge of the benefactor's identity.

At six o'clock there was a rapping at the front door and the woman from the office went to open it. It was the guard who looked after the main gate entrance.

'Stay out of trouble,' said the governor without looking up from his paperwork.

The yellow headlamps shone in her face as the doors in the outer wall were pulled closed behind her, and she stood shivering in the putrid smock and worn leather boots. The silhouette of the driver came towards her, and she recognised the old tweed jacket with pockets that bulged from where he'd walk with his hands inside them.

Tears came and she dropped to her knees.

'Come here.' Thomas pulled her up and into his arms, and for a brief moment, as bats swooped in front of the headlamps, she let him hold her.

'I'm sorry.'

'Sshhh, don't say anything.'

He made sure she was comfortable before closing the passenger door of the unfamiliar car. She looked around it.

'Who's is this?'

'Robert Walsh lent it to me after I told him I was picking you up.'

He drove them through the streets back towards Cork and neither of them spoke. They passed boats on the river, with lights flickering behind dirty portholes. She hugged herself to get warm and assumed Thomas must have made the payment using Alice's parents' money. Of course he would need to keep it quiet. However he'd managed it, she was grateful to have left the gaol behind.

'Let me ask you one thing. Why didn't you go to the office as arranged?'

She let out a big sigh. 'I couldn't simply sit back and leave it to others. I know you think I'm rebellious for the sake of it, but it means so much to be part of the movement.'

Thomas left the lights of Cork behind and the quieter roads lay ahead of them. Lanes that lead back to Queenstown. 'Well, it's a good job you didn't go to the office.'

She turned to look at him. 'What do you mean?'

'They were broken into the same day the politician arrived. Someone went through it, smashed the furniture to pieces, emptied files of papers into the streets. Mrs Walsh was beside herself that you were inside at the time.'

'Oh my God,' Emma whispered. 'Who would do such a thing?'

'Someone who disagrees with the movement, and there are plenty of people who fall into that category.'

They drove on in silence for a while.

'I promise I won't do anything else that worries you. I am sorry, really.'

'You're bad for my heart, Emma.'

The smirk was tiny but definite.

'When my mother gave me her blessing to follow the cause, something in me was fired up.'

'I wondered if it had something to do with her.'

'Before her letter, I felt like I was only pretending to be part of something big. Because I had to hide it, you know? Whereas now, she's there in spirit with me, and I had to see what it felt like. I wanted to be able to write home and tell her that I'd marched and protested for her too.'

'And now you can.' He turned for the final approach down the hill and passed the cathedral, its spire half-built and reaching up into the darkening sky. 'Perhaps just miss out the part where you were arrested.'

She chuckled, safe in his car, safe in his care, their baby safe in his fortress. 'Yes, she doesn't need to know every tiny detail.'

Chapter Thirty-One

The newly formed *Titanic* Celebrations Board had been meeting weekly.

In three days' time, Queenstown would host a grand party in the harbour and on the morning of 11th April, the big ship would sail west as so many before her had done.

But this voyage would be special and Alice was ready.

Humming, she turned left and right in front of the mirror to survey herself in one of the new dresses she'd had specially made for the trip. Hollywood was calling and she'd never felt more secure about her future. Alice had cut out and pored over a newspaper article on the new ship. The *Titanic* had been designed to serve the rich and famous, and knowing that she would soon be dining with them during the six days at sea was verging on more excitement than she could handle.

Downstairs in the drawing room, her husband had been joined by Robert Walsh, Patrick and a further five members of the TCB to discuss the town's arrangements.

'It's the steerage lot we'll have to keep an eye on, not those travelling First,' Thomas said in response to concerns about drunk passengers causing trouble on the tenders, trying to gain access to the ship without paid-for tickets.

He had only that morning been able to concentrate on matters in-hand. For the previous few days, he'd been terrified Emma had landed herself in serious trouble, even when Mrs Walsh had tried to assure him that Robert was pulling strings in the hope to get Emma released. He didn't care what string they pulled, only that Emma was back at the hotel and safe.

'Hell!' Patrick exclaimed.

Thomas turned to see his wife standing in the doorway.

Robert Walsh stood up. 'Good evening, Alice. How resplendent you look.'

'Thank you, Robert.' She glided to the head of the table, where she took Thomas's face in her hands and kissed him on the mouth to a ripple of applause and hearty murmurs of approval. 'I'm sure my husband loves me enough to persuade you all to squeeze me in at the party? I'd love to sing for the town and I've never before performed on the bandstand.'

'I'm sure we can arrange that.' Robert studied the agenda. 'It will be an honour to have you.'

'Thank you, Robert,' she said, and sashayed her way back to the door, passing behind their chairs and trailing her fingers along each of their shoulders.

Thomas said nothing. She closed the door quietly behind her.

'Shame she didn't buy *you* a ticket to New York.' Patrick raised an eyebrow.

Thomas had no intention of sharing his thoughts with Patrick or anyone else. 'I'm going to enjoy the extra business the event will bring. You know what I think about pomp and ceremony. Couldn't imagine anything worse than a week of forced socialising.'

'Blimey, remind me not to invite you onto the rowing team next year,' said Robert. 'We love a bit of pomp and fizz.'

Thomas changed the subject. 'Have we got a list of passengers yet? The tenders will need to know that they've got everyone as they'll only go out to the ship once.'

'Yes, there's a copy here.' Robert slid a piece of paper across the table.

The meeting went on for another hour, before it was brought to a close and the men filtered out. Thomas opened a window and leant on the outside sill, breathing in fresh air.

'You alright?' Patrick asked.

He closed the sash window halfway. 'I need a whiskey.'

Patrick poured them both a glass from a tray on the sideboard. 'What is it? You look like you've seen a ghost.'

'It's just dawned on me.'

Patrick waited.

'I don't love my wife.'

Patrick glanced at the closed door then whispered, 'What the *hell* are you talking about?'

'I know what love feels like, and I don't feel it with Alice. Even looking like she does tonight.'

Patrick sat back down in his chair and scratched his scalp. 'What's got into you? It's not that American?'

Thomas walked slowly round the room and said nothing.

'Bloody hell, I'm right, aren't I? I thought last summer was a flight of fancy and you'd got it out your system. She's just another woman, Tom.'

Thomas turned and faced his friend. 'That's where you're wrong. She's far from "just another woman".'

'You've got it bad, but it'll pass.' Patrick downed his whiskey and got up to pour another.

'She's pregnant.'

Patrick spun round. 'She's *what*?'

'And it's mine.' He put his own glass down and tried to steady his nerves.

His friend moved to stand next to him. 'I don't mean to be crass, but… can you be sure?'

Thomas turned on his friend. 'Give me some respect or… get out.'

Patrick held his hands up. 'I'm sorry, it had to be said.'

'Hell, it did.'

'There are single girls who travel in such fashion and—'

'That's enough. You know very well why she came to be here. Take my word that she is the good person I know her to be. She'll return to New York sometime in May, as soon as she's well enough to travel. She'll have the baby soon after, and Patrick…' Thomas put his head in his hands, 'it's breaking me apart. I'll never know the child, nor see Emma again.'

Later that evening, after the tables were cleared, Thomas went outside with his pipe. Patrick's question haunted him. What *was* different about Emma? From the moment she walked through the front door of the hotel, she had caught his attention. And now she'd captured his heart.

His own mother had been a determined woman who'd held the family together even in the early days when her husband had preferred a relationship with the bottle. His father had ended his sorry excuse for a life with a particularly long drinking session after losing the latest in a long line of jobs. Thomas and his mother had gone on to keep their boarding house pristine, right up to the day Victor had come knocking with his offer.

The back door to the hotel opened and closed. He turned and watched Emma walk across the grass towards him. The faint edge of her profile was highlighted as a cloud moved away from the moon.

'I've always wondered what falling in love felt like,' he admitted.

'Why did this have to happen?' She slipped her hand into his.

'Do you regret it?' he asked.

'Of course not. I wanted adventure. I got that and much more, which is something poor Martina will never get to experience. I admit returning to New York with a broken heart and an extra person to think about wasn't on the cards.'

He squeezed her hand. 'Close your eyes, there's something I want to show you.

'What is it?'

'Just close your eyes.'

She did as she was told and he led her forward a few steps and lifted the cover from the rowing boat. 'Okay, open them.'

It took a moment for her eyes to focus in the dim light. The little rowing boat looked like new with a fresh new coat of white paint.

He waited.

She leant closer.

'Oh, Thomas!' she gasped. Her fingers followed the letters he'd so carefully painted next to the letter 'A'. 'This is just… the most beautiful thing anyone has ever done for me.'

He turned her to face him. 'I needed a reason to save this old girl and put her back on the river. You gave me that reason. This summer, *MARTINA* will once more be able to enjoy exploring.'

'Thank you, Thomas. Thank you for being you.' Emma reached up and took his face in her hands and kissed his mouth. 'I will always love you.'

As he held her in his arms, he knew she meant it.

Neither of them saw the curtains fall slowly back together at one of the bedroom windows.

Chapter Thirty-Two

'Where's my fur?'

Clive opened one of the many leather carry bags Alice liked to travel with. 'Will this do?' he asked, holding up a cream feather boa.

'Are you joking? I need the purple one to go with this dress, are you blind?' She stalked across the room and peered into the second bag. 'Where the hell is it?'

Clive looked around the room. 'When did you last wear it?'

'God knows.' Alice paused, then snatched the cream boa from his hands. 'Probably left it in The Colonel's drawing room last week, when I was waiting for *you*!'

The ends of the boa slid through his fingers. A handful of feathers tore from their moorings and floated in defeat to the carpet. She fiddled with the garment until she was satisfied with her reflection in the mirror.

'Right. I have to go.' She made her way down into the hall and called through into the dining room, 'Thomas? Are you coming to watch?'

Thomas was wiping perfectly clean bottles at the bar. 'If I can get away.'

Alice slammed the front door closed behind her.

'Is she singing dressed like that?' Aoife, with a handful of cutlery, paused at the window to watch Alice cross the road. 'She'll freeze.'

'We'll take a wander over once we've set up for breakfast.'

'Oh, good, I'd like to watch her.' Aoife moved more quickly to finish the task. 'How many are boarding the ship tomorrow?'

'A little over a hundred.'

'I wish I could see the ship close up.'

'There'll be photographs in the papers soon enough.'

The newspapers had been reporting on the *Titanic*'s progress since her departure from Liverpool two days earlier. She'd steamed first to Cherbourg and then to Southampton but was due off Roche's Point the next morning. They even printed one of the lavish five-course menus being enjoyed by businessmen, statesmen and their wives who'd been onboard since the start of her maiden voyage.

The entire population of Queenstown were out at dusk. Emma's breath curled in the cool air as she followed Aoife's progress through the crowds moving towards the bandstand. People were drinking and laughing, eating and singing. Politics forgotten. Many were dancing with partners and with strangers. Children ran around, pilfering bags of hot chestnuts from the little carts which had set up along the quay.

A band were playing, the men with white sashes diagonally across their uniformed chests. Emma recognised one or two of the sailors from her afternoons volunteering in the Home.

Thomas had his hands in his pockets and his body language was cool. Emma had two more weeks before the doctor would sign her fit to sail.

'There's something else I need to thank you for,' Emma said quietly, hoping to gain some warmth between them. They stopped at the railings at the harbour's edge.

'Oh?'

'For helping me to understand I wasn't responsible for Martina.'

'I'm glad you see that now.'

Water lapped against the wall, dark green seaweed trailing on the surface like strands of wet hair. The sun had already set, but there were purple remnants of afternoon sky near the horizon. Green and purple. A timely reminder that the suffrage movement was now well and truly established in the little town.

'What about you?' Emma turned and leaned back against the railings.

'Don't worry about me. I'm doing what I set out to do – run the hotel.'

People started to sing along to a tune they recognised.

'But you could do that anywhere, you know.'

'Emma, don't let's do this again.'

'Come to America with me at the end of the month.' She leant closer so no-one would hear. 'Leave all this.'

'Emma, that's impossible. We both know I can't do that.'

'I do know, and I don't like it.'

He led her away from the crowd and down the slipway where small boats were launched each morning into the sea to go fishing. Two boys were catching crabs with bits of stolen bacon tied to lines of string.

Thomas spoke quietly. 'I have to stand by my wife.'

Emma felt sick with the injustice of it. 'But she hates you!'

'She doesn't hate me, even if it looks like it sometimes. Beneath it all, we're still friends.'

'I think I might move out. From the hotel.'

'What? Why?'

'It's becoming impossible to live in the same house. Yes, I chose to have this baby alone, but I thought I'd be home long before now. Every day I look at you, I imagine us together, which is ridiculous. I'm fully aware it can't happen; I was expecting to feel a bit sad, but the reality of this is… it's just too hard to see you every day.'

She could tell by the look on his face she'd hurt him.

'Please don't do that. Don't go.' He confirmed her thought.

'I think Mary has a spare room. People are already starting to talk.' Emma looked round, then took his hand and lifted it to her lips and kissed it. 'I'm sorry for my outburst. Thousands of women have brought babies up alone before me when they've lost husbands in wars or to illness. I'll cope. I know I will. John would tell me, if he was here, that I could do this, and I know I can.'

The boys had moved further down the slope, embarrassed by the adults' behaviour.

'I've turned sentimental since being pregnant, and as hard as I tried not to, I've fallen in love with you.' She took a step back. 'See? I've said it twice now. Matters of the heart always get in the way of good decisions. Martina warned me of that.'

The band stopped playing and Alice went up the steps to talk to one of the musicians before searching the crowds for the face she most hoped to see. There were too many people and the saxophonist was giving her instructions.

She was halfway through her first song when she noticed Thomas alone and leaning against the rails. At least he might be listening, even if he wasn't watching.

The crowd cheered when the song came to an end and called for another. Alice kept them entertained for nearly an hour. Landlords from the public houses were moving amongst the crowd, topping up cups and tankards with ale and wine. Even a slight drizzle had not deterred the revellers' desire to celebrate such an historic event. Tomorrow would be for goodbyes, but tonight, every man, woman and child hailed the shipping company for bringing such excitement to their port.

Alice was helped down from the bandstand and accepted the offer of Clive's jacket. She made her way through the crowd to Thomas.

'I need to talk to my husband.'

Clive followed her progress through the crowd. 'Don't get cold. Your voice will suffer.'

'Ah, good.' Alice ignored him. 'That silly girl is speaking with Mary and her useless son. Thank God he will be steerage, Clive. I couldn't bear to be associated with him on deck!'

When Alice weaved through the edge of the crowd and reached the railing, Thomas was no longer there. She stood on tiptoe and searched the crowd again.

'For goodness' sake, where—'

She spotted him over near the road.

'Let me through.' Alice separated two men who had linked arms and were singing their own version of one of her songs. 'Let me through!'

'Watch it, Madame, or I'll have to spank that backside of yours!' one said, and both men roared with laughter, before one stumbled and fell. The other looked back for him, momentarily confused that his friend had vanished.

'Thomas! Wait!' Alice called. She caught up and moved to stand in front of him. 'What was all that about?'

'All what about?'

'I saw you two earlier, coming back from the slipway.' She pointed at Emma a few feet away.

Thomas nodded at passers-by who had gone silent and slowed their progress. He made to walk on, but Alice had other ideas, poking him in the chest. 'I asked you a question.'

'Don't make a scene, Alice.'

Alice saw no reason to hide what was happening any longer. 'Aoife! Aoife! Where's that girl, Emma? She mustn't be anywhere near my husband. I've seen her trying to seduce him in our own garden.'

Some of the crowd gasped.

'You're being ridiculous,' Thomas said.

'Oh, you think so?'

Clive caught up and intervened, steering Alice towards the road. 'Let's get home, shall we? You've got a big day tomorrow.'

Back at the hotel, tempers were taut.

Alice walked in and threw her boa on the ground. 'Thomas, I've never been so insulted.'

Thomas paced the hallway. '*You've* never been so insulted!'

Emma and Aoife entered the hallway together as Alice shouted at the top of her voice, 'The whole town is out to watch me sing and my own husband scurries off behind a wall to do God knows what with some American whore.'

'Alice!' Clive and Aoife chimed in unison.

'She didn't mean that, Emma,' Thomas said.

'Yes, she did.' Emma looked at the floor. 'And she's right.'

Alice clapped. 'First thing you've said which makes sense.'

Emma started up the stairs. 'I'm going to pack. Mary said I can have her room and she'll sleep in the parlour on a camp bed. Harold's going to help us sort it.'

'But Harold is sailing tomorrow,' Aoife pointed out.

Emma kept climbing.

Thomas walked to the bottom of the staircase, but Alice blocked his way. 'Let her go.'

'Alice. For God's sake, stop this.' Thomas grabbed her arm.

'Stop what? It's rather fun, watching you squirm.'

'This hatred. What have I ever done to you?'

She pulled her arm free from his hold. 'How long have you got?'

'And what's that supposed to mean?'

'You've been a disappointment from the day I married you.' She walked up three stairs, then came back down. 'You may look shocked, Thomas, but I had rather hoped that I had married a man. A *real* man. But no, you're too pathetic to know how to be one.'

244

'You're never around long enough to know *what* I can be.'

'I have a career to nurture.'

'It's my guess that you don't in fact need or want a husband. I was convenient – a set-up to meet your father's wishes.'

'They sound like the tramp's words, not your own.'

Thomas prayed Emma hadn't heard, though she'd have to be deaf to have missed it. 'Stop referring to Emma in that way. She'll be going home soon. All her suffrage work has been important.'

'Huh! Women shouldn't need to march and vandalise property to make their point. They simply need to learn the art of seduction.'

Emma came back down the stairs carrying her carpet bag. 'I'll have my trunk collected tomorrow. It's all packed.'

Aoife moved to help her.

'Aoife?' Alice said. 'Are you sure you know where your loyalties lie?'

'Alice, please. She can't carry this up the hill.' Aoife walked with Emma to the door and looked back. 'I'll be back soon.'

There was a moment's silence until the front door closed behind them.

Alice stared at her husband. 'Why are you looking at me like that?'

'You rely on looks and sex to get what you want. Suffragettes don't.' He wondered if he'd gone too far, but Alice had a thick skin.

'Pah!' Alice said. 'The government are playing with them. This will be a five-minute wonder, you'll see.'

Thomas grabbed his jacket from the hat stand where he'd hung it only a few minutes earlier and opened the door.

Alice called from halfway up the stairs, 'It was me who told her to go, by the way.'

He stopped, the doorknob cold in the palm of his hand.

'Yes, I told your little harlot that she was treading on dangerous territory and that if she wanted to be left alone in her final days in this town, she would do better to seek alternative accommodation.'

Chapter Thirty-Three

Thomas knocked on the door and waited. He'd walked the roads of Queenstown until three in the morning and knew it was a ridiculous time to call, but Mary wouldn't hold that against him. He stared at the black panes of glass. Perhaps the morning would be a more sensible time to call.

He walked the town for another hour before finding himself back on the front steps of the hotel. He looked up at the cathedral's silhouette. Tell-tale signs of a new dawn filtered slowly through the deep blues of night.

Upstairs, he knocked gently on Emma's door, praying she might have seen sense and returned while he'd been out. There was no reply and he pushed the door open. The curtains were drawn and the bed had not been slept in. As his eyes grew accustomed to the light, something else struck him as strange.

The room had been cleared of all Emma's things, including the trunk. She'd not had time to clear a year's worth of living in the few minutes there'd been the altercation on the stairs.

He crossed the landing and knocked on Aoife's door.

Aoife opened her door a little way and whispered through the gap. 'Thomas?'

'Aoife.'

'Can I help?'

'Where's Emma? I'm worried.'

She looked down. Her toes poked out from beneath her nightdress. 'I *do* know where she is.'

His heart raced as he waited for her to expand. When she didn't, he pleaded with her, 'Tell me, Aoife, you know I only want what's best for her.'

'She told me not to.'

He sighed. 'I admire your loyalty, really, I do, but I need to know where she is for the baby's sake. Aoife, you must want the baby to be safe. Emma is vulnerable.'

She looked up and seemed to take forever before deciding to speak. 'She's gone to stay with Eva.'

'Eva? How on earth did she get there?'

'Lower your voice,' Aoife pleaded. 'She has made many friends, Thomas. I believe she packed her things this afternoon, before we went to watch Alice.'

The fight suddenly left him and he leant against the landing wall, a hand across his brow.

'Go to bed and get some sleep. We have guests needing their breakfast tomorrow. It's a big day,' Aoife said, and closed the door.

He laid in bed and thought about the ultimatum his wife had delivered and groaned as Emma's outburst on the quay suddenly made more sense. She'd known she was leaving the hotel and had tested his resolve to see if he'd consider joining her. He turned over and closed his eyes. At least he could relax a little now he knew where she was. The car had been returned from the garage, fully mended, and after breakfast service, he'd drive to Eva's and talk Emma into coming back to the hotel.

It was gone ten before Thomas started the car's engine. Aoife had barely looked at him all morning. He was sorry he'd forced her to reveal Emma's secret plan but relieved Aoife had seen sense. He'd make it up to her.

He drove through crowds making their way to the quay to watch the departure. The *Titanic*'s foghorn had been a point of discussion amongst locals for weeks. Some believed they would need ear protection while others said the captain wouldn't waste fuel firing it up as she was moored out in the bay.

Thomas no longer cared about any of that and, once clear of the town, he drove as fast as he ever had. Seeing Emma was more important.

He remembered the way to Eva's workhouse and hoped to get there in less than the hour it had taken before. More carts than usual were meandering their way towards the port, full of families wishing for a glimpse of a ship they could only ever dream of sailing on.

A few miles outside Queenstown, Thomas was able to gain some speed. He pulled on the steering wheel to round a sharp corner but didn't anticipate a flock of sheep scattered across the road.

He slammed on the brakes.

The wheels jammed and steering was futile. The car travelled across a bumpy verge before skidding to a halt. One of the newly replaced headlamps crunched against the stone wall.

His fingers still gripped the wheel long after the car had stopped and he exhaled slowly, then swore under his breath.

In his rear-view mirror the farmer was waving his crook above his head and yelling. Miraculously he had missed all the animals, but the bang of burst tyre against a rock in the grass had been unmistakable.

The farmer drew level with the window and rattled his stick against the glass. 'What you think you're doin'?'

Thomas wound the handle to lower it. 'Did I catch any of them?'

'No, for the love of God, ye didne', though why you're hurtlin' along these lanes in one of these tin machines is beyond me.' He shook his head and walked off, whistling his collie to gather the startled animals.

By the time Thomas had changed the wheel for the spare, an hour had passed and it was almost twelve o'clock when he finally parked the car outside the workhouse. He wasn't sure how Emma would react to his arrival, but he had an explanation ready as to why he was there and how Aoife wasn't to blame.

He knocked twice before at last he heard footsteps on the other side. He pulled his jacket straight and planted a smile on his face.

'Thomas!' Eva's welcome was one of surprise. 'Come in, come in. What are you doing out this way?'

She stepped back and indicated for him to follow her.

'I… um…' He hesitated. He had expected animosity, perhaps a door being slammed in his face. 'I've come to see Emma.'

She frowned, confused. 'I'm sorry?'

'I've been informed she came here last night as she needed… well, she wanted a break from the hotel for a few days.'

She stared at him and cocked her head to one side. She was good at acting the innocent, he'd give her that.

'I'd rather not play games, Eva. I've searched the whole of Queenstown.'

'Thomas, I'm sorry. I have absolutely no idea what you're talking about. Emma isn't here, I assure you.' Her face couldn't have shown more sincerity if she was taking part in her own Confirmation. 'What's happened, Thomas?'

He flopped down on a wooden stool just inside the door and heard his own voice crack. 'I can't find her.'

'I saw Emma at a meeting last week and she was fine. Talking about the *Titanic* and the party you were planning. I'd have been there, but old Alfred needs round-the-clock care now.' Eva touched Thomas's wrist. 'In fact, I'm surprised you're not down at the harbour seeing everyone off.'

He leant back against the roughly plastered wall and stared at the ceiling. 'I just want to find her.'

'Is she with Mrs O'Connor?'

'No.'

'Well, surely she'll be in the crowds somewhere. Isn't your Alice travelling today? First class, I heard.'

Thomas kept his mouth closed. He didn't trust himself to say something he might regret. Evidently the gossip of their failed marriage hadn't yet reached the countryside. It was only a matter of time.

'I'll get us some tea.'

He followed her to the kitchen and watched dazed as she clanked cups down on the draining board. She turned to face him.

'I dread to think what a first-class ticket will have cost. Mary's boy Harold managed to save for a third-class ticket, she told me. Must be so proud, although a bit teary today, I bet.'

Thomas snapped his head in her direction and gasped.

'What is it?' Eva's hand flew to her chest.

'Mary's son's not going!'

Not for the first time, Eva looked confused. 'What? Why?'

'He sold his ticket. Hell!' He ran for the door and left it open.

As he drove back the way he'd come, he mumbled under his breath the whole way, praying the sheep would not be on the lanes.

Counting down the miles, he kept his eye on his pocket watch. It was twenty minutes after one o'clock. The roads went on forever and he thumped the steering wheel with the heel of his hand.

He couldn't deny she'd set him a trap and he'd fallen head-first into it. If Emma had assumed he would have stopped her boarding a tender, then she was right.

He swore again.

He'd been away from Queenstown for nearly three hours, and as he drove over the brow of the hill and down beside the cathedral, he slowed the car and stopped. Near Roche's Point, silhouetted against the calm of the sea, the *Titanic*'s four funnels were distant, glinting in the sun. She had already raised anchor and was on her way. From his viewpoint, the two black shapes of the tenders returning to harbour were almost back in port.

He dragged his sleeve across his eyes before continuing his way down the hill and on past the hotel. The crowds were still ten deep, but he parked and got out. He fought his way through to the kiosk of the White Star building.

'Hello, Thomas, wasn't it great?'

'Can I get a list of who's gone?'

'Who's gone?'

'The passengers who left here.'

'Sure.' The clerk twisted the logbook round for him to see through the small arched window.

Harold's name had been crossed out and been replaced with a name he'd hoped not to see there.

Thomas turned away.

He was too late. Emma was on her way back to a life in New York. A life without him.

'You can write to your wife, you know,' the clerk called after him. 'Mail only takes a week.'

Chapter Thirty-Four

Alice would never have guessed the sound of a ship slicing through water could be so loud. For nearly three days she had watched the waves hitting the gigantic hull far below. She was too high up for the sea spray to reach her, but she found the repetitive fountain of white froth oddly relaxing.

From deck seven, she had a great view. The coast of Ireland had long gone, as had her anger at Thomas. She'd been disappointed that he'd not been around to wave her off, but she supposed after the fiasco on the harbour, they were never going to part on sunny terms.

The white railings were cold but the polished wooden runner at the top was wide enough to lean on and slightly warmer where the sun had warmed the varnish. She still had much of the ship to explore but her favourite part was dressing for dinner each night.

Two children and their governesses were starting a game of quoits at the other end of the deck. 'Clive, look at this.' She summoned him over.

Clive had been struggling with seasickness since they'd left Ireland and frequently had to retreat at speed to his cabin. This amused Alice, considering how level the ship remained while negotiating the nautical miles. He pushed himself up with a grunt from his deckchair and took a tentative look but quickly returned and put a newspaper over his head.

Alice laughed. 'Oh, you stay there. I'm going for a walk.'

She went towards the front of the ship, which she'd been reliably informed was called the bow, and stopped to speak with dignitaries she already recognised from the dinners. She passed tables set up with games of chess and backgammon, parasols held aloft by uniformed stewards to keep the sun's glare off the players who sat with faces deep in thought and fingers on stems of delicate glasses full of sherry. Up the steps to the next deck, she was delighted to find the same quartet practising with whom she had flirted the previous night.

She spent some time chatting with them before going inside through double wooden doors in which were portholes of glass ensuring collisions could be avoided with someone coming the other way.

She turned left into a lounge.

Two rows of button-backed leather chesterfields divided the room, and each had a walnut coffee table placed before it – adorned with newspapers and ashtrays – ready for anyone wishing to relax. She moved through panelled corridors, beneath ornate glass lamps hanging from the ceiling, electric bulbs sending shimmers of light onto the patterned carpets. She pushed open more double doors into the dining room.

'Good afternoon, Madam, we will be serving dinner in an hour, but can I offer you a drink from the bar?'

Alice checked a clock on the wall and decided half past five was the perfect time for an aperitif. 'Thank you, why not?'

The waiter led her to the bar.

Divine smells from the kitchens wafted through as she sipped a cocktail. She studied a copy of the menu printed on fine guilt-edged card and her mouth started watering at the thought of oysters, a choice of consommé and poached Atlantic salmon with mousseline sauce.

She declined a second drink as she needed to get back to her cabin to change for dinner. Clive would have done so already and be waiting for her. But when she finally located the corridor with their berths, there was no answer when she knocked on Clive's door. She guessed he must be sleeping.

She opened her own cabin door and revelled in the detail. No expense had been spared. On one side of the luxurious suite, a round table and four chairs gleamed, while on the other was a three-quarter size bed draped in velvet-fringed throws and silk pillowcases.

She re-set her hair and changed her outfit. A clever mirror at the dressing table tilted and she brought it closer to re-apply her red lipstick. The sumptuous carpet beneath her feet was far thicker than anything they had at The Admiral, and hanging on the walls were an assortment of fine landscapes.

Dinner would be served in fifteen minutes and she was surprised Clive hadn't knocked on her door. She clipped cut-glass drop earrings to her earlobes and turned her head to catch the reflected light from an ornate lamp on the wall.

She left her cabin and knocked once more on Clive's cabin door.

She stood back as a young steward in a snowy-white jacket walked down the corridor towards her with a pile of towels between his hands.

'Thank you, Ma'am,' he said, and walked on past.

After a second or two, Alice called after him, 'Excuse me, I don't suppose you've seen my manager? We're due at dinner.'

The boy turned around. 'Yes, sorry, I assumed you knew. He's been taken ill and gone down to D Deck.'

'Where's that?'

'It's the hospital cabins. He was found on deck, collapsed. Dehydration, I think they said.'

'Oh, God, how do I get there?'

'It's starboard side, Ma'am. Go to D and follow signs from second-class dining.'

Alice held up the silk hem of the golden dress she'd earmarked for the evening and hurried down to the central part of the ship. With help from staff and friendly passengers, she found her way and was allowed to enter the room where Clive was asleep. His usual blotchy face was the colour of ash.

'You look terrible,' she whispered at what looked suspiciously like a corpse.

'Thank you.'

'Hell. You're awake? I thought you'd died.'

'Again, thank you.' He opened an eye, bloodshot from heaving 'til there'd been nothing left in his belly. 'They say a few hours on this stuff and I'll be as right as rain.'

A bag of clear liquid hung from a hook on the wall at the head of his bed. It was attached to him via a tube in the back of his hand.

'So, you'll not be joining me for dinner.' She laughed.

'Not tonight.' He smiled and shooed her away.

She left Clive to sleep and improve and started her progress back to the elegant dining room. Along the corridor she was stalled for a moment while two nurses decided on the best medication for a patient. They were stooped behind open cupboard doors which obstructed the corridor.

'This tonic should do the trick, if you're sure it's only exhaustion?'

'Stressed and tired, that's what she is.'

'Fine. Take it, but for God's sake, keep it hidden 'til you get there. We're only meant to treat first and second class.'

'That's hardly fair. Steerage can fall ill, too.'

Alice was getting impatient and was about to interrupt them when she heard something that snatched the breath from her lungs.

'They've got a doctor down there, but he won't have access to of all this, and if she's seven months pregnant, the poor girl will need something to give her a boost.'

'And what's the passenger's name? I'll keep a note in my diary.'

'Emma Quinn.'

Chapter Thirty-Five

'It's cold out here and the wind's getting up. Wouldn't you be better resting in your cabin? You look awfully pale.'

'Are you a nurse?' Emma took in a cloak and the uniform beneath it.

The girl smiled and nodded. 'Just having my break and thought I'd take a stroll here. It's quieter than the upper decks.'

Emma closed her eyes again and tried to ignore the wooden slats of the deckchair digging into her back.

'Can I help you back to your cabin? Your baby will prefer it if you're comfy.'

Emma became aware of fingers on her forehead and forced her eyes open. She looked into the kindly face.

The nurse supported her and together they made their way slowly to the little cabin, just big enough for a single bed, a tiny dressing table and one chair. The walls were simple white-painted cladding and there was a small plain wall light near the pillow for reading. In the moments she was not thinking about Thomas, she had to admit the space was adorably cute.

'That's it, you lie down there. You look shattered.'

Emma wanted to cry but had no tears left. 'I'll be alright… just need sleep.' She curled up and faced the wall.

The nurse unlaced Emma's boots and covered her with the bedding. 'I'm going to speak to Sister. She's a whizz with pregnant ladies.'

An hour later, the nurse returned and quietly placed a brown glass bottle on the dressing table. 'One gulp of this twice daily until the bottle's gone. It's just a tonic but should help with your energy levels.'

Emma rolled over. 'That's kind of you.'

'You're welcome. And when you feel strong enough, get some fresh air, but don't get cold out there.' The nurse opened the wardrobe door to fetch an extra blanket from the shelf. 'Your wardrobe's empty, where are your clothes?'

Emma rubbed her face with her hands and sighed. 'I left in a hurry.'

'I'll see what I can do.'

After the nurse had gone, Emma unscrewed the bottle's cap and took a long swig and immediately followed it with a glass of water to take away the taste.

She'd found the euphoria of her dramatic departure had ebbed away within hours.

Now all she felt was desolate.

She'd skipped all offered meals because heartache had stolen her appetite. The only vision she allowed was that of her mother at home, waiting to welcome her. She knew from her mother's letters that things had changed in Manhattan. Although details were scant, it seemed her father had become absent during the winter for weeks at a time and her mother and Henry lived mostly alone. A deal had been struck for the sale of the grocery shop and her mother had been left with no choice but to move.

Within an hour, the tonic was taking effect. Emma took her time walking to the dining area. Long rustic tables with benches down each side filled the entire space, people had congregated, chatting in loud, excited voices to compete with singing from other groups. Some played cards; others sat around drinking.

She took a plate of bread and cheese, sat at one of the tables and ate.

The bread stuck in her throat as she read a plaque on the wall. It told her that a certain 'Thomas Andrews' had been the *Titanic*'s ship-builder. Her eyes were drawn to the letters of the name. She averted her eyes from the reminder. The innocent man who'd helped design the ocean liner now carrying her across the seas – *the Ship of Dreams*, she'd heard it called – did not deserve to be the reason for her sorrow. He wasn't the Thomas who had altered her life's path forever. Leaving her Thomas behind was going to be harder than she'd assumed.

Raised voices in the corridor outside her cabin woke her just after eleven. She swung her legs off the bed and poked her feet into her boots. She made her way to the lavatories and listened to snatched conversations of people rushing back and forth past the bathroom.

Hit something, I think…

Just relax, everyone…

It's alright, Mabel, this is the Unsinkable Ship, Uncle Archie told me…

Go back to your beds and rest, there's nothing to worry about…

Where's Mummy…

Get those sausages prepared for breakfast and into the fridge...

Fred's the best crow's nest spy there is...

Are we going faster, dear...

Bloody hell, it's cold out there...

What the hell is that noise...

Herbert, let's go up on deck. See what the fuss is about...

Emma finished in the bathroom and pulled the sides of her coat around her belly. She took another swig from the bottle she'd put in her pocket.

Outside, the temperature had plummeted since she'd been on deck the previous afternoon.

With each breath, her lungs ached with the cold.

People ran up and down, calling out names of loved ones.

A steward was blowing a whistle trying to calm everyone down. He stood on an upturned box and blew his whistle again, then flapped his hands with his palms facing down. 'Everyone, please listen to me. Stay calm.'

Someone near the front called out, 'What's happened?'

'The ship bumped into a small iceberg, there are many in these waters, as you can see. Please, there's no reason for this ridiculous panic. Just go back to your cabins and try to sleep.'

The passenger persevered, 'What's that's goddamn grating noise I keep hearing?'

Emma waited for the steward's reply, but he was ignoring the American's questions and had moved on down the deck, repeating his request for calm.

Looking out into the night, Emma could see nothing. The lights from the ship reflected in the surrounding water, but when she looked to where the horizon might be, the inky watery depths merged into a sky speckled with stars. Her breath swirled in front of her and the wooden rail was covered in a layer of sparkling frost. For half an hour, she got steadily colder, watching agitated passengers arguing and crying.

When one of the little white lifeboats was lowered down on ropes from a deck high above them, passengers became hysterical. Men and women who a few hours earlier had been dancing and singing without a care in the world were demanding to know where they should go to wait for one. The steward was losing control fast. No-one was listening and at one point a burly man ripped the whistle from the steward's hand, hurled it over the side and pulled him close by his lapels.

'I can't see any lifeboats on this deck? Where are they?'

'It's okay, sir, can you let go of my jacket, please? There are plenty of lifeboats. I'm not sure why they are being deployed. Let me go, and I'll report back to you.'

'You'll do better than that, you pompous piece of shit. You'll get a boat for me and my family and row it yourself. The name's O'Brien, don't you forget it.' The man threw the steward onto the floor. 'Telling us to go back to bed, for God's sake. I knew this was serious.'

Emma walked to the metal staircase she'd seen, but her way was barred by more stewards.

'Why can't we come up?'

'You'll get your chance, once the passengers up here have been loaded.'

'Are we all getting off?' She shivered. 'Is the ship going to sink?'

'Just… wait there, please, Madam,' the steward stuttered. 'We will call you up when it's time.'

Try as she might to remain calm, Emma's heart was battering her chest.

She cradled her belly and made soothing noises and hoped her baby could hear her.

The sea below was becoming littered with the white wooden ovals of lifeboats, some only half full, others crammed with women and children. For an hour, no-one allowed anyone up to the deck where they could board the lifeboats, and for the first time, Emma realised with horror that there might not be enough boats to take all the passengers. She watched over the side as people in the boats jostled for space and called up to others still on the ship.

The man called O'Brien from earlier had gathered his family around him and was issuing instructions to them, their faces concentrating on his every word. 'Right, we've got to look after ourselves before it's too late. I'm going first, and I'm gonna catch both of you.'

'You mean we got to jump in?' The boy was no older than eight or nine and grabbed his father's sleeve.

'Yes, my son. I'm going to save you, you hear? Jane, take him now while I go.'

'Is this safe?' the wife asked, and pulled her son close.

'This bloody boat is going down, you mark my words. No way they'd have used the lifeboats if it wasn't. Don't take a genius to see there aren't enough.'

His wife nodded.

Emma watched as he climbed up the railings, stood for a moment on the top, before leaping over the edge. His wife screamed and the boy started to sob. Emma looked down at the littered surface of the sea. The father disappeared through a tiny white circle of froth before coming back up, his mouth open in shock.

His arm waved, his voice lost amongst the panic closer to them.

Emma rushed to help the mother who was trying to persuade the boy onto the rail.

'I don't want to, Mummy!' he cried. 'I can't do it.'

'Cherub, you can.' She cupped his face while he sat on the top, his arms gripping her shoulders. 'You're my strong boy.'

'Tell him again,' Emma said.

The wife's tear-streaked face turned to her. 'Do you think? I'm throwing him to his death, surely?'

Emma shook her head, the Joseph Cobb factory elevator coming to mind. 'I think your husband is right about this ship. Don't wait to find out, have faith in him. The boy's strong like his dad.'

'Oh God!' cried the woman as together they helped him up and steadied his boots on the rail.

The father waited, calling and splashing the surface so the boy could see where he was.

With a gentle push, the boy fell away from his mother, who screamed again.

They watched his body make a splash and the father swim towards him. He put up his arm, telling his wife their son was alive. They saw his little body in the big man's arms.

The ship's lights flickered and all went out.

The wife grabbed Emma's arms. 'Now we go. This is it,

we've got to jump.'

'Go on, you go join your family.'

'You're coming too?'

'I'm seven months pregnant. If I jump, I'll kill the baby. I can't.'

'I can't leave you,' the woman cried, and Emma pulled her into a hug.

'Don't think about me. Unhook your skirts, they'll drag you down in the water.'

The woman did as Emma suggested and climbed onto the rail before looking back. 'Good luck, and thank you.'

She was gone.

Emma watched the three of them making negligible progress towards the lifeboats.

Other people were jumping and she closed her eyes. But it was no good; she could still see the factory women hurling themselves from the factory windows, falling to their death on the concrete below, just as folk were doing now. The surface of the ocean, from this great height, was as hard and unforgiving. The sum of human catastrophe was increasing with each minute and once again, she was powerless to stop it.

She fought her way against the flow of people, back to a space beneath the metal staircases. Tucking herself away, she sat with her knees against her chest. The shivering made her teeth chatter and she could no longer feel her hands.

She tilted her head and listened. A different sound filtered through the screaming and the ship's metallic struggle to stay afloat.

Music.

Very distant, but the distinct sound of string instruments.

Perhaps she was hallucinating. She closed her eyes and covered her ears with her hands.

'Let me down these steps, right now, you insolent little man.'

'I'm sorry, Ma'am. No-one's going down or coming up those stairs.'

'You didn't hear me. If you don't let me down these stairs, I'll knock you out.'

Emma opened her eyes.

The exchange taking place at the top of the steps sounded just like Alice barking orders. She'd know that voice anywhere. Emma looked up in time to see the steward fall sideways and someone bustle their way down.

When the woman reached the bottom of the stairs, she paused.

'Alice?' Emma ventured.

'Emma? Is that you?'

'Oh my God, Alice, is it really you?'

Alice pulled Emma to her feet. It was so dark, they couldn't see each other, but Emma fell against the woman she'd come to know so well.

'Right, you're coming with me.'

'But I'm not allowed up there.'

'You're a bloody suffragette, or have you forgotten? You don't follow rules, remember?'

Emma allowed herself to be led back up the stairs amid others who'd now spotted the route was no longer being guarded. Alice steered them towards the doors leading inside and they stood behind one of the potted palm trees.

'Why have we come back inside?' Emma said.

'Because we're going to swap clothes and you're going to take my ticket.'

'*What?*'

'You're going to get in a lifeboat and save that baby.'

Emma stared at Alice in the dark. Occasionally torchlight brought her features into view. 'I can't do that.'

'You bloody well can. That's Thomas's baby, I take it?'

She nodded in the dark and whispered to confirm, 'It is, yes.'

'Right, well. You're going to save it and I'm going to help you.' Alice pulled the simple dress Emma had been wearing since the night of the party up over Emma's head. 'I've never known how to make up for taking fatherhood away from Thomas. I've never wanted children and have spent years being victimised for it.'

'Oh, Alice.'

'Listen. I've seen the happiness you've brought my husband these last few months, even if I have been fighting it. But you know why, don't you?'

'No.' Emma put her feet into the boots Alice was holding.

'I'm jealous of you.'

'Jealous? You're jealous of nobody.'

'You don't know me, Emma. Only what I allow you to see.'

'What do you mean?'

The ship lurched to one side and vases full of flowers thudded on to the carpet.

'I'm jealous that I'll never live the life I really want to live and you can.'

'I don't understand. I thought your touring was the life you wanted.'

'Quickly, put this dress on. Put it on backwards, with the buttons down the back. Put the coat on next. You'll look perfectly first-class from the front!'

'Alice, I don't know what to say.'

'There's nothing you can say. Just promise me you'll try and survive and bring that baby into the world. I know Thomas would be proud if he ever were to find out you'd been able to do that.'

Alice pushed a hat down onto Emma's head and fixed it with a pin.

'What are you going to do?' Emma said.

They made their way back outside, gripping each other's hands. In the vague light, Emma looked at Alice wearing Emma's dirty dress and scuffed boots, her hair free and blowing around her face.

'There's no point in going on. The acting is all an illusion.'

'An illusion?'

'I love Aoife. Always have.'

Emma stopped. 'Aoife?'

Alice pulled her forward. 'Yes, Aoife. No man has ever captured my heart like that girl has. What's the point in my survival? My whole life is a lie and I can't see it ever changing.'

'Alice, I'm not leaving you,' Emma said.

'That won't be our choice.'

They made their way to the end of the deck where a steward was checking his list.

Alice leant close and spoke quietly so only Emma

would hear her. 'Now it's you who needs to lie and you'll be just fine.'

Emma felt something sharp appear in her palm and looked down. Alice's first-class ticket was scrunched up, the name and sex clearly stated, but no further form of identification.

Alice pushed her towards the steward who held a board on which he was ticking names from a list with a pen. Another steward was holding back anyone else who wasn't first class. They let Emma through and forced her to let go of Alice's hand.

Alice stepped back.

Emma looked from the steward and back at Alice.

Alice was smiling. 'Go on. You're Alice Murphy! You can conquer the world if you only believe in yourself.'

The steward took the ticket in Emma's hand and helped her in. 'That's it, step inside quickly.'

She clambered in the lifeboat and someone pulled her down onto a narrow bench across the width of the boat. A boat that reminded Emma a little of the rowing boat with Martina's name on the side.

The steward with the list stepped inside. 'Okay, that's it. Hold on tight, everyone!'

He pulled on the ropes.

Alice was standing a little way along the railings, waving.

Emma thought she heard *Good luck!* on the wind but couldn't be sure.

The ropes moved and their descent to the ocean's icy surface had begun.

'Wait!' Emma stood up again, and the other passengers

shouted at her, ordering her to sit back down.

The steward turned to face her. 'What's wrong?'

'I need my friend with me. I can't have this baby without her help.'

'But she's third class. This boat is for first-class passengers only.'

'I don't care about class.' Emma thought on her feet. 'She's a midwife, for God's sake. She saves babies' lives. Are you going to deliver this baby if it arrives early, and get your hands covered in my blood?'

The steward went a funny colour and pulled a different rope. He called to Alice, 'Hey, you! You're a midwife?'

Alice nodded.

'Right. Get in here, quick.'

A few minutes later, the boat bumped against the water and tipped and swayed on the swell.

Emma and Alice gripped each other's hands.

The surface was dotted with blocks of ice, not all of them frozen water.

Stewards in each lifeboat attempted to allocate rowing duties to the stronger passengers. Some had manoeuvred their boats into the darker and quieter waters, away from the majestic but tragic shape of the *Titanic* tilting in the sea.

Everywhere Emma looked, people cried out or whimpered as their energy was sapped. Every lifeboat had been deployed yet hundreds of people remained onboard.

The lifeboats were full.

She turned to Alice, her teeth chatting and clicking. 'Whatever happens, I think you're amazing. If we do survive this, I'll never know how to thank you.'

Alice pulled Emma in close and whispered in her ear, 'I'm not amazing. I'm a coward. I've spent my life trying to please my father and look where that's got me.'

'Alice, you saved my life.'

'No, Emma, you saved mine.'

Chapter Thirty-Six

For three days after the *Titanic*'s departure, Thomas existed in name only. He ran the hotel in body, but his mind was elsewhere. He was polite to guests, but behind closed doors, he was a mess, certain only of one thing – as soon as Alice returned from Hollywood in a few months' time, he would make it up to her and they could somehow try and rebuild their marriage.

At four o'clock in the morning of the fourth day, unable to sleep, Thomas went down to his office. Having gone to bed feeling confident there might be a future with Alice worth fighting for, why had he woken a few hours later feeling so wretched?

Aoife finished spring-cleaning Emma's room and found a handkerchief under the bed which she placed on Thomas's desk. He found it later and folded it carefully before pressing the cotton to his face. A faint smell of perfume crumbled the wall he'd spent four days trying to build. He laid his head on the blotting pad, minutes ticking into hours.

A blast of cold air reached his ankles and the front door banged and woke him from his trance. Aoife ran to the office doorway carrying a newspaper which she pushed under his nose before putting her hands on her knees to catch her breath.

'Slow down, Aoife, you'll have an accident.'

'I had to run,' she gasped. 'It's awful.'

He took the *Daily Mail* and saw nothing untoward on the front page.

'It's on page five…' Aoife tried to catch her breath as Thomas found the headline.

TITANIC ACCIDENT
NO LIVES WERE LOST!
Titanic being towed to Nova Scotia by the Virginian

'What's this?' Thomas stood up and read the column. 'What do they mean, "accident"?'

'Something about an iceberg… they're all talking about it in town.'

Thomas read out loud, '*At 2:15am on the night of 14th April, the* Titanic *struck an iceberg. Radio operators managed to secure the services of two boats sailing close by – the* Parisian *and the* Carpathia – *and all of the* Titanic's *passengers have been transferred safely onto them.* Thank God!' He looked up from the newspaper. 'I must go. She'll be terrified.'

'Alice?'

'I'm going to the harbour to buy a ticket for the next crossing,' Thomas said, ignoring her. He rushed from the room.

'But you don't know where the *Titanic* is being towed to!' Aoife called after him. Thomas slammed the front door and broke into a run, weaving through horses, carts and children kicking an old leather football across the road.

A big crowd had gathered outside the White Star shipping building, reporters with notebooks and pencils poised, eager to hear what the big men of the shipping company were thinking.

The shutters were closed at the ticket office, but Thomas knew another way in.

The back door was also secure, but he banged on it with his fist. A couple of reporters had followed him, keen for an update.

'Are you someone from the company? What are your thoughts on this accident? Will you be able to repair the damage? What will it cost?'

Thomas ignored them and kept hitting the door.

Finally the door opened an inch. The clerk recognised Thomas and opened the door enough for him to slip inside before he closed and bolted it behind him.

'Sorry about that. Been hell keeping them out all morning.'

'I need a ticket. For the next sailing to New York.'

The young man hesitated but then moved to his desk. He flicked through some papers in a ledger and ran his finger down a list.

'There's one leaving tomorrow, a cargo ship. It's not taking general passengers.'

'I don't care. Sell me a ticket. Whatever it costs.'

'I can't, Thomas. It's for goods only. Unless…'

'Yes?' Thomas waited, hopeful.

'If you take hotel papers, as if you're planning business meetings with hoteliers at the destination, I might be able to wangle it.' He pulled the book of tickets from a drawer and proceeded to complete a form and tear off a boarding ticket. 'It's an early departure, 8am.'

The barrage of booming voices outside was growing louder.

The clerk stood bolt upright and gasped. 'Oh, God! I've just realised why you want one. Your wife was on the *Titanic*. I'm so sorry. I'm sure she'll be fine, sounds like they've got it all under control.'

Thomas took the ticket. 'Let's hope so.'

Two days into the crossing, Thomas's bad mood took a turn for the worse.

He'd spent the morning sitting on a bench near the radio operations room, attempting a crossword from an old newspaper, when activity from the men inside became frantic.

He listened through the open window.

'Quiet!' the captain ordered, while his radio operator monitored incoming messages.

Thomas held his breath as muffled wording was jotted down and checked before being repeated out loud.

'The *Titanic* sank, sir. It never *was* being towed to safety. She went down at the point of impact with the iceberg, four hundred miles south of Newfoundland.'

'Bloody hell!' The shock in the captain's voice echoed across the deck.

'Early hours of the fifteenth, sir. That was Monday. I'm afraid the original reports were untrue.'

'Christ, are there any survivors?'

Thomas dropped the newspaper to the floor; the pencil rolled away across the deck; his lips were dry.

'Yes, a few hundred, it seems. Rescued by the *Carpathia* and taken on to New York.'

'Right. Thank you, William. Keep ears open for any more news. You three, come with me. We're going to have to work on an announcement for the crew.'

Thomas heard them leave the operations room and felt the pit of his stomach surge like the waves that slapped against the side of the ship. He moved to the railing and looked over. A lone seagull bobbed on the surface and he watched it get left behind.

Being sick over the side of a ship in the wind was never going to go well.

'Bit seasick, are we? I'll get a cloth and a bucket.' A young ship hand had come down the steps from an upper deck, his clothes covered in oily smudges.

'I think it's done. I'll just go and…' Thomas looked at the railings.

'No, you go and lie down. I'll sort it.'

Thomas staggered away from the rail, stepped over the rusting lip of the doorway and went along the narrow corridor, gripping a metal handrail as he made his way to the narrow cabin he'd been allocated.

The very ship Queenstown had celebrated now lay at the bottom of the ocean.

He knew from paperwork on his desk a few days before that nearly two and a half thousand people had been on board when the *Titanic* set sail across the Atlantic.

If what the operator had said was correct, that hundreds had died – even those in lifeboats – what possibility could there be that she was among them?

He stood at the little tin basin and stared at his tired reflection in the oval mirror. This was all his fault. Emma might have still been safe at the hotel and planning her next federation meeting had he been less of a fool.

Over fourteen hundred souls were still classed as 'missing', according to the captain's announcement, while the *Carpathia* would be arriving at Pier 54 in New York sometime within the next twenty-four hours. He'd gone on to confirm that their own arrival was still three days away.

Thomas chewed his nails and counted rivets around the door, unsure how he could possibly endure three days of not knowing who the survivors were, or where they'd been taken once the *Carpathia* had docked.

He didn't later recall how he made it to the dining room, and couldn't have described what he'd had for dinner. But consuming it would keep him going long enough to start his search.

Rumours of who was to blame for the tragedy continued to trickle through the crew for the remainder of the voyage. Thomas heard about a night watchman in the *Titanic*'s crow's nest who'd not been concentrating. Another that the *Titanic*'s Captain Smith – and one of those still missing – had ordered the ship maintain too high a speed for iceberg-filled waters.

Like some torturous game of roulette, a list of confirmed dead was pinned up daily in the dining area. The sketchy information came across the wireless as authorities in New York made steady progress identifying those who had been pulled from the icy waters of the Atlantic or those who had made it to New York but died within hours of arriving.

On the final day of his crossing, Thomas knotted the handkerchief one more time and held his breath as he read both lists. Neither bore the names Alice Murphy or Emma Quinn.

The captain of the cargo ship gave Thomas a map of the city before they docked and he spent his final hours in the tiny cabin studying the strange road network, with its straight lines and crossroads.

He circled in pencil the location of St Vincent hospital which, according to newspaper reports, had taken in a large number of survivors.

He would start his search there.

Chapter Thirty-Seven

Thomas walked across a harbour so enormous, he couldn't see from one end to the other. Everything they said about America was true. It was unimaginably vast. And noisy. And smelly, even more so than the little harbour of fishing boats back home. Here, great clouds of fumes billowed across from the ships moored where the edge of the Atlantic nudged its dark water against the concrete of the east coast of the promised land. The aroma of hardworking men filled Thomas's nostrils as he made his way towards a coffee house he'd been told to look out for.

Reporters with notepads rushed this way and that, hoping for a human story. Hundreds of relatives mingled with workers, waiting for news that each ship's arrival might bring.

He stepped around piles of empty crates piled the size of houses and saw huge lettering painted on wooden doors on the side of a building: 'JOE'S CAFE'.

Through steamed-up windows, men stood three-deep against the counter. He went inside, the draw of fresh coffee awakening his tired body.

The *Titanic* was the word on everyone's lips.

He paid for his drink with some nickels the captain

had given him. *They'll start you off, you'll need to find an exchange when you get there.*

He found an empty stool by the window and sat down. The folded map he'd practically memorised was safe in his inside pocket. A copy of yesterday's *New York Times* had been rolled up and wedged between the window and a wooden plank fixed as a shallow bench on which to rest a cup. He pulled the paper free, its edges damp and curled from condensation.

The front page showed photographs, one showing the *Titanic*'s lifeboats, tethered together in the water at Pier 59. The article reported how passengers had crowded into the small boats, climbing in to escape the freezing waters. Many had capsized, tipping their panicking occupants to their icy death.

He ran his finger over the empty grey husks in the picture and prayed.

The list of dead passengers was much longer than those the operator of the cargo ship had been given. He read slowly and carefully, sipping his coffee.

Neither Alice nor Emma was listed. But Thomas did see a name he recognised.

He spilt his mug of coffee and it scalded his thigh. 'Hell.'

'Okay, man?'

Thomas put his hand up. 'Thank you, yes. Tired.'

'First time over here?'

He nodded.

'Here, you have mine.' The stranger passed Thomas his mug of coffee.

'There's no need, really.'

'It's bad times here right now, we're all helping each

281

other. That's what we do here. You enjoy that and take yer time.'

Thomas thanked the man, turned back to the paper and took a deep breath.

Clive Harrington was part of a huge number listed as 'Dead on arrival at Pier 54'.

Thomas could smell disinfectant mixed with death long before he was inside the hospital.

The double doors were jammed open to allow room for the continuous stream of people going in and coming out. Children in sullied bandages limped their way inside; adults hobbling on crutches moved around the entrance and leant against the wall outside. Shell-shocked faces and bedraggled bodies in torn clothing wandered in and out of the hospital, gripping the arms of friends, perhaps strangers.

With his heart in his mouth, Thomas walked inside. The area filled with people and noise. His body ached from lack of sleep and his clothes smelt of a week at sea. Behind a desk two women conferred about a patient before the older one looked up at him.

'You from the *Titanic*?'

'No, but I'm looking for…' He toyed with the names on his tongue. 'Miss Emma Quinn.'

'We're still registering everyone, I'm afraid. Poor souls still coming in, too. We thought after the *Carpathia* lot that would be it, didn't we?' She looked back at the younger nurse. 'Our lists are not in alphabetical order, we haven't been able to keep up, but you're welcome to check the log we started three days ago.'

She passed him a book in which names had been scribbled in the order survivors had arrived. He checked each one carefully. His life seemed to revolve round reading lists in the hope of finding names.

'You may need to check the hotels in the area, sir. Some have opened their rooms for those who didn't need medical attention.'

'I see,' Thomas said.

The younger girl was no older than Aoife and she indicated the book. 'I hope you can read my writing?'

He nodded. 'I can.'

Behind them, two men entered the building carrying a stretcher.

The nurse called out, 'Room 13, and do we have a name?'

The first bearer shook his head. 'Not yet, he's not spoken. He was found gripping a log basket, his fingers entwined with those of a dead boy. Two days. It's a miracle the man's alive.'

'I hope you find who you're looking for,' she said to Thomas with a wan smile. 'Our porters have worked non-stop. It's been a horrible week, but when relatives come in, like you, it's lovely to see some of their faces light up.'

He turned the page and tried to focus eyes full of grit. When he read a woman's name amongst the men, his heart would miss a beat, as if the list was taunting him with a cruel twist of fate and the woman listed was really Emma with mistaken identity. That she might be lying in a bed in this very building, with the wrong name on the board clipped at the end of a bed, left him feeling sick, and if she was unconscious, how would they know what to call her?

A doctor came to the desk and leaned over to speak with the nurse. 'Lisa, can you add this man to the log, please?' He handed her a piece of paper and then looked at Thomas hunched over the logbook. 'Are you okay?'

'I was just hoping to find my... hoping to find out if my friend might be here.'

'Your friend may be at The Jane, if they weren't badly injured. But can I just check what class of ticket they sailed with?'

Thomas swallowed and recalled Mary's delight that her son had managed to save enough money to buy his ticket.

'Third class. And she was pregnant.'

The doctor pulled him to one side and spoke quietly. 'I have to tell you most of the survivors that we've seen here were first-class passengers. I don't think the others had much of a chance. I'm so very sorry.'

Chapter Thirty-Eight

He followed the doctor's suggestion and made his way towards a hotel on Jane Street. *Only twenty minutes away,* the doctor had assured him.

The relief on learning Emma was not in St Vincent's had been short-lived. Once more, the fear of the unknown messed with his mind and he briefly debated about turning round, the option to remain ignorant holding some small appeal.

It started to rain and the thin coat he'd grabbed when he left Ireland was not waterproof. Puddles were collecting quickly and vehicle tyres swished through them, sending spray onto pathways double the width of those at home.

The streets were so busy, they made Cork City look like a village. He stepped backwards into a shop doorway to allow a huddle of women to go past, the hems of their skirts soaked dark with rainwater, wooden boards on posts held high above their heads:

JOIN US MAY 6, VOTES FOR WOMEN

And another:

FIGHT THE DICTATORS

He didn't fight his body as his knees gave way. He'd give anything now, he realised too late, to see Emma marching with these women. Sliding down a wall of green tiles in the doorway, grief overwhelmed him. Just to know her heart might still be beating in her young and perfect body would be the greatest gift God could give him right now.

After ten minutes' sitting on the damp doormat, he pushed himself back up and raised his collar before stepping back out into the sea of people.

Vehicles queued three deep in each direction. Never had he seen roads so full. Or straight. The traffic loomed away into the distance.

Conical turrets decorated corners of gable-roofed apartment buildings. Looking up, he lost count of the number of floors some of the blocks boasted. Posters plastered to the sides of buses invited people to '*SEE THE ODDITIES IN BARNUM'S MUSEUM!*' and '*TAKE A TRAM TO CONEY ISLAND!*'.

He must have taken a wrong turn. The road names differed from those on the map. He stopped and looked about, and pedestrians in a hurry cursed him for getting in their way.

The rain fell harder and it trickled down his neck.

His feet were soaked.

'Get on outta here!' a shop-keeper shouted from a doorway to his left.

Two young boys with bare feet and faces covered in oozing scabs ran out into the street. Thomas moved out of their way, but one caught his eye.

'Hey, mister, you got a nickel?'

'Don't give them anything,' the shop-keeper warned.

They ran across the road, weaving between the trams and buses.

'Were they homeless?' Thomas asked.

'Probably, and sick. From one of the orphanages, I shouldn't wonder.'

Thomas was so wet that worrying about shelter was a waste of time.

'Come in out the rain, you're not from round here, are you?' The shop-keeper closed the door behind them, the noise of the street fading. He offered Thomas a filled roll containing some sort of meat and waved away the handful of coins.

'So, where ya from?'

'Just arrived today. Ireland. I came to search for someone.'

'You're looking for someone on the streets?'

'No,' Thomas said, and took a bite of the roll. 'She was on the *Titanic*, and her name is not on the missing lists and she's not in St Vincent's. I'm going to check The Jane Hotel next, if I can find it.'

'You're not far from The Jane.' He pointed through the shop window. 'You go up here four blocks and take a right into twelfth. You can't miss it.'

The plaque outside the hotel on Jane Street told him he was about to enter the American Seaman's Friend Society Sailor's Home and Institute. He pushed open the double doors and took off his wet coat. Drops of water fell to the floor and collected by his feet.

There was no-one at the desk, and not wishing to wait, he started walking down a corridor, reading the names on pieces of paper pinned to every door. Some had names crossed out and a new one written beneath. At the end of the corridor was a set of stairs which led to the first floor. He went up and along that corridor.

A nurse was pulling a sheet over somebody's face in the first room and then stood back, her hands together in prayer.

Thomas reached for her arm as she came out into the corridor. 'Excuse me, sorry to bother you. Do you know if there's an Emma Quinn here, please?'

She shook her head and looked shattered. 'We've had over two hundred come through in the last three days, she's certainly not on this floor, that I do know.'

The smile did not reach her eyes.

He watched her walk away, before calling after her. 'She was heavily pregnant.'

The nurse stopped and turned back to face him. 'We have a small maternity unit set up on the fourth floor, you might try there.'

Thomas stubbed his toes more than once racing up the flights of stairs.

Up and round, up and round. How many floors was that? He continued up one more flight, leaping the steps two at a time. Breathing hard, he hesitated for a moment at another set of double doors, each labelled with a brass number four. Behind them came the unmistakable cries of a tiny baby.

He followed the sound along the corridor and stopped near a room with an open door. He leant back against the wall for a moment and tried to calm himself. His chest was tight, as if he'd been holding his breath. He realised in fact that he had, for eight long days.

When he heard the voice, he grabbed the edge of the door for support. If it was Emma, would she refuse to see him? Hadn't she told him on the harbour slipway there was no point in their union? He found himself rooted to the spot, wondering what he'd been hoping to achieve. He waited, willing her to speak again, sure his mind must be playing tricks.

There came a second voice. Another woman was in the room, someone older.

'Darling, she'll be fine.'

'I want to see her!'

There was no doubt the first voice he'd heard was Emma's.

Her panic stirred something primal in him, and he moved towards the doorway. Urgent footsteps marched down the corridor towards him and Thomas stepped back.

The doctor went into the room.

Thomas wondered if he should follow. Emma was asking... no, she was *begging* the doctor for something.

'No-one else needs it, so don't you dare take it away!'

'I told you last night, Miss Quinn. Weaklings such as yours... it's a waste of resources. Eight weeks early is unfortunate, and you'll go on to have more babies, I'm sure.'

'Shut up!' Emma screamed.

The older woman pulled the doctor out into the corridor by his sleeve and Thomas stepped even further back into the shadows. She mumbled something and the doctor replied, 'It's for the best to let this little thing go in peace. Who are we to interfere with God's will?'

'God's will? You idiot! She's given birth prematurely due to shock.'

'I'll be back.' The doctor stalked off down the corridor, and the woman walked back into the room. Thomas clenched his fists, took a deep breath and moved into the doorway.

To the right, a red-haired mother sat in a bed gazing at the face of her suckling baby, and on the other side of the room, Emma stood staring out a window, her back to the room.

Her hair lay in tatty strands down her back. She wore a crinkled white linen gown and the older woman rubbed her back in slow circles.

The redhead glanced up and gasped at Thomas's presence. Emma heard her and spun round.

Her eyes were bloodshot.

It took only three steps to reach her, to take her in his arms and hold her close as she sobbed in disbelief into his wet clothes.

For an age they stood and cried, supporting each other.

When he finally pulled back, he relished her hands on his cheeks as she whispered, 'You're really here?'

'I'm really here.'

She started to sob again. 'The baby came early…'

He pulled her back towards him and promised himself he would never again let her go. He wondered if she could hear his heart thumping against his ribs. 'It's okay… ssshhh.'

Her sobbing slowed and she wiped her face and sighed. Then she reached for the older woman's hand. 'Thomas, this is my mother. Mom, this is Thomas.'

'Hello.' He held out his hand.

The woman was pale and drawn. She sat on the edge of the bed and patted a space beside her. 'Call me Maggie.'

He sat down.

She took his hand and held it. 'Thomas.'

He waited while the grandmother of his baby thought about her words. 'I should despise you, a married man falling for my daughter, I know I should. My own husband left me in January for another woman and I certainly despise him.'

Thomas couldn't bring himself to speak.

'But the last twenty-four hours, my view on the world has changed.'

He couldn't have said it better himself.

Her green eyes were sad. 'Two days ago, I didn't even know Emma had left Ireland. When I received the telegram that she'd been aboard the *Titanic*, and was one of the survivors, I came straight here. She's been through too much trauma for one young soul – it's only been a year since that blessed fire.'

'I know,' Thomas said, glancing up at the beautiful young woman standing in front of them, silent tears running down her cheeks.

Maggie hadn't finished. 'I will never again try and advise her how to live her life, or be anything other than supportive in her decisions. So, my dear Thomas. I have heard a lot about you these last few hours and it's a complete honour to meet you—'

'No, the honour is mine, you have a remarkable daughter.'

Maggie blushed and patted his hand. 'It's in the blood.'

'Oh, Mom.' Emma stooped to hug her mother's shoulders and then sat beside Thomas.

'As I was saying.' Maggie stood and placed her hands on her hips. 'I am only now interested in supporting Emma, and women's rights in general. So, where will I find that damned doctor?'

'Do you need to?' Thomas asked.

'Hell yes I do. Because if he turns that incubator off and kills my granddaughter, I will personally see to it that he never works again.'

Chapter Thirty-Nine

Alice sat quietly in a corner of the dining room of a ship headed for Ireland. She stretched her right leg on the bench in front of her, while the stump of her left fizzed and stung behind the bandage, just below the knee where the surgeon had placed his saw.

The simple clothing she'd been given at the hospital was perfect to help her merge into the background and remain unnoticed. Recent events had stolen more than a limb.

Previous desires to become a famous movie star had disintegrated when their lifeboat had been ambushed by too many desperate to climb aboard. Thinking she was being clever, Alice had hooked her foot into a curled rope in the hull beneath the bench on which they'd been sat to secure her place. As more people climbed aboard, the boat had tipped sideways, its cargo a mash of thrashing arms and legs. Alice's plan had nearly killed her when she was dragged under, but the rope had unfurled itself just enough to release her from a watery grave.

A waiter delivered a tin plate of spam and bread and a mug of water. She was one of a tiny group of passengers returning to Ireland who'd been on the *Titanic* and survived. Most had chosen to stay on American soil, joyous to be alive and in the land of their dreams when so many had not made it.

There was only one place she wanted to be.

Only one person she wanted to spend her second chance at life with.

Nothing else mattered.

It had always been Aoife. For a while, Thomas had tried hard to be a dutiful husband. She prayed that the letter she'd scrawled while on the *Carpathia* would get to him and absolve him of any responsibility for her happiness. Or lack of it. They would work out the finer details over time, like the management of the hotel. If Thomas wanted to stay in New York with Emma and his child, then Alice knew he should do that. In fact, she'd discovered she was genuinely happy for him.

She shook her head to rid herself of the vision of Emma floating away, motionless at first in the inky waters before her pregnant belly had in fact helped turn her to face the stars. Alice had not felt the break in her ankle due to numbness, and for what seemed an age had tried to find Emma the help she needed. *Save that woman, she's pregnant!* Alice had shouted, and eventually, a lifeboat had made its way over, passengers using their hands as paddles.

A ship called the *Carpathia* had come to their rescue, scooping up survivors hanging on to life in the small white wooden boats. The crew plucked from the surface hundreds of bodies as hard as the blocks of ice which surrounded them. The corpses were stored together on a deck beneath covers which Alice avoided as she hobbled amongst the injured in search of Emma two days later.

'You can't see her,' a nurse told Alice in front of a closed cabin door. 'We're trying to keep the room sterile due to the baby. We've no proper maternity equipment aboard, only basic first aid.'

'Well, can you give her this?'

The nurse had taken the folded piece of paper with little knowledge that the information on it would alter the lives of at least four people, and a fifth who had taken only her first few breaths of life.

Alice had spent her life thinking she could have it all. The career on the stage, the spotlight and adulation of directors across Europe. A love affair more passionate than any she'd feigned on stage or in the beds of agents past and present. She'd also banked on always having a secure financial future in the shape of the hotel, and the service of the man chosen by her father to be her husband.

But now, with the closeness of death still only a few hours behind her, Alice had woken up. Living and breathing were her spotlights now. Seeing and hearing the lines she would treasure. Touching Aoife would be the only audience she needed. This was what mattered now.

Even though the world would never allow their union, Alice's experience had changed her, and although she hated to admit it, for the first time, she'd begun to reflect that there may be a need to fight old-fashioned bureaucracy. And that meant men, the very beasts she'd spent her adult life pursuing and manipulating. Men led the church and the church forbid women to be together.

For the time being, Aoife would live in the hotel full time and they would hide their relationship from prying eyes. Alice had known others who had managed similar situations. Aoife was not her first female encounter, although she would certainly be her last. Perhaps Emma's fight for suffrage did have the potential to change the world. She wiped a tear from her cheek and tried not to think of all the wasted months she'd spent hating the girl. Perhaps she would never see the law change to allow two women to be recognised as a couple, but the fight should start somewhere.

The cabin was cramped and for three days she'd shared the space with a family of five. The father had made eyes at her on more than one occasion. In the past, Alice would have responded, and encouraged it in case there might be something in it for her, but since their journey back across the Atlantic had begun, and her thoughts had turned to Aoife, Alice no longer felt the need to pretend. When she'd shaken her head at the husband that morning, turning away with revolt in her eyes, she'd felt liberated.

Chapter Forty

Emma sat at the window of her mother's small apartment overlooking a street which ran parallel to Central Park. The baby slept, little snores drifting out from a Moses basket in the corner of the room.

Thomas knelt in front of her. 'You okay?'

'I'm happy, but am I allowed to feel happy when there's been such tragedy?'

He kissed her hand. 'Life is precious and can be snuffed out in less time it takes for me to light my pipe. Of course you're allowed.'

'I'm sorry about your marriage, Thomas. Are you cross with Alice?'

'How could I be cross?'

'With her wanting the hotel in her name.'

'It's the right thing to do, Emma,' Thomas said. 'I'll write to Patrick and he can draw up some paperwork. She will have my shares and although we can never be officially divorced, she and I will be able to live separately. I, here with you.'

'Will you write to her?'

'Yes, of course.'

'She has a heart of gold. She saved my life, Thomas.' Emma stared out of the window and saw her mother turn

297

the corner a few yards along the street, returning with some shopping. 'We talked and she told me things.'

'On the *Carpathia*?'

'No, on the *Titanic*, in the moments before she saved my life. On the *Carpathia* I went into labour and they took me down to someone's cabin. I never saw her again.'

Emma sipped her tea and heard the front door of the little flat open and close.

Emma looked at him. 'And have *you* decided what you're going to do?'

He turned to look at her. 'Whatever it takes.'

'What do you mean?'

'To keep us together, Emma. If you want to stay in America, then I will stay too. I can find work.'

'It's where Nana came to live and it's where I want to spend my life. It's also where I want to set up the Soldiers' Home, close to the docks.' Emma stood and moved to the cot. 'And it's where I want to bring up Martina. I feel I'm home here.'

She fiddled with the edge of the tiny sheet and tucked it more firmly beneath the little mattress. The baby's lips opened and a bubble of spit grew to the size of a pea before bursting.

Thomas appeared behind her and placed his hands around her waist, gently pulling her into him. 'I love you, Emma, and my home is wherever you are.'

Epilogue

Three years later...

'How's your parlour coming along? We need to leave soon to meet Daddy.' Emma bent down and kissed the top of her daughter's head. Martina was arranging furniture in the doll's house, her pretty blonde curls tamed into plaits. Outside, the November air was cool, the sky cobalt blue.

'Nearly done,' Martina replied, and placed miniature plates on a table no bigger than a pouch of tobacco. She bent the pipe-cleaner man – who wore a brown felt suit – into the correct position and sat back on her heels. 'There. He's cooked a welcome-home dinner for his wife, and it's a special day.'

Emma could see the trouble the little man had gone to – the table was laden with a feast. 'What's special about it?'

'His brother is coming home from the army.'

'Oh, now that *is* special.' Emma turned away and brushed imaginary fluff from her jacket. She went to the mirror hanging above the fireplace and checked her reflection.

A diagonal row of buttons ran from her left shoulder to her right hip, accentuating the fit of the jacket. Warm enough to endure the freezing winters of the east coast but stylish that the young American women wearing them could feel smart. Emma had been inundated with orders when she'd first worn her own and had gone on to make seventeen more.

'Okay, I'm ready!' Martina jumped up and pulled at the hem of her coat which hung from a high row of hooks near the front door.

Emma helped her into it and bent down to do up the buttons. At three, her daughter was still smaller than other children her age, but her friendly outlook and grasp of the world around her more than made up for the effects of a premature birth.

'Where are we meeting him?' Martina asked as she jumped down the front steps two at a time, pausing between each jump to gauge the drop.

'At the bridge.'

'I love the bridge.'

'Morning, Lilian!' Emma waved to a woman near the flower stall on the corner.

Lilian was arranging buckets of narcissi and pots of colourful pansies but stopped to wave back. 'I presume you'll be at the meeting tomorrow?'

Emma laughed. 'I'm not missing this one. In fact, save some of those pretty little daffodils, will you? Bring them to decorate the table. I'll pay for them there.'

'Right, you are.'

As they weaved their way through excited crowds, Emma noted the front pages of all the newspapers, stand after stand, full of the day's momentous news. She stopped and bought one, in case Thomas had not had time.

The women of New York had finally won the right to vote, and in every direction, groups had gathered to sing and chant about their success. Times were changing and it was there in black and white, on the front pages.

The breeze chilled her skin, but she didn't care. She couldn't keep the smile from her face as they turned the final block and Ellen skipped along beside her. Ahead, the majestic towers of Brooklyn Bridge were bathed in sunshine.

'There's Daddy, I can see him!' Martina pulled free from Emma's hand and ran with her pigtails bouncing against her back. Thomas bent forward and held his arms open wide.

'Daddy, I've finished my table-setting. Can I show you?' She yanked his hand to go back the way they'd come.

'Later, little one.' He tucked a strand of hair behind her ear, blown loose from a plait.

Thomas kissed Emma's cheek. 'I think a small celebration lunch is in order, don't you think?'

Emma grinned. 'So you've seen the papers?'

'My dear, I've bought extra copies and had staff place one in every bedroom.'

She laughed. 'All of them?'

'Every single one.' He kept hold of Martina's hand.

They reached the middle of the bridge and stopped to let Martina watch boats on the water below. Emma leaned her head against Thomas's shoulder and stared at the horizon across the deep expanse of the Atlantic which had nearly taken her life. She respected – more than feared – the ocean.

'Well, Mr Murphy, I believe you will have the most well-read hotel guests in all of Brooklyn.'

'I bought extra copies. Thought perhaps you'd want them for your meeting tonight.'

Thomas was referring to the tea shop Emma had opened up for soldiers and sailors who arrived home from warzones but who wanted a day on neutral ground, to unwind, to talk, to calm their nerves before returning home to well-meant love and smothering by their families. Some of them slept for whole days and nights, and the staff Emma had employed made sure the men were well-fed, refreshed and never drunk when they left the premises. Emma's café had become the talk of the neighbourhood and she was planning to open more, with the help of others along the coast.

'Has anyone ever told you that you're amazing?' She kissed him.

He grinned. 'Been at least two days.'

Acknowledgements

There are many people without whom this novel would not exist. In no particular order I'd like to thank;

Playwright, Beth Flintoff, for rekindling my love of writing when she came to speak to a group of ladies at the Ipswich Lighthouse Women's Aid – the venue for self-esteem workshops I attended in 2017 – while she researched her play, *The Ballad of Maria Marten*.

I rediscovered a love of reading through The Fiction Cafe Book Club, and a particular shout out to founder, Wendy Clarke, who witnessed me develop from reader to writer in 2017. Kiltie Jackson's 2018 birthday card message '*Always believe that you can, for then one day you will.*' remains on my pin-board even today and I adore her almost as much as her cat, Princess.

I joined the Romantic Novelists Association and made new friends and met tutors. On my first writing retreat, Julie Cohen was instrumental in teaching me our novels often need to begin further into a story than we initially believe. I've never forgotten that. And later, Alison May's detailed critique of the first draft of Maid of Steel helped to steer this novel in the right direction. I removed two characters because I didn't have a sensible answer to her question; '*What is their purpose, exactly?*'

I want to thank my friend, Hannah Buxton. She travelled with me to Ireland in 2019 for a girlie weekend during which she poured both wine and helpful ideas into early ideas for this story. We returned in 2020 with a crammed itinerary for a research trip to nail the project down. It took us from the old suffragette meeting rooms in the city of Cork to St Colman's cathedral in Cobh, the bandstand on the quay and the Heritage Centre. Thanks for spotting *SOLDIERS HOME* carved in quiet letters in stone above a doorway which led to an important thread in Emma's story.

My weekly accountability partner, Karen Storey, who keeps me on the straight and not-so-narrow every Monday morning. And a group of writing buddies known as Bar-babes (Julie Morris, Emma-Clare Wilson, Jennifer Kennedy, Sandra Forder, Emma Jackson and Katie Wells) so named after an additional table had to be set up in the bar at a summer writing conference!

Creative writing studies with Anstey Harris taught me a lot more than how to knit a quality sentence. Members of the Best Seller Experiment podcast-following and their Academy for unwavering encouragement and particularly Mark Stay and Mark Desvaux for their enthusiasm and encouragement to do things our own way. Mark Stay's edit helped to fine-tune this story and made it shine brighter than it had before. My beta readers for their comments; Angela Nurse, Rosie Moore and Aaron Brooks.

The team at The Book Guild for responding to my submission so positively and giving my story a chance to be read, and a special thanks to Chelsea Taylor for the beautiful cover. Sophie Hannah for her Dream Author Coaching content. So much of what you teach reinforces the self-esteem study I did five years ago, so your presence in my support-team is priceless.

To my offspring, Bonnie and Don, who were still living at home when I began this book and never moaned that the house was a tip. And finally to my number one fan, the husband who brings me teas and coffees and plates piled high with toast, who believes in me and who stood by me while I found myself.